MW01717280

Warm Regards
From Hoddy

FLIGHT SURGEON & INTERN

Francis John Haddy, M.D., Ph.D.

Noble House
Baltimore, Maryland

Flight Surgeon & Intern

Library of Congress
Cataloging-in-Publication Data
ISBN 1-56167-859-7

Library of Congress Card Catalog Number:
2004093765

Published by

Noble House

8019 Belair Road, Suite 10
Baltimore, Maryland 21236

Manufactured in the United States of America

Introduction

The time was 1947 and I was serving two years on active duty in the Army Airforce, paying back the federal government for allowing me to complete medical school at the government's expense during World War II. I had recently received orientation as a medical officer and was on my way to Panama for my first permanent duty station, exact site still unknown to me.

Terry, my wife of 14 months, was in the fifth month of a rotating internship at the Minneapolis General Hospital in Minneapolis and was currently on the Obstetrics and Gynecology Service with her good friend, Elaine McKenzie. She lived in the nurses' quarters while on duty and in her family home in St. Paul when off duty, traveling between the two sites by street car.

My father, mother, and sister Juanita were in Lebanon, visiting my father's family for the first time since my parents immigrated to the United States in 1911.

Rio Hato Airfield
Republic of Panama
10 November 1947

FRAN

The B-17 lifted off the Albrook Airfield airstrip in the Canal Zone and headed up the Pacific coast at a low altitude. I watched what passed below through an open cargo door while lying flat on my stomach. There was the Pacific Ocean to the left, jungle on the right, and a thin strip of beach in the middle. All three were beautiful. After a flight of about thirty minutes, we approached our destination, Rio Hato Airbase. I knew not what to expect.

This had been a busy day, full of surprises, at least one at first glance not so pleasant. The day really started at 10:00 a.m. when our Army personnel transport ship, the *Pvt. William Thomas,* docked in Cristobal, a city at the Atlantic end of the Panama Canal. We (enlisted men, dependents, and ten replacement medical officers with whom I had trained and traveled) immediately disembarked ship and boarded a train which took us across the Canal Zone to the Pacific side. The trip bordered the Canal most of the way, providing interesting sight-seeing. I was surprised to see the country so mountainous. It was easy to understand why building the Canal was so difficult, even though much of the distance was natural waterways in the form of lakes. The underbrush was very thick, resembling the densest jungle, to a large extent because this was still the rainy season; in fact, it rained much of the way across. Had we arrived in Panama a little later, we would have been in the six month long dry season, and the foliage would not have been as lush. The Canal with its locks was always nearby but never close enough for detailed inspection.

We arrived in Balboa, the city at the Pacific end of the Canal, at about 12:30 p.m. Balboa was about one and a half miles from Panama City, which was just outside the Zone and which we did not enter. We were met by Army vehicles and driven the one and a half miles to Albrook Field. At the time there were three large airbases in the Canal Zone, Albrook, French, and Howard. Albrook was massive and very beautiful. The buildings were modern and permanent. It certainly was superior to any of the Panamanian cities we saw during our train trip.

We were taken to the bachelor officers' quarters (BOQ), which was part of the Officers' Club at Albrook. After being assigned to rooms, we immediately ate and then went to the administrative building to fill out forms and receive our work assignments. It was then that the ax fell.

"Haddy, you are going to Rio Hato," an officer said.

"Man, what and where the hell is that?" I said.

I soon found out. They "just happened to have" a plane leaving for Rio Hato Field, so I rushed, retrieved my bags, and hopped on the plane, thus accounting for my viewing scenery on my stomach from a low flying B-17 bomber. Rio Hato was about seventy miles up the Pacific Coast in the Republic of Panama. We approached the landing strip at 4:30 p.m. As we did so, I reflected on the assignments of my nine medical officer travel companions. Two were immediately flown back to Puerto Rico, from whence we had just come by ship (example of Army efficiency), and the rest were assigned to French, Albrook, and Howard Fields in the Canal Zone. Why couldn't I have been so fortunate? I was told that Rio Hato was primitive relative to the Canal Zone, no place for a recent bride.

I was twenty-five years old at the time and had just received the M.D. (Doctor of Medicine) degree from the University of Minnesota. Leading to the degree were grade schooling in two Southern Minnesota small towns (Walters and Kiester), high schooling in one of them (Kiester), pre-medicine training in two institutions of higher learning (Luther College, Decorah, Iowa; and the University of Minnesota, Minneapolis, Minnesota), medicine training in an excellent medical school (University of Minnesota), and a 15-month rotating internship in a charity city hospital (Minneapolis General Hospital - MGH). Medical school training was accomplished as a member of the United States Army during

W.W.II and thus generated two years of obligatory active service as a medical officer following the internship, which was accomplished as a civilian in the reserves. During that period, I married a medical school mate, Theresa Eileen Brey ("Terry").

I finished interning at MGH on June 30, 1947 (Figures 1a and 1b), and was soon returned to active duty to begin my payback obligation, which could have been anyplace in the USA or overseas, wherever US troops were stationed. I was told that the active duty would begin August 16th, with about four weeks attendance (25 August 47 to 19 Sept 47) at the Medical Field Service School, Brooke Army Medical Corps, in Fort Sam Houston in San Antonio, Texas, where I would be taught to be a proper Army medical officer. Since Terry was about to begin her 12 month rotating internship at MGH and I hadn't seen much of my father and mother while in medical school and during internship, I decided to visit them. My parents and some of my siblings lived in Los Angeles. Thus, I decided to spend some of July and August in Los Angeles. Not only could I reconnect with my family, but a driving trip out with a classmate and fraternity brother and a train trip back would be relaxing after a stressful five years and would provide great sightseeing, something enjoyed but missed. Furthermore, my father, mother, and sister Juanita were planning a prolonged trip to Lebanon in the fall, narrowing the window of opportunity to see them.

It turned out the stay in Los Angeles was a bit long because I very soon started missing Terry, a prelude to a more prolonged and painful separation as a result of my assignments.

Figure 1a and b- Terry and me in front of the Minneapolis General Hospital on June 30, 1947, the day I completed my internship and she began hers. The building to the right in the lower picture was the home of the *Minneapolis Star*.

The assignments were in rapid succession, over the period from August 16th to November 10th, schooling in Fort Sam Houston, several weeks in Camp Kilmern, NJ (a holding area for personnel assigned overseas), several weeks more in New Orleans, LA, a ship trip to Panama via Puerto Rico, and finally assignment to Rio Hato. Except for a short furlough after the Fort Sam Houston experience, my recent bride, Terry, and I were separated for the entire August 16th to November 10th period, with more to come.

Minneapolis General Hospital
Minneapolis Minnesota
10 November 1947

TERRY

As I was landing at Rio Hato, Terry (see Figures 1a,b), my bride, was taking a terrific razzing. She, along with two other women interns at the Minneapolis General Hospital, had been featured in a story on women in medicine in the Sunday edition of the *Minneapolis Star* (located just across the street from MGH).

My wife, Terry, and her close friend, Elaine McKenzie, rotated through the various specialties together, and were currently on the Obstetrics and Gynecology Service. A second friend, Christine Furman, was on the Dermatology Service. The story was accompanied by photographs. One showed Terry being gowned by a nurse in a surgical suit just prior to a gynecological procedure (Figure 1c). Elaine stood in front of her, pointing. Another showed Christine entering an ambulance and showing a bit of leg in the process (Figure 1d). When Terry arrived at work in the morning, one of the maids on Station F, a Mrs. Schneider, was waiting for her. She excitedly handed Terry the newspaper clipping and said, "This is for Dr. Haddy," meaning me. Mrs. Schneider had worked in the interns' quarters a year earlier, when I was an intern. "Be sure to tell Dr. Haddy that I sent it," she said.

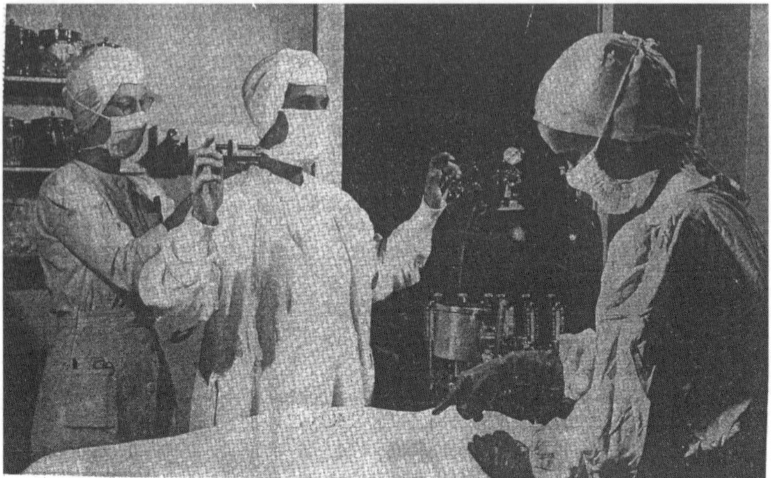

OPERATING ROOM—Typical of the new crop of women physicians are these two Interns at General hospital who demonstrate their preparation for assisting at operations. Dr. Theresa Haddy, second from left, is gowned by Nancy Hoetger, left, a graduate nurse. At right is Dr. Elaine McKenzie. Both Dr. Haddy and Dr. McKenzie are specializing in obstetrics and gynecology, both are married and plan to combine their careers with marriage.

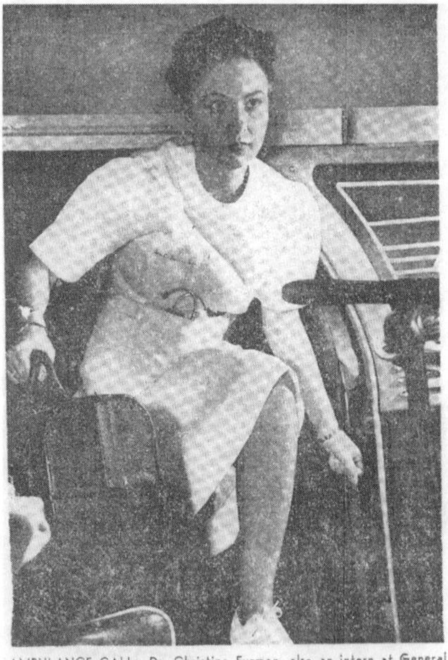

AMBULANCE CALL—Dr. Christine Furman, also an intern at General hospital, enters an ambulance on a call. Dr. Furman's husband is a medical student at University of Minnesota and, like her two colleagues, she will juggle marriage and career.

Figure 1c and 1 d- From a Sunday edition of the *Minneapolis Star*, November 1947.

The razzing commenced later on rounds. The "skin men," including Christine, passed the "gyn men," including Terry and Elaine, in the hall. As they went by, Drs. McAfee and King, both "gyn men," did a little pantomime — King took off his white coat, put it on backwards, and McAfee pretended to help him "gown" for surgery. Christine received even worse razzing from the "skin" men, who had a reputation for being great jokers (they took pride in their ties, which were usually patterned with bugs, and competed to see who could sport the most repulsive or startling design), for revealing so much of the largest organ in the body. The skin, by the way, is the largest organ in the body. The newspaper story implied (mistakenly) that Terry and Elaine were OB-Gyn specialists. Some of Terry's colleagues told her that I would divorce her for choosing OB, or at least demand a separate bedroom when I read this part of the story. What they meant was that my sleep would be disturbed regularly because of the many night calls that obstetricians receive.

No chance. I was totally in love with my wife. Terry and I had met over a cadaver four years before, in a gross anatomy class as freshmen students in medical school at the University of Minnesota in 1943. I had seen and admired her earlier, while taking physical chemistry as a third year pre-medical student, but had not met her. In gross anatomy, four students were assigned to each cadaver. My cadaver co-workers were Ethel Erickson, Richard Frey, and Robert Goldish. Ethel was one of five women in our class of 104 students and a good friend of Terry's. Ethel was a bit older than the rest of us, having trained and worked as a medical technologist before entering medical school, and she was a motherly, matchmaking type of woman. Somehow she surmised that Terry and I would make a good pair. She grabbed my hand and pulled me into the next room, where Terry was dissecting another cadaver with three other students. There stood Terry on one side of the cadaver, and there I stood on the other, both of us in greasy white gowns, with Ethel at the head, formally introducing us to one another. It was effective, because we soon started dating and were married three years later on September 21, 1946, while Terry was a senior medical student at the University of Minnesota and I was a rotating intern at MGH. I completed my internship June 30, 1947, and Terry started hers at MGH the next day (Figure 1a and 1b).

A rotating internship was one in which the intern moved from one specialty service to another, usually after four weeks, and included such specialties as internal medicine, surgery, orthopedics, pediatrics, obstetrics, gynecology, dermatology, emergency medicine, and contagion. The total length of an internship was typically twelve months, which was the case for Terry. (Mine was 15 months because of a wartime alteration of the schedule.) Adaptation (from medical student to intern) for Terry was not difficult because she had worked at MGH during her junior and senior years in medical school and, in contrast to many classmates who went off to other cities, she knew the city in which she interned. Some services, e.g. OB-Gyn, were split between hospitals, e.g. MGH and St. Mary's (a private hospital with many deliveries), in order to ensure an adequate experience. The new hospital environment complicated adaptation a bit, but not seriously.

Terry's first service, beginning July 1st, was internal medicine. Her supervisor (resident) was Dr. Frank Gouze, a fine internist, teacher, and person. He had supervised me one year earlier when I interned on the Internal Medicine Service. Chief of the service was George Fahr, sometimes called "God" (second in command was called "Jesus Christ"). Her next service was "receiving" for two weeks. This would correspond with the emergency room, emergency medicine, and admitting today, except the intern also rode the ambulance and hoped that the police got there first. She then went on OB-Gyn, two weeks of which were at St. Mary's Hospital, which had more deliveries. Eight more services followed and the internship ended on June 30th. A rotating internship contrasted with a straight internship where the intern would stay on a service, e.g. internal medicine, for the whole year. A straight internship was elected when the student had already decided to specialize. The term internship is not usually used today where most students specialize and stay on a service for the entire three to five years of a residency. The first year of post-graduate training is called Year 1 of the residency rather than internship.

Rio Hato Airfield
Republic of Panama
10 November 1947 (cont.)

Rio Hato

The B-17 landed uneventfully at Rio Hato. I was met at the plane by an ambulance sent by the medics to pick me up. They took me to the Officers' Club and briefed me on my new surroundings. They told me that Rio Hato Field was an American Army Air Force base (the Air Force was not yet an independent service). It was a B-29 bomber base in the Republic of Panama built during the war to help protect the Canal. There were other air bases at some distance from the Zone for the same purpose, e.g., in Columbia and in the Galapagos. Rio Hato had an Army personnel census of 800. However, there were considerably more people than that counting dependents and the approximately 580 Panamanians working at the base. As I had seen from the air, Rio Hato Field was situated on a beach, and I was told it was the best bathing beach in Panama. It certainly looked nice from the air.

Almost all of the buildings on the base, except for the Officers' Club, were temporary barracks-type construction. The foliage around them was pretty, however, not the jungle type I saw around the Canal. I was told that it was "cooler here, but not much. It rained like hell most every afternoon. Everyone bitched like hell when they heard they had been assigned here, but strangely enough, once they got here, didn't want to leave." I was skeptical. My cursory glance told me otherwise. There were no large towns around the base, only Panamanian villages. I was told that they were really primitive. The Officers' Club was nice; it was the only nice building in the area, on or off the base. I decided I would spend a lot of time in it.

The medics then took me to the BOQ (Figure 2). It was a two-story structure, and I was assigned a room on the ground floor. It was primitive, intended for transient officers, but it would have to suffice for several days until a permanent one on the second floor could be cleaned for me. The next day was a holiday, you see.

All buildings on the base, including the BOQ, were open, i.e., screened on all sides to keep the bugs out and roofed with large overhangs to keep the rain out. I could see that most of the occupants of the BOQ had mosquito nets over their beds. I was told they had had five cases of malaria in September. I saw warning signs all over the place, i.e., "stay indoors at night to avoid malaria" and "use your mosquito repellent, it may be sticky but relapsing malaria sticks worse." My net was still on its way in my barracks bag.

I was told, "There are no government quarters here for married couples. They rent quarters near the base from private landlords." What they were like I was not told. I saw many wives at the officers' club. I wondered how this would impact Terry's arrival when she finished her internship at the end of June. I got the impression the command was reluctant to send me to Rio Hato because I was married, and off quarter rental for married couples were hard to find. But they said that in 6-7 months there would be a possibility that I'd be sent back to the American Zone again since they needed an officer for internal medicine and noted my preference for that specialty on one of the forms I had filled out. I hoped that would be the case. Not that this was too bad a place to bring a wife - there were many there - but the American Zone would be much nicer. I was certain we'd enjoy ourselves more.

Most everyone went down to the Canal Zone on weekends or holidays for excitement. They either flew or drove. There was a good road leading to all the larger cities in and around the Zone, about 76 miles distant.

Figure 2- Rio Hato Airfield BOQ as viewed from the front of the dispensary.

There were three other medical officers at Rio Hato. One was said to be of Lebanese descent like me, but I hadn't yet met him to confirm. There was a dispensary with some bed patients, but I was told that all serious cases were flown to the US Canal Zone because "they don't have too much equipment here for major medicine." I heard that another medic, Lt. Breck, who traveled all the way from Fort Sam Houston to Camp Kilmer, to New Orleans, to Puerto Rico, and then to Panama in our group of ten might join us in Rio Hato. I hoped so. At least I would then know someone from before my arrival at Rio Hato.

Mail had been a problem. I had asked about mail at Albrook Field just before flying to Rio Hato and, lo and behold, I found three letters from Terry. I read them at least five times apiece. They were awfully sweet. I agreed that it was tough being apart - awfully tough, but I tried to reassure her that time would pass quickly and we'd soon be looking back on this unpleasant separation. Then we'd be glad she stayed home. After all, she needed to finish her internship, too. I was certain that more letters would show up soon. The three letters were written on the 26th and 27th of October and the 4th of November. Some others were probably sidetracked temporarily, understandable considering my circuitous recent travels.

One of Terry's letters contained a letter from my sister Juanita, who was in Lebanon with my father and mother, visiting my father's family. This was my parents' first visit there since emigrating in 1911. Juanita was my only unmarried sibling, and, as predicted, attracted many Lebanese suitors.

After writing a letter to Terry, I went upstairs in the BOQ, where two officers were holding an open house. Girls came in freely at any time, escorted by their dates. It turned out to be quite a "rugged" party. Drinks, laughter, songs, and off color jokes flowed freely. It reminded me of a fraternity party. I left early and turned in reflecting on Army marriages. I had been surprised by the behavior of some of the married women, who were traveling to join their husbands, with the enlisted men and male officers on the voyage from New Orleans to Panama. There was free admixture of men and women, and liaisons were not infrequent. This wouldn't happen to us. We were too much in love.

Rio Hato Airfield
Republic of Panama
11 November 1947

My Boss, A Tour Of Panama, And My Work Schedule

I felt a little better about the entire situation the next morning after having had a good day off. I was awakened about 10:00 a.m. by Captain Namay, the senior medical officer. He asked if I wanted to drive down to Panama City with him and his wife. Of course I said yes. He happened to be of Lebanese descent (confirming what I had been told the previous day), as was his wife. He said, "It's funny that the only two Lebanese in Panama end up in the same dispensary." I agreed.

He first drove me over to the little bungalow they called home. It wasn't luxurious, but adequate. They paid quite a price for it, since it was rented from a civilian landlady. Mrs. Namay was pleasant, and nice looking, too. Both of them were from Charleston, West Virginia. They had married six months previously, just before coming to Panama. They knew quite a few Lebanese people with whom I was slightly acquainted, some of whom were distant relatives. So we got along fine. Not that we wouldn't have anyway, but our common background speeded up the process a bit.

We drove the 75 miles to the American Zone on a good, new, paved road, built by the Americans for the Republic of Panama. The roadside was beautiful - tropical foliage interspersed between little villages of straw-roofed huts. Once in the vicinity of the Zone, we went sightseeing. We drove through Panama City and Balboa. About two hours of the day was spent shopping in downtown Panama City, which was just outside the Zone. I was impressed with the things to buy — alligator bags and shoes, snake skin bags and shoes, silver jewelry, and many other items. I considered whether they would interest Terry. After having a drink at a hotel, we went to Albrook Field for dinner. None of this took much time because distances were not great. On the way back to Rio Hato, we picked up two US soldiers who had lived in Panama most of their lives. They proudly offered Panamanian history (of questionable accuracy, I suspect); much of it concerned an English knight-pirate named Henry Morgan who conquered the area sometime in the sixteen hundreds. We, in fact, drove through the ruins of "Old Panama," which included cathedrals and other buildings destroyed by fire after Morgan took over.

We got back to the base about 8:00 p.m. and, after going to the Club for some cigarettes and turning in my laundry, I wrote to Terry.

The trip was enjoyable for several reasons — congenial company, a new car, and talk about Terry (that was fun). Mrs. Namay was one of those persons who gray early. She looked nice partially silvered on top. She did a bit of back seat driving. Dr. Namay took it very calmly, though. I thought to myself, lucky Terry doesn't do that because I doubt if I'd take it so graciously.

Another reason for feeling a bit better was that I now knew what to expect in my work schedule. Namay told me I'd have enough work to keep me busy most of the day. In fact, the dispensary had enough work to keep four medics busy most of the day. That included much one finds in a general practice, a lot of pediatrics, some prenatal work (not deliveries; they were sent out), a lot of skin, etc. He said they also had a small library. I should expect to be at work at 7:00 a.m. each morning; the work day started early and ended fairly early. Finally, I thought Namay, the chief, had a good impression of me. Everyone seemed very friendly. I guess they had to be friendly. There wasn't much else to do.

I had to check in at headquarters the next day, to fill out a lot of forms. I also planned to apply for Terry's transportation, housing, and an ice box, so that everything would be set when my baby came home.

One negative. Namay verified that regulations said I couldn't go back to the States for a year, but he also said, "We can get around that." He thought a Mexico City meeting was a good idea.

It was damp in Rio Hato — particularly that time of year. Clothing became moldy very easily, I was told. To combat the mold, people kept a special light burning continuously in each closet; this did the trick. The days were warm and sticky. I feared Terry wouldn't like that. Strangely enough, it cooled off beautifully at night in this part of Panama. I slept under a sheet and wool blanket the first night.

I hoped Terry would write often. I was going to need her letters. I decided to tell her that again.

Minneapolis General Hospital
Minneapolis, Minnesota
12 November 1947

MGH OB-GYN

While I was getting settled, Terry was again having a busy but educational time. While the previous day was a holiday (Armistice Day, now known as Veterans' Day), and she had done little else but think about our separation, the evening before had been busy indeed. She had admitted only two patients, an OB (obstetrical) and a GC PID (gonococcal pelvic inflammatory disease), but they had kept her up until 5:00 a.m. The OB was a multipara (one or more previous deliveries), so she called the anesthetist and delivery room personnel and set her up in the delivery room when the cervix dilated to 6 cm. However, the head presented in a persistent posterior (backward) position and therefore progress was very slow; the cervix did not become fully dilated and thus ready for the baby to be delivered until four hours later. Terry was razzed for keeping all those people waiting around for hours. The patient was also unusual for another reason; she began to bleed from a premature separation of the placenta near the end of the first stage of labor. Dr. Baker did a very smooth Scanzoni's maneuver (a method of forceps rotation of the fetal head when it is in the posterior position of the occiput) and delivered the baby quickly. The baby and the mother were just fine. The patient with a PID was a prostitute. This was not unusual at MGH, but it was rare to find one who would admit it. They usually called themselves hostesses or something similar.

Terry was getting a liberal education. Many of the women who came in on the OB & Gyn service had sordid histories. Another of her patients had pediculosis pubis (genital "crabs"). When Terry told her the diagnosis, she asked, "Is that bad?" So many of the poor girls she was seeing, she said, had nothing upon which to build a foundation of security and happiness.

Terry reported in her letter that the weather was very cold. There was snow on the ground, and more snow kept falling. It was pleasant to sit indoors by the fire and look out at the snow covering the trees and lawn. She wished, though, that I was sitting by the fire with her.

Rio Hato Airfield
Republic of Panama
12 November 1947

The Dispensary

Today was my first day of work and I learned a lot. I was at the dispensary at 7:00 a.m. and Capt. Namay immediately showed me around. The building was a wooden two story structure (Figure 3). The bottom floor consisted of two examining rooms, an emergency room, an x-ray room (for chest and bones only), a laboratory (for blood counts, smears for malaria, and fecal parasites only), several administrative offices, and a sleeping and reading room for the corpsman on call at night. One of the offices contained

Figure 3a-Rio Hato Airfield dispensary and one of the three ambulances in 1947.

Figure 3b- Rio Hato Airfield dispensary with four of the corpsmen in 1947.

a small library of medical books. Most of them were printed in 1942 or 1943. The dispensary also received medical journals each month but they were kept only ten days, after which they were sent on to another dispensary in the Zone. Upstairs was a dentistry suite and, surprisingly, about twenty beds. This dispensary was actually a small temporary hospital, although its beds never filled up. We only kept the less serious cases — the rest were sent on to the Zone by plane or ambulance.

Seven a.m. was sick call for soldiers and 7:30 a.m. was sick call for civilians but patients kept straggling in all day. I was actually quite pleased with what I saw. There was much more than I expected because dispensaries are rarely so complete. The reason, of course, was that fully staffed and equipped hospitals were 75 miles away. There were two female nurses, about 20 corpsmen, and four medical officers working at Rio Hato.

When the tour was over, Namay negotiated a jeep and driver to take me around the base to "check in." I went to about ten different offices to complete the administrative requirements. Lots of red tape - finance (allotments and pay), personnel, postoffice (five cent U.S. airmail stamps were OK in either direction; I was using ten cent ones temporarily just because I had some on hand), officers club, billeting, SI (I hadn't a clue) and S3 (ditto). When I finished, I had the driver take me to the PX, where I bought a few articles - socks, tobacco, khaki trousers (to be delivered), etc. After that I went to an officers' meeting which occurred every Wednesday at 10:30 a.m. Boring. Wednesday afternoon was off for most everyone on the base. So I didn't do any medical work my first day.

In the afternoon I walked down to the beach (Figure 4) which was only about 200 yards from the BOQ. It was really terrific. I knew Terry would like it when she saw it. The sand was the finest I'd ever seen and the breakers were nice and gentle. I hoped to spend a lot of time at the beach as soon as my footlocker containing my swimsuit arrived.

I then moved from my temporary room of the BOQ to one

upstairs. It had taken some time to clean it; that's why they didn't put me in it right away. It was far from deluxe but adequate for a bachelor. Again, it was a small square room with a closet in which a light burned continuously to keep the mold out of the clothing. One outside wall was entirely screened.

The walls between rooms were paper and didn't reach to the ceiling (like a cow's stanchion) so that my room was not really separated from other rooms. I could throw things over the walls at the other fellows. A sink, bunk, desk, and chairs completed the room.

I was told to shake out all items of my clothing before putting them on. Scorpions sometimes found them to be a comfortable home and didn't appreciate having it invaded by a hand or a foot. Their stings could be nasty.

I filled out application forms to get Terry to Rio Hato and also forms to get on the married officers' quarters list immediately — five copies! I'd probably be at the top of the list by July — but the quarters application was only for the U.S. Zone 75 miles away. I applied just in case I was moved there; we would then need government quarters. In Rio Hato, married officers' quarters were negotiated privately on the concerned person's own initiative.

I had one of the corpsmen type a letter requesting application blanks from the Mayo Clinic for a fellowship in internal medicine. I also asked Terry to find my premedical and medical school blue prints (grade transcripts) and a photograph, which I knew I would need for the application. Premedicine blue prints were split between two schools. I attended Luther College in Decorah, Iowa, for two academic years and one summer session (1940-1942). I then completed my premedical training at the University of Minnesota in Minneapolis, Minnesota (1942-1943), in order to obtain credits in physical chemistry, a requirement for medical school, which was not available at Luther College. I entered the University of Minnesota Medical School in April of 1943 and, with continuous attendance, including summers, graduated in March of 1946. It was these transcripts I needed to apply for a

Figure 4- The beach and pier at Rio Hato, just 200 yards from the BOQ.

fellowship (residency) in internal medicine at the Mayo Foundation (the education and research component of the Mayo Clinic) in Rochester, Minnesota, following my army experience, whenever that would end.

World War II was being fought at the time of my premedical and medical school training and the military services decided to induct all of the male medical students via one of two mechanisms, the Army Specialized Training Program (ASTP) and the Navy V12 Program. The students destined to be in the ASTP were one day in April 1943 taken to Fort Snelling, issued uniforms, and sent back to medical school later that same day. I was living in Pioneer Hall at the time, a men's dormitory. We were subsequently housed in a girls' dormitory (Sanford Hall), a grade school (Motley School), Pioneer Hall again, and then, during our junior and senior years, allowed to live wherever we wanted, including fraternities and hospitals (for clerkships and externships). During this entire period we were in uniform and received the pay of a private first class as well as the usual other benefits but were allowed to function as medical students as long as we maintained the proper grade point average. The women in the class, including Terry, were not part of any such program and therefore paid the entire cost of their education themselves. This accounted for the fact that Terry graduated a year after me; she dropped out between the sophomore and junior years to make money to pay tuition. The benefits received by the men generated a pay back provision of two years of active duty and accounted for my being in Panama in 1947 following my internship and the receipt of my M.D. degree.

I concluded I would like Rio Hato more than I initially thought. I was happy about the dispensary. It would keep me busy. The beach was terrific. I didn't seem to mind the heat much at all, though it was now cooler than usual. Every one was friendly. Believe it or not, on Wednesday afternoons (which were free of scheduled work), they flew personnel in a special plane down to the Zone just to play golf. The colonel was a golf addict. They had tennis courts and archery. The country side was really beautiful. But it was damp all the time and the quarters were pretty punk. However, I now felt better about Rio Hato than I did when I arrived. Terry might like it. I wished my baby was in Rio Hato now.

I didn't have to pay for my room at the BOQ. The government was supposed to supply "adequate quarters" for its officers. Ours were considered "adequate" for a single man but inadequate for a married man. So I didn't pay. It cost me about $45 a month to eat at the officers club (Figure 5), however. At that time all of the officers were eating in the enlisted men's mess at 30¢ a meal because the dining room in the club was being fumigated (overrun with roaches). We were told we'd be back in the Officers' Club in a week.

I was reading periodicals in the dispensary after dinner when a patient came in with throat trouble. Namay was on call but rather than have him come over from his home, I saw the young man — my first patient! I thought he was a bit neurotic, however. I continued to read my EKG (electrocardiogram) book in my spare time; to date I had covered about half of the 500 pages. The medics said they were going to make me the "EKG man" when the machine returned from the repair shop. I laughed but secretly thought I could do it better than anyone else at Rio Hato.

Namay said he would put Terry to work on the peds (pediatrics) cases when she comes down. I didn't know if he was serious but he said he'd sign her up as a typist but use her as an M.D. That way she'd make as much as I. I really missed her.

Figure 5- Officers' Club.

Minneapolis General Hospital
Minneapolis, Minnesota
16 November 1947

More OB's And A Perineal Laceration

It had been several days since Terry had written me and she felt like such a heel. She had planned to write a long letter but her next letter was probably going to be short — just long enough to tell me she loved me.

Life had been rugged these last few days. Dr. Baker was a wonderful teacher and a nice guy, but he did keep Terry and Elaine on the jump. Terry had only eight to nine OBs during the month but most of them had been unusual in some way. Yesterday she had a III° laceration. She didn't feel too responsible because Dr. McCaffrey stood behind her and kibitzed every inch of the way. She told him that she thought the episiotomy was too small and should be made larger, but he said "no" and so the baby went on to emerge from the birth canal and its head ripped the vaginal mucosa. Well anyway, she guessed Baker said "laceration" to her at least four times during her next delivery. Elaine and Terry didn't feel that they were doing very well on OB.

Sleep had been very scarce. Yesterday Terry shopped with her mother who bought a black dress with silver sequins. Terry bought a little gold chain on which to hang her ring while scrubbing for surgery. She also looked at watches with a sweep second hand, which is essential for a physician. She then went to bed at 8:00 p.m. and slept the clock around.

Terry's next letter to me was in fact short — just long enough to tell me she could write on for pages about her love for me and to reassure me that I never need worry about her while I was gonc.

Beirut, Lebanon
6 November 1947

My Parents in Lebanon

Terry enclosed a letter sent to us at her home. It was written by my mother on 6 November 1947 in Beirut, Lebanon, where my father and mother and my sister Juanita were negotiating their ship passage back to the USA on the 15th of November. They had just attended a wedding in my father and mother's home village,

Figure 6-My father and grandmother in Lebanon just prior to his return home to Hollywood.

Ain Arab. The celebrating started three days before the wedding and was still going on. They planned to return to Ain Arab for final farewells which would be particularly hard on my father's mother since she was aging and realized that this would be the last time she would see her son.

In the letter, my mother said she hoped Terry could meet them in Cedar Rapids, Iowa, where they intended to stop to see relatives on their way home to Los Angeles. Cedar Rapids was not too far from Minneapolis; they would call Terry when they made that stop.

Hollywood, California
6 July 1947

My Trip To Hollywood

I had last seen my parents in July, just after completing my internship at Minneapolis General Hospital. I had traveled to Los Angeles for a visit, knowing that I faced two years in the service, potentially any place on the globe. After that visit, the Army placed me on active duty, first in Texas then sequentially in New Jersey, Louisiana, and Panama. The Los Angeles trip and visit was from 6 July 1947 to 28 July 1947 and I traveled there with my medical school classmate and fraternity (Kappa Chi of Phi Chi) brother, Lyle Jacobson. Lyle was in the Navy V12 program in medical school and had just completed his internship at Detroit Receiving Hospital. He too was being placed on active duty, in his case in the Navy. He was to report for induction in San Diego. Lyle had a not-too-new Ford sedan which he decided to drive to San Diego. He asked me to accompany him. We and three other fraternity brothers had driven the very same vehicle to Los Angeles once before (over Christmas vacation, 1945) attesting to its maturity and to Lyle's and my immaturity with respect to judging the car's probability of surviving the proposed trip. Sure enough, the motor overheated and blew a water hose while climbing mountains in

Wyoming, and the generator started screaming and stopped functioning between Las Vegas and Los Angeles (I brought the generator partially back to life by using Vaseline hair oil as a lubricant). I was really impressed by the food, shows, gambling, and glitter in Las Vegas, particularly the Flamingo Club, formerly owned by "Bugsy" Siegel, the gambler who was shot shortly before we arrived.

We reached my parents' home in Los Angeles about 3 p.m., 10 July 1947, cleaned up, and ate with them and Juanita on the back verandah. Relatives and friends dropped by in the evening and later, Juanita drove Jake and me about Hollywood, showing us the sights. The next day Jake left for San Diego. He made quite a hit with mom and dad. They liked him a lot. Jake thought the family market was really quite wonderful. He was especially taken with the liquor department supervised by Joe, my brother. Joe took us with him when he made several deliveries to elaborate residences in the Hollywood hills, including one owned by Wallace Beery, using my brother-in-law John's impressive Buick convertible. Jake liked that and he liked my family as well. In fact, three days later I received a phone call from Jake and two of his friends. They had driven up from San Diego for some recreation and joined us at my sister Lucille's apartment. We partied there until 11 p.m. and then we four boys went down to Earl Carrol's for a floor show and dancing. The club was known for its out of town trade; about 90% of the customers were from places other than Los Angeles.

This was Terry's and my first separation since marrying in 1946 and we both found it difficult and unpleasant. It was soon obvious that I had planned too long a stay in Los Angeles and too many stops on my way back home. I had many close relatives in Los Angeles, in addition to my parents, including a brother and three sisters, and they entertained me royally. That helped but did not lessen my missing Terry.

One evening at my brother Joe's house, I tried on his extensive army wardrobe. His uniforms fit me perfectly and he gave the clothing to me. What a saving that was for me. My brother had been an officer in a tank destroyer unit during WWII and had been released less than 2 years previously. The uniforms were therefore still in style and in excellent condition.

I tried to find time to write a manual for premedical students concerning medical school applications, ethics, and other matters and in fact wrote a forward and a chapter on medical ethics. Social activities with relatives didn't leave quality time for concentration, however, and the book didn't progress further.

Time was spent arranging my parents' passage to Lebanon and my travel back to Minneapolis. I received more detailed travel orders from the Army while in Los Angeles. A telegram said I was to report to Fort Sam Houston, San Antonio, Texas, on August 21st for temporary duty until further assignment. I therefore made train reservations on the City of Los Angeles leaving Los Angeles on Sunday July 27th and arriving in Cedar Rapids, Iowa, on Tuesday morning July 29th, where I had a sister Vernita. The plan was to then go to Kiester, Minnesota, my home town, Albert Lea, Minnesota, near my home town, and finally Joice, Iowa, where I had another sister, Beatrice. I hoped to have Terry meet me in Joice, from whence we'd travel back to Minneapolis together.

I spent some time with Dr. George Nicola, a young surgeon and a relative. At one time he'd been team physician for U.S.C. and had taken me on the football field with him. I thought he was interested in me as an eventual partner.

Minneapolis General Hospital
Minneapolis, Minnesota
8 July 1947

First Service, "Tarry" Stools, Graphology

While I was in Los Angeles, Terry was adjusting to her rotating internship at MGH and to her first service, internal medicine. She seemed to be happier at MGH than at the University Hospital where she had worked as a medical student.

She occasionally encountered patients that I had seen when I interned on internal medicine at MGH the previous year. One such patient was an elderly man with "tarry" (black and sticky) stools, which suggested bleeding from high up in the gastrointestinal tract. However, his hemoglobin and x-rays of the stomach and duodenum were normal. Dr. Fahr, chief of service, complained in conference about "incompetent interns (me) who don't know what a tarry stool is!" The patient was sent back to x-ray for fluoroscopy of the aorta and esophagus. Dr. Gouze, the resident physician, thought the patient might have an obstructing esophageal lesion.

Dr. Gouze looked at the handwriting on my history and physical examination, filed in the patient's chart, and said that the handwriting indicated I was a "vigorous, ambitious person with definite ideas of my own." It also indicated that I was changeable but not temperamental (I hadn't heard that before, though a Minnesota multi phasic test several years earlier indicated I had a borderline psychopathic personality). Dr. Gouze said graphology was one of his hobbies. Besides being a nice person and an excellent internist and teacher, he also had a sense of humor. He gave Terry a bottle of vitamin-yeast tablets to send to me. He said that after taking them I "could float along instead of walking."

Minneapolis General Hospital
Minneapolis, Minnesota
15 July 1947

MONEY PROBLEMS

Terry said she dreamed of me the night before last. She dreamed that I came home unexpectedly and woke her out of a sound sleep to tell her that my orders had come and that I'd been assigned to an airport in Iowa, only 50 miles from home. She only wished it were true. So did I.

Both of us worried about money. The intern salary at MGH was $15 per month plus room and board and I was essentially unemployed until I was placed on active duty. Terry needed $5-

$10 for dry cleaning and money for her train fare to Joice. I sent her $10 cash and a small check. I also received from my father $600 in war bonds and my life insurance policies.

Minneapolis General Hospital
Minneapolis, Minnesota
16 July 1947

"Tarry" Stools Continued

Terry again said her internship was fine. She really liked it at MGH and she was sure that she'd continue to do so. She said the elderly patient with the black "tarry" stools and negative occult stool blood test had an esophagram and a large cancer was found in the lower portion of the esophagus. He must really have had melena (blood in the stool). She guessed the laboratory could be wrong. As usual, Dr. Gouze was right. He was flying high for another reason. His wife had a baby girl yesterday. They had hoped for a boy, but he was going to keep the girl "because babies are hard to get."

Minneapolis General Hospital
Minneapolis, Minnesota
22 July 1947

Complex Schedule

Terry's letter to me said she was sorry but she was unable to meet me in Joice, Iowa, at my sister Beatrice's home on my return from Hollywood. She also said she would write a letter of explanation to Bea. Terry had just found out that her next rotation (service) would be "receiving" (emergency room) for the first half of August and then St. Mary's Hospital for the second half of that month for OB. Her schedule was complicated. She had a free 24 hours every fourth day. The first day she worked from 8:00 a.m. to 6:00 p.m. The second day she worked from 6:00 p.m. to 8:00 a.m. She then had 4 hours to sleep. Following that, she worked from 12:00 noon until 12:00 midnight. She would then take second call (in reserve behind the intern on first call) from 12:00 midnight until 8:00 a.m. of the fourth day. Then the cycle would repeat itself. It looked to her like it would be almost impossible to break away. She would hate to ask anyone to take her extra calls. In addition, she'll be new on the service and wouldn't even know which part of the rotation would be her beginning. In a letter to Terry on 26 July 1947, I expressed my disappointment but I knew that being on receiving made it difficult. I knew how hard it was to get a substitute on that service. I encouraged her to write Bea an explanatory letter; I would do likewise. In fact I would probably decide to skip Joice all together, allowing me to get home early (Wednesday or Thursday). I would be able to stay home until August 19th at least because I didn't have to report until the 21st.

Hollywood, California
23 July, 1947

MORE GRAPHOLOGY

I joined friends and relatives on a trip into old Los Angeles to Alverado street, the first street constructed in Los Angeles. It had gradually turned into somewhat of a Mexican carnival. Very pleasant. I had a lady read my handwriting. She told me I began writing left handed but now wrote with the right hand but did most everything else with my left, that I was interested in either engineering or medicine. Pretty good, eh? She advised me to specialize. Ha!

Minneapolis General Hospital
Minneapolis, Minnesota
24 July 1947

MYELOMA

Terry stayed at the hospital overnight so that she could attend journal club and hear Dr. Gouze speak. She didn't want to go home in the dark (the area around MGH was not safe for unaccompanied women to walk after sunset).

She also said that a patient I had seen last year was presented at conference. The patient had pleomorphic multiple myeloma, a disseminated plasma cell cancer characterized by widespread lesions of the bones. She overheard someone say that my job of originally writing up the case was well done.

Minneapolis General Hospital
Minneapolis, Minnesota
25 July 1947

Clinical Skills

Terry wrote her last letter to me in Hollywood and said a medical school classmate and fraternity brother and fellow member of ASTP, Andreen Sylvain Midthune ("Andy"), had called to say he and Odd Arvid Eide (another classmate, "brother" and ASTP member) also had to be at Fort Sam Houston for a month of instruction on August 21. Andy said he might be able to get his dad's car and then we could all drive together. He and Carol, his wife, were traveling to Minneapolis on August 10 and would contact us at that time.

Terry felt good about her clinical skills. She had seen a fresh flame hemorrhage in an eye ground during a fundiscopic examination. Dr. Gouze congratulated her for picking it up! He had talked about transfusion reactions that night before and it was instructive. George Fahr, a famous internist and staff member, was there and as usual had much to say during the discussion period. Fahr was coauthor with Einthoven in Germany on the first paper to describe the electrocardiogram. (In the early nineteen hundreds, studying medicine in Germany was very much the thing to do.) Fahr was a great and critical teacher and once berated me on rounds for saying the patient "had a coronary" instead of saying he had a "myocardial infarction." He said "of course he had a coronary—everyone has a coronary (artery)." However, he later agreed to write a letter of reference for me when I applied to the Mayo Clinic for a fellowship and expressed interest in my observations on malaria.

Hollywood, California
26 July 1947

Chaos

I spent the day with dad making arrangements for his trip to Lebanon. What a mess! It was no small matter arranging passage for three, particularly because the time was so short. I also packed for my trip home. This also was no small matter since I had to include all of Joe's army clothes in a footlocker lent to me and I had to check all the luggage 24 hours before departure.

John Haddy, my brother-in-law (married to my oldest sister Elizabeth), took Elizabeth, Selma (my mother's sister), Juanita, Donald Shaheen (my cousin) and me to the Outdoor Greek Theater in Griffith Park (just below the observatory) to see and hear Blossom Time. It was a light opera with Schubert's melodies, beautifully done, and I enjoyed it immensely. But it made me lonesome for Terry; anything that moved me, even a little, made me think of her.

John, George (my sister Lucille's husband), Joe, Donald and I went to a baseball game — Hollywood played Las Vegas.

The Haddy household was in an uproar. Dad had just heard that, if he, mom, and Juanita wanted to go Lebanon, they'd have to leave from New York August 13th. Arranging passports, business, finances, clothing, household, etc. in the short time left generated a lot of activity, much of it confusing. Everyone, including me, was tense. I decided it was time to go home.

That time was fast approaching. The next night the entire family gathered for a farewell barbecue in my father's back yard and the next day I boarded a train for Cedar Rapids, Iowa, where my sister Vernita lived. She was a twin to my sister Juanita in Los Angeles. From there I went home to Terry.

Rio Hato Airfield
Republic of Panama
14 November 1947

First Sick Call

After finishing my first day of work in the dispensary, I thought I was going to be completely satisfied professionally. I had taken sick call in the morning with Capt. Nunnelley (Namay took his car to the Zone for some maintenance work). We started at 7:00 a.m. and finished about 11 a.m. It was a lot like a small private practice. We saw infants, children, women, soldiers, Panamanians, fly boys — everything you would ever want to see. I dealt with gynecology, pediatrics, ear, nose, and throat, minor surgery, and lots of dermatology, just in this one morning. Even a fracture. And plenty of psychiatry. And praise be, there was no administrative work for me. There was a medical administration officer, Captain Phillips, to handle the paperwork. He was not a medic (physician). Of course, Namay had some administrative chores since he was the chief. But Nunnelley and I had none. I didn't meet the fourth medic. He was in Peru temporarily with another doctor. We were expecting still another medic, bringing the total to five soon. The more the merrier, I figured.

Nunnelley was a fine fellow. He trained at LSU in Louisiana. He was a bit hypomanic but pleasantly so. Everyone loved him. He was interested in psychiatry and internal medicine. Since Namay and Alpier (the guy in Peru) were "cut and dried" surgeons, Nunnelley said he was glad I came to help him hold up his end. The guy had just got a new Buick convertible, almost exactly like the one Elizabeth and John Haddy (my sister and brother-in-law) had in Los Angeles — it was super. Nunnelley took me for a ride and promised me more. I thought he might turn out to be my Panama pal, especially since Namay was quite reserved and seemed all business.

It was nice having the dispensary so compact. For example, I saw a classical case of tinea cruris ("jock itch"), scraped some of the scales from the lesion on to a microscope slide, sent upstairs for some 10% NaOH from the pharmacy, stepped across the hall into the laboratory and prepared the slide and read it under the microscope. I actually found the fungus — the boys were quite impressed when I said "would you like to see some Epidermophyton infunoli fungi?"

I spent an hour at headquarters finishing the check-in process and after lunch I waded through a line of prospective customers to get a haircut (there was an inspection the next day). After that I went back to the dispensary and saw a couple more patients. The nurses and corpsmen were giving infants and children their routine shots so, of course, the mothers had to kill two birds with one stone and see the doctor about Willi's cold, too. But mainly, we spent the afternoon doing things of more interest to us, including seeing the few bed patients upstairs in the "hospital."

I thought I should receive a large batch of mail from Terry soon. I had outdistanced it in my travels but it should have almost caught up with me by now.

Nunnelley, of his own accord, said he'd sure push the idea of putting Terry to work in the dispensary — with pay of course. I thought that would be fun, Terry and me working together. I had no doubt that we would work something out, even though Nunnelley would be gone by then (he was due for discharge in March). Namay also thought the idea was workable.

I was on night time call. Taking call in Rio Hato was nothing like taking call at MGH. We had no seriously ill patients in the "hospital," so only accidents and sudden severe illness generated calls. The corpsmen took care of minor problems that came up at night or tried to delay treatment until sick call in the morning.

It got very warm in Rio Hato during the day but I was actually chilly at 7:30 p.m. while writing a letter to Terry. I told her I slept under blankets each night and the coolness of the night was one reason why Rio Hato was preferable to the Zone. As isolated as Rio Hato was, I had yet to hear of an officer who didn't like living at Rio Hato. That wasn't true for some of the enlisted men.

However, the officers wouldn't trade the Zone for Rio Hato. I thought I was going to like Rio Hato too, thank heaven. I told Terry to keep looking forward — straight at our meeting in Mexico City. That was our goal and we would make it. One could do anything with the correct amount of incentive and Terry was many times more than enough.

Rio Hato Airfield
Republic of Panama
18 November 1947

Settling In

I was gradually getting used to work in the Rio Hato dispensary. Saturday morning was rather slow. We didn't hold sick call until 11:00 a.m. on Saturday in order to keep as many malingerers away as possible. Formation and marching were held that morning and if sick call were held at 7:00 a.m., as usual, we would be flooded with low back aches, headaches, etc. By holding sick call at 11:00 a.m., we avoided most of them since formation was over by then. However, dependents kept slowly dribbling in all morning at a speed that just kept us comfortably busy.

Fungus infections were very commonplace, reflecting the very warm, damp environmental conditions in Rio Hato. Otomycosis (fungus infection of the ear canal) was probably the most common fungus infection. The treatment was creosote and thymol on a cotton wick placed in the ear canal. The other medics said it worked well. Then, of course, athlete's foot was common, as was tinea cruris (jock itch).

I was following a case of chronic glomerulonephritis in a young, married woman who had had two caesarean sections for toxemia of pregnancy and who was finally sterilized a year previously. She was now hypertensive (elevated blood pressure) and had much albumin in the urine, indicating kidney damage. She was about two weeks past her period, which had always been regular, calling the sterilization procedure into question in my mind. I decided to do urinary concentration and PSP (phenolsulfonphthalein) tests of kidney function as soon as I could get the laboratory geared up to run them. I thought since I was going to be at Rio Hato awhile, I might as well start some new procedures.

While writing to Terry Sunday evening, I was interrupted by a call from the dispensary. I was taking calls for Nunnelley since he went to the Zone to get his car checked. The case was most probably malaria, the second case of malaria we had had since I'd arrived at Rio Hato. I made some blood smears since he was at the height of his fever, but I couldn't see anything abnormal on them with the microscope. But clinically he had malaria, a disease endemic to Central America, including Panama. It is caused by intracellular protozoa of the genus Plasmoduim (P.). Examination of blood under the microscope reveals them in the red blood cell. There are four types, P. falciparum, P. malariae, P. ovale, and P. vivox, usually transmitted by the bites of infected anopheles mosquitos. Malaria is characterized by prostration and periods of high fever, shaking chills, sweating, anemia, and enlarged spleen, which may lead to death, often from its most severe complication, cerebral malaria. P. falciparum malaria has the highest blood levels of the protozoa and was the most severe form of malaria, sometimes called malignant malaria, causing death due to plugging of the little blood vessels. This was the type seen most often in Panama. When I wrote George Fahr, the well respected internist at MGH, requesting a letter of reference for my application for a fellowship at the Mayo Clinic, I mentioned that falciparum malaria was the commonest type in Rio Hato. He found this interesting and commented on it in his return letter to me (Figure 28).

On the other hand, I was told that there were no cases of yellow fever, the plague that prevented the French from completing the canal. Yellow fever ("yellow jack") is an acute destructive infectious disease of warm regions marked by sudden onset, prostration, fever, albuminuria (protein in the urine), jaundice, and often hemorrhage and is caused by a virus transmitted by a mosquito (Aëdes aegypti). Walter Reed and his colleagues conquered yellow fever by destroying the breeding grounds of the mosquito, thus allowing the canal to be built.

I was also told that the Caribbean venereal disease rate was among the highest of all the army theatres, a fact which later led us to heroic measures in an attempt to reduce it.

Nunnelley was certainly an interesting fellow. He was bursting with energy — a typical hypomanic. But he was also refreshing and witty. He was about 30 years old and well educated, having spent five years in college before going to medical school. He told me he was divorced, but he didn't elaborate. It seemed to me that it would take quite a women to keep up with him! He was just like a kid over his new car, which was understandable. It was a beauty. The two of us had fun Saturday afternoon. After polishing his car, we went swimming at our beach. As advertised, it was terrific, though a couple of breakers caught me unawares and hurled me to the sand a couple of times. If you didn't keep your eyes open, the breakers nearly drowned you. I saw a lot of stingrays in the shallow water, some half buried in the sand. I had to watch were I stepped. I was told stings were painful and hard to treat since they frequently became infected.

Nunnelley gave me a very good book to read, *The Fountainhead*, by Ayn Rand. I found it was about young, struggling, New York architects, very long, and captivating. I couldn't keep away from it, reading most of the previous evening and the next day. I asked Terry to read it. I was anxious for her opinion of the book. Nunnelley was fast becoming a good friend.

Namay, on the other hand, was more reserved and was little to be seen outside of working hours. Perhaps this related to his newlywed status, something with which I could understand and sympathize.

I told Terry, tongue in cheek, that I was broken-hearted because Iowa beat Minnesota in football, an unexpected result based on past performances. Maybe Minnesota was lucky up until they met up with Iowa. Sporting events back in the States were followed closely on the base, a tonic for boredom and homesickness. Eating also helped. The meals at the Officers' Club were excellent, in marked contrast to the food we had been eating in the mess. We switched back to the Club yesterday. There was a wild parrot flying around the Officer's Club at all times. It scared us to death with is incoherent shriek when we weren't expecting it.

Thus far I found life at Rio Hato quite pleasant, except for my longing for Terry. I saw that my life was going to be sedate. I had lots of time to be alone, to think, and to do whatever I wanted. I enjoyed that, I found. But there were moments — only moments — when I felt shut off and lonesome. As long as I kept busy reading and puttering around in the dispensary, I thought life would be livable until I saw Terry again. I told Terry to try to determine when she could get some time off so I could start to plan that most enjoyable and exciting meeting.

Figure 7-Terry.

Minneapolis General Hospital
Minneapolis, Minnesota
17 and 19 November 1947

OB—Terry's Background

Terry was still being educated in the behavior of women on the OB-Gyn service. Abortions, spontaneous and induced, were frequent. In one of her letters to me, she called it the OB and AB service and said the service was making her lose faith in women, too, referring to my observations on the ship to Panama. On the 19th, Terry did a D&C (dilation of the cervix and scraping the uterus) by herself and found it to be "fun." She hadn't delivered more than four or five babies by herself, but she hoped to have a few more. There had been a little fussing on the OB-Gyn service the previous day. They had a laparotomy (opening the abdomen to explore organs) to do and they got started late. The patient had very difficult veins. Elaine started the intravenous solution while Terry scrubbed. It took Elaine some time, through no fault of hers, and Drs. Baker and McCaffrey, the resident physicians, both blew off a little steam. Elaine went up to her room and we were both rather cool to them for the rest of the day. Baker later apologized to her. Terry thought both of their resident physicians would be a little more courteous in the future. In her opinion, they had both done an uncalled-for amount of nagging over small details.

Like me, Terry was confident of her skills as a physician, and almost always slept soundly, rarely suffering anxiety over past or imminent professional activities. She had trained under excellent teachers in a reputable medical school and she was raised in the tradition of high quality medical service. She attended grade school and high school in Wabasso, Minnesota, where her father had an active general practice and her mother worked alongside him as a nurse. Her father had graduated from the University of Minnesota in 1910 and her mother received her certificate in nursing from Rochester State Hospital, a psychiatric institution. Her father was in general practice in Wabasso, a small town in western Minnesota, for approximately 30 years. He provided high quality medical care, not hesitating to refer patients to the Mayo Clinic when he encountered problems outside his expertise. He served as Terry's role model and encouraged her to apply to medical school when she expressed interest, even though women in medicine were few in number. He died prematurely in 1940.

Terry said many people at MGH asked about me every day and she responded by telling them about my new post. Dr. Baker had some good things to say about my abilities and, according to Terry, he was usually not very free with compliments. Dr. Litman said his brother was stationed in Panama and that civilian doctors were in demand there, especially pediatricians. Dr. Binder told her to remind me to take my atabrine. Terry said she didn't think she would care too much for a yellow husband, but if it was in my best interest, she guessed it would be alright. The fact of the matter was, we didn't take atabrine at Rio Hato, but depended more on spraying, screening, and Bug-Off.

Rio Hato Airfield
Republic of Panama
17 November 1947

A Cloudburst Of Letters; Wanting; Eyes

I felt wonderful; I had received five letters from Terry, all written some time ago (Oct 20, 22, 24-25, Nov 7-8). I thought they were beautiful, particularly the one written on November 7th while at the hospital in which she demonstrated the depth of her sentimentality in explaining how hard it was to be apart. I responded by saying it was also hard for me. It seemed that life was just one continuous want, always striving to create something. Never completely satisfied. Reaching one goal and immediately wanting another. It was enough to generate a neurosis in even a stable person. But, then, perhaps life wouldn't be interesting if we stopped wanting something. Even so, I thought that once Terry was with me again I'd be as near satisfied as any person could be!

Monday was a busy day. Namay and I worked sick call continuously all morning and I was on call alone all afternoon and was really kept busy. I feared I got a little irritated with a child when I looked back on it. I always did when I was too busy. I wondered if the mother noticed.

I diagnosed another case of malaria in a Panamanian citizen even though I can't speak Spanish. I found it on a blood smear on a slide, too. It was a P. vivax. Namay told me that 75% of the malarias in Rito Hato were caused by P. falciparium but that, in contrast to what the textbooks said, the cases were not malignant at all. I tried to convey this to Terry and added that the cases were few and far between and that I was at minimal risk.

I received a letter from the War Department requesting a complete examination of my eyes. Namay said they'd do it here. He said, "Want to get out of the Army bad? We'll fix it." I thought that wasn't a bad idea but I wasn't certain he was serious. As it turned out, the eyes figured importantly in my eventual premature discharge. The fact of the matter was that I had no central vision in my left eye due to a macular scar caused by a chorioretinitis as a child. This was detected at the Mayo Clinic shortly after I was able to verbally describe the problem, perhaps when I was five or six years of age. It lay dormant ever since. The eyeground findings were impressive and consequently I was subjected to many funduscopic (ophthalmoscopic) eyeground examinations by my fellow students while in medical school. It had also been detected and noted on every physical examination given me by the Army.

It was a beautiful day. I would have loved to have gone swimming but instead had to attend a lecture on military jurisprudence between 4:00 and 5:00 p.m. There were nine lectures to go, one a day. I did not look forward to them.

I learned that by February 16th I would have eight days of leave coming. I thought that would be a good time for our projected meeting, perhaps in Mexico, and asked Terry to try to find out what service she was scheduled on at that time.

I was on call again Monday night and would also be on call on Wednesday night. However, after that I was free for four nights. I didn't think that schedule was bad but, then, Namay took it easy on me because I was the new kid on the block. While writing Terry in the evening, I was called to the dispensary to see a young man complaining of a sore throat. He had gingivitis (Vincent's angina, trench mouth), an infection of the gums and nearby tissues due to a bacterium and spirochete, hardly an emergency. On the other hand, the young man had a lot of psychological overlay, a common condition at Rio Hato.

Minneapolis General Hospital
Minneapolis, Minnesota
20 November 1947

Night Call At MGH

Tonight was Terry's night on call. She had already had two deliveries, a perineal repair (surgical repair of a rectocele and cystocele, i.e., relaxation of the perineal floor, often due to multiple childbirths) and an incomplete abortion — "time to quit for the night." Contrary to her prediction, Dr. Baker was not nicer. He had been "just like a bear" for the last two to three days.

Her letter to me said "seven months and ten days until I start on my way to you! I'm counting the days darling. Here's hoping that it will seem like a short a time as possible for both of us. If I can get through that lonely, sentimental, Christmas season — why, I'll be over the hump. But it's so lonely without my sweet husband!"

She also said that if I should happen to receive a package marked, "open on December 25" that <u>means</u> open on December 25th.

She told me she had received a letter from my sister Lou in Los Angeles containing family names we had drawn (by proxy) for Christmas gifts. I drew Gene Haddy, married to my sister

Vernita, and Terry drew Elizabeth, my oldest sister. The maximum was $10 and that generous price rather floored Terry "because we'll have to try to make our gifts nearly that price." She suggested a set of 6 steak knives (about $8-9) for each.

Terry had just read about the princesses' wedding. She said it must have been lovely but not nearly as romantic as ours.

Rio Hato Airfield
Republic of Panama
21 November 1947

Night Call At Rio Hato; Mess Hall Inspection

It was raining again. Everything was wet because the humidity reached 100%. The writing paper was limp as a rag. The bed sheets felt almost wet. But it was nice and cool.

I was catching on to my work. Both Nunnelley and Namay were helpful and thoughtful. They didn't make me take night call for a while until I knew people and the job better. That was nice. I did take call on Thursday night but only because Namay's car was gone. He lived quite a distance from the dispensary while I lived in the BOQ, less than a block away. I was called at 10:30 p.m. to see an infant with an upper respiratory infection and an enlisted man with pneumonia. I admitted the enlisted man to our upstairs "hospital" and was in bed by 11:30 p.m. There were no calls after that.

I found I was a real amateur at reading thick and thin blood smears for malaria, but I was learning. Reading the thick smears was the hardest of course.

In the afternoon, Namay took me around with him inspecting the mess halls, food sections in the NCO (non-commissioned officers') Club (Figure 8), food sections in the Officers' Club, PX kitchen, bakery, and meat shop. He was quite a stickler for detail but of course had to be in tropical Rio Hato. Everything had to be spotlessly clean because food spoiled quickly.

Figure 8- Non-Commissioned Officer's Club.

Gastroenteritis due to food poisoning could put the whole base out of action if the medics weren't careful. Namay was proud of the fact that he hadn't had an epidemic. I could see why. He really made them keep things spotless. The fumigation process in the officers' club dinning room was complete and consequently I was allowed to eat there the next day. Apparently it truly was overrun with cockroaches, which was why I was happy to leave the enlisted men's mess.

Minneapolis General Hospital
Minneapolis, Minnesota
22 November 1947

More Ob; Living Alone; Take Care; Mum's The Word

Terry said my letter of Sunday arrived today, taking six days. She didn't think that was too bad and wondered how frequently I had received her letters and whether I had yet received those back numbers. She thought I was developing a wonderful talent for letter writing. She liked it when I described the place and people. It gave her a better understanding of what I was doing and should make her feel more at home when she arrived in seven months.

She was on call, sitting in the little office on station C. They had had one new patient, a primipera (first pregnancy) in inactive labor, but she had been running around all evening anyway. Dr Baker had been just as sweet as he could be for the past two days, and he'd had much more reason to be nasty then he'd had before. He was really a very excellent teacher when he wanted to be. He "played scrub nurse" for her the day before — something that most residents wouldn't do. Elaine and she had decided that he must have family troubles. He apparently loved his wife very much, but Terry bet that she's a bit difficult to keep in hand. Terry said he said some very nice things about me.

Terry took quite a beating around MGH at mealtime. She was assured that I was supporting another woman down here in Panama. Dr. Brigham also quoted her a passage from the Bible that says, "It is not good for man to live alone." Terry said to me that it isn't good for women, either, darling, and that she missed me more than she could ever say.

She thought we could take our vacations in February or March. She didn't know how she would work it out, but believe her, she would. It depended partly on how many new interns started in January. She heard that Don Sutherland would start a medical residency at that time. Don was a friend of ours and Terry liked him personally. She also heard that George Lund, a classmate of mine, was going overseas to the European Theater.

Terry wanted me to be very careful not to get malaria. She said "take good care of yourself for me. And your rather inclined to athletes' foot too. I married a fine physical specimen, without any reflexes (my knee reflexes were a bit small) and I want him to stay that way — except I wouldn't mind a little more subcutaneous tissue (I was a bit thin)."

She hoped my fellow officers and their wives would like her when she arrived in Panama because she wanted them to feel comfortable around me and her. She asked me not to say too much about her being in medicine; she found that, for some reason, it put her at a disadvantage right away. She'd rather be thought of as my wife.

Terry delighted in keeping me abreast of University of Minnesota athletics. She knew it made me happy when the Minnesota football team won, which it did 21-0 when it played Wisconsin on a cold windy Saturday in the green grass turfed Memorial Stadium at the University of Minnesota.

Rio Hato Airfield
Republic of Panama
18 November 1947

EARS, PID, EYES, LABOR, AND A NEW RUMOR

I was tired because the day had been quite busy. Ears, ears, ears! I also had picked up an acute pelvic inflammatory disease in a young woman, though I made the stupid mistake of thinking a distended urinary bladder could possibly be a tumor of some sort. Out of practice, I guessed. I found the organisms (gonococci) myself on a slide, so I felt better.

Namay showed me how to do eye examinations on air force personnel in a long narrow room upstairs in the dispensary. The examination was more exhaustive than the usual service eye examination. I found it complicated, i.e., testing for various eye deviations such as esophoria, exophoria, and heterophoria, and for convergence, accommodation, visual fields, etc. on a complicated machine that I didn't understand. Perhaps I would soon, though. He said he'd also teach me refraction, too, if I liked.

In the evening, a woman, wife of a flyboy, presented in the

early states of labor. We bundled her on a plane, sent a nurse along and sent her to Fort Clayton in the Zone. We did the prenatal care at Rio Hato but all deliveries were in the Zone. I told Terry about this system "just in case she was interested." Then I added "however, I'm not suggesting..."

There was a rumor circulating about the base that most medics of our type (temporary, not regular army) will be discharged soon. As far as I was concerned, it was a rumor until I saw the order. The rumor included those in before May 1947. That disqualified me from the rumor.

It had been a beautiful day. Warm with occasional showers. I hadn't suffered from the heat yet. I turned in early because getting up at 6:00 a.m. after a hard day required it.

Minneapolis General Hospital
Minneapolis, Minnesota
24 November 1947

QUESTIONS

As requested, Terry sent me my blue prints (transcripts) from the University of Minnesota Medical School so that I could apply for a fellowship in internal medicine at the Mayo Foundation in Rochester, Minnesota. She could not find my Luther College premedical records or a proper photograph. She said she would keep looking and if need be, would send her "own precious picture that I carry in my billfold (sob!)". She also said she "felt proud when she looked at my medical school record."

Terry received a letter from the Minnesota State Board of Examiners asking why she hadn't registered her medical license and requesting her to send her $2 fee for this year. She said she would "get busy and do that little thing."

She had a number of questions for me. "How's my baby? Tell me how the weather is and what kind of clothes I should bring. Will I need a warm coat? Will I need warm pajamas? Will we need blankets and should I plan to bring our own? Do you think that I will need to buy any furniture to bring along? Do you ever get to wear civilian clothing? I guess those questions will fill up a little space in your next letter. Honey, have you a swimming suit there? Please take good care of yourself for me. I won't be happy again until I'm with you and we're making our home together."

She was on night call. She decided that it would be nice to be off of OB & Gyn. It was a very good service, but it was so hard on one's sleep at night. Then too, she was becoming neurotic for fear she would have a "precip" (a sudden explosive delivery that could damage the perineum and baby). She'd already had a III° laceration and, even though the patient got a good result from the repair, she was afraid of having any more complications.

Rio Hato Airfield
Republic of Panama
18 November 1947

BURNED BABY; CAPT. ALPIER; EARLY DISCHARGE; DREAM

I was a very busy OD (officer of the day) last night, so busy I didn't get a chance to write Terry. An officer, a lieutenant., brought his 2 year old baby boy into the dispensary because a cup of hot grease had spilled on his chest and abdomen and then had run down on to his right foot, causing 2nd and 3rd degree burns on about 20% of his body. I dressed the burns, gave him plasma intravenously via a tiny arm vein, and then had him flown down to the Zone. One of our two nurses is a qualified flight nurse and she, as usual, accompanied the patient on the flight.

Capt. Alpier, the fourth medic in the dispensary, returned from Peru today. He had been there a month replacing another physician. I met him today for the first time. He was a very nice small fellow, a surgeon by character and by actions. He brought back a lot of sterling silver items which he bought for a total of $308 and which would have cost $1000 in the States. Among the items were a large tea set, large candle holders, cocktail shakers and glasses, ash trays, demitasse spoons, etc., all silver. Doctor and Mrs. Namay saw the items and asked Alpier to send to Peru for $300 worth for them also. Silver was much cheaper in Peru than in Panama — and it was cheap in Panama also by States standards. I asked Terry to tell me what she thought of it. Perhaps we should buy some for our home before we left Panama.

The rumor concerning discharges was true. Any medic inducted before May of 1946 was eligible for discharge before December 31, 1947. Both Nunnelley and Namay were inducted in April of 1946. That would reduce their two year terms by three months. However, they thought they would stay until March 1946, since all of their plans were based on that date. While the new ruling didn't apply to me (I was inducted after May 1946) it did suggest that my tour of duty might end before I had served the entire two years of the current requirement. Furthermore, I had a complete eye examination scheduled for Monday November 24th down in the Zone. I would fly down and back. Perhaps my eyes would be very tired that day. I knew they were borderline in any case since Washington wouldn't go to all the trouble of scheduling a special examination if they weren't borderline. Namay was at first going to do the examination at Rio Hato; I wondered why he changed his mind and arranged an appointment for me in the Zone. I didn't ask. It wasn't because he couldn't do it. He was qualified and had all of the equipment here, upstairs in the dispensary. Perhaps he didn't care to be "involved" because of a conflict of interest. He did ask me initially if I wanted him to get me out of the Army. I just laughed. I asked Terry whether my attitude was unpatriotic.

I had the oddest dream last night (Wednesday). I was back in Kiester (my home town in southern Minnesota) inside our former home there. I was to be married. Preparations were in full force. The girl was Mildred, my high school infatuation. The ceremony was to take place at 2:00 p.m. At 1:00 p.m. I suddenly thought, what am I doing? This is the wrong girl. There's Terry (she had been in my dream just before). So one hour before the wedding I marched up to everyone, announced the wedding was off — "the wrong girl." That's all there was to the dream. That's a mean trick to play on a girl, but I thought entirely justified under the circumstances. After all, she was the wrong girl. Terry was the right one — and always would be.

Today I received two sport pages that Terry had addressed to Camp Kilmer, New Jersey. They were obsolete but I enjoyed them very much nevertheless. I said, "What a nice wife I have. Thinks of Pappa's interests." Mail was slow and irregular. I had no letters since the five came all at once.

I smoked a pipe. I didn't use a tobacco pouch in Rio Hato. With the high humidity, the tobacco stayed moist even when out in the open.

I finished *The Fountainhead*. It certainly was an unusual book. I again asked Terry to read it and give me her opinion. While interesting, I couldn't evaluate it with respect to quality. I was also still reading my text on electrocardiography.

My footlocker and barracks bag hadn't yet arrived. I was still living out of my old suitcase and getting along very well.

Minneapolis General Hospital
Minneapolis, Minnesota
26 November 1947

Insurance; The Brey Home; Breakfast Dishes

It had been 3 days since Terry received a letter from me and she was lonesome and wondered whether I was receiving her letters, how long they took to get to me, and how often mail came in and went out of Rio Hato.

She had paid Louis Schaller the premium on my life insurance policy, and he had called to acknowledge receipt of the check ($99.37) and to greet me and to ask for my address. Louis Schaller was an insurance agent who worked closely with professional fraternities at the University of Minnesota. Most of the fellows in my fraternity, Kappa Chi of Phi Chi, had a small policy with him. Terry thought it was nice to have the premium paid, but it seemed the money did fly. With Christmas coming "I'll be using even more of your hard-earned cash."

Dr. Gouze's band was playing at the Seven Seas bar every Wednesday night. Terry said she would like to go and hear him sometime. His brother, who was a musician, wrote the words (but not the music) to "She's Too Fat for Me." What a talented family. Both Terry and I had had Dr. Gouze as our internal medicine resident and were impressed with his physician qualities.

Dr. Brigham asked Terry for my address. He wanted to ask me about some people he knew in Panama. He had spent four years there and seemed to know a lot about it.

The OB Gyn service had been rather slow recently. There was no elective surgery on the Gyn service because of Thanksgiving and probably would be none until after Christmas and New Year's Day. Of course, the babies kept coming. The last several days had been particularly busy with deliveries — about three or four per day.

Terry was on call the night before Thanksgiving Day. Elaine relieved her at 3:00 p.m. on Thanksgiving day so she could go home for Thanksgiving dinner. Mrs. Jolly ("mama") the mother of two of Terry's female medical schoolmates (Betty and Ruth Jolly), Terry's Aunt Ann Daub (her mother's sister), and Terry's mother were guests. Terry's mother worked as a psychiatric nurse in the State Hospital in St. Cloud, Minnesota, and regularly spent time in the family home in St Anthony Park, across the street from Langford Park, in St. Paul, Minnesota. The family home was a large Victorian house built about 1885 by members of the Pillsbury milling family. An ancient-milling stone still lies half buried in the driveway. The Brey family acquired the house in 1946, in part because its proximity to the University of Minnesota would simplify the higher education of the six Brey children.

Terry got off work promptly at 5:00 p.m. on Tuesday, November

25th, leaving her time to shop. She took our little radio to Donaldsons for a tube, bought some stationery for letters to me, and then again looked at yellow, black-eyed Susan, breakfast dishes that she had admired for a long time. She told me that she had decided to buy them because it would make her feel good to have something she liked so well for our home. She hoped that I was looking forward to our own little home as much as she was.

Rio Hato Airfield
Republic of Panama
21 November 1947

WEDDING; BOWLING; FIRE; COSTA RICA

Today was a little different; we had an elaborate wedding on base. One of the "fly boys" married a girl who works in the administration office. The wedding was very military—white dress uniforms, guard of honor, etc.—quite different from the usual wedding. Afterward, there was an impressive reception at the Club. Everyone got partially stoned and the party raged on late into the night.

After the reception, I accompanied the medics bowling team to the bowling ally. The team was composed of the two nurses and three enlisted men, all from the dispensary. Our team won. The bowling alley was nice, better than I expected for a base like Rio Hato.

Two days ago, a married sergeant's house burned down. The couple lost everything except what they were wearing, and they were not wearing much because it was mid-day and consequently very warm. Everyone on the post chipped in with cash to reimburse them (I gave $2). This generated a lot of money. A nice gesture. I doubted you would find such uniform participation at a civilian air base.

My footlocker and barracks bag finally arrived, but I hadn't yet picked them up from the quartermaster's. I needed to do that quickly and place them in my dry locker before the contents got moldy. Mail delivery was also pretty slow. Mail came to the base four days a week—not on Wednesday, Saturday, and Sunday.

A pilot offered me a ride to Costa Rica the following week. He said the trip would interest me—the people were truly Spanish and merchandise was of good quality and reasonably priced. Costa Rica was a couple hours flying time up the coast. He also said flights to the States would begin again in January and that it shouldn't be hard to get a ride.

It was warm and muggy again. We had at least one hard downfall a day—just a short shower. But it managed to keep the humidity up.

Minneapolis General Hospital
Minneapolis, Minnesota
27 November 1947

THANKSGIVING A.M.

Terry had trouble falling asleep last night—something out of the ordinary for my wife—not because of on call responsibilities but because of loneliness. She sat up most of this night with a multipara who just wouldn't progress. The pregnancy was complicated by anemia. After breakfast, she thought it a good time to write me. Early this morning she had drawn blood from three policemen who came in at 4:00 a.m. Since she had to be up anyway, she did it willingly—particularly because they were blood donors for the OB-Gyn service. Afterward they invited her out for a bite to eat. She told them that she couldn't leave the hospital because of her responsibilities.

Thanksgiving morning was beautiful—snow on the ground and big soft white flakes falling through the slightly cold air. She bet that they didn't even celebrate Thanksgiving in Panama. If they did, it couldn't be the same. She went home at 3:00 p.m.

Rio Hato Airfield
Republic of Panama
22 November 1947

Snakes; Breast Feeding; Smoking; Swimming; Girl Friend Transportation

Each Saturday morning everyone on the base congregated in the theater for an orientation class. The commanding officer usually provided advice and the latest administrative news. In addition, a guest lecturer was usually present. This Saturday morning a gentlemen with a Ph.D. in Entomology gave a very interesting talk on Gatun Island, which is in Gatun Lake, a part of the Canal. From listening to the natives one would think there were many dangerous snakes in Panama. There were in fact some poisonous snakes but in a three year period, there were fewer than 200 snake bites in Panama and a very small percent of those bites were fatal. More people were killed by lightning than by snakes. Snakes were only seen in the underbrush where sane people did not go. Bushmaster, coral, and fierre delance were some of the common names for the poisonous snakes.

We held sick call at 11:00 a.m. as usual on Saturday and had quite a large number of patients. There were many cases of upper respiratory infection, something one wouldn't expect in this climate. However, the climate relieved my nasal discomfort. I had some symptoms but much less then in Minnesota. Except for days when the humidity was high, the heat wasn't bad at all. In fact Nunnelley and I got goose pimples when we swam. And I always used covers while sleeping.

Alpier was officer of the day (OD) Saturday night but went out for dinner. He told me to take care of any emergencies while he was gone. I received one call — a young woman who had been breast feeding her baby for months and then recently decided to stop. Now she had congested painful breasts. I told her to express them and stop gradually. She was in lots of discomfort but this wasn't exactly my idea of an emergency. I also saw a monilia vaginitis at sick call Saturday a.m. It was developing quite an OB-Gyn practice.

I was smoking too much in Panama. I was convinced that was what made my hands and feet so cold. I had done a lot of reading on the subject. The literature said smoking causes peripheral vasoconstriction with a decrease in skin temperature, an increase in blood pressure of about 10 mm Hg (both systolic and diastolic), tachycardia (increase in heart rate) of about 10 beats per minute, increase in cardiac output, and depressed st segments and sometimes depressed and inverted t waves on the electrocardiogram. There was no proof that these changes indicated harm (exercise can cause similar changes) but I asked Terry what wife wanted a man with cold feet and hands? And my tongue burned and I had a pretty punk taste in my mouth in the morning and an a.m. smokers' cough. For why? I wondered if I could quit.

In the afternoon, I listened to short wave football broadcasts between cat naps and reading. Following that, Nunnelley and I went swimming. Our beach was terrific and I told Terry so in my next letter. I had never seen a nicer beach for swimming. Not commercialized at all. In fact, it was exactly as nature had fashioned it. Never crowded. In fact, except for an occasional native straw hut (Figures 9-11), we had the whole beach to ourselves. I told Terry she'd love it if she ever saw it, and I was thinking today, wouldn't it be fun to have our own bungalow here. We would go swimming, come home, take a shower (to get the sand and salt off), and then — eat!

There was a big formal dance at the officers club tonight. I told Terry I wished she were here so that we could go. There weren't enough eligible women on the base for all of the officers. A lot of them had girl friends in the Zone. On occasions like this, the Army flew the girl friends up to Rio Hato for free and gave them quarters to stay in overnight and then flew them back the next day. Nice, huh?

The collection for the couple whose house burned down generated $6-700. Pretty good, eh?

I missed Terry very much. Every little thing I did that was the least bit different made me think of her and how much more fun it would be if she were with me. But I guessed that day would come.

I decided to hold my Saturday night letter until Monday and add a few lines on Sunday. The letter would not leave the base until Monday in any case.

Minneapolis General Hospital
Minneapolis, Minnesota
28 November 1947

Bloody Footprints; Boyfriend; Royall Storey; Mrs. Jolly

Terry had not received mail from me for foue-five days. She thought my letters must have been held up and she hoped her letters weren't that slow in reaching me. She was getting desperately lonesome for word from me.

Yesterday, Thanksgiving Day, was a lovely day at home. Alois, Terry's brother, came by the hospital for her at 3:00 p.m. She wasn't quite ready because she had just finished a delivery. She hurried to meet him and when they stepped outside, her shoes left faint bloody prints in the snow. The look on Alois' face was something to behold. Terry was a bit astonished herself at what she had accomplished

Terry had another laugh, when Alois came for her, the hospital operator told her that her "husband" was calling for her and the nurses' home operator said that her "boy friend" was calling for her. Well, the news must have gone around because she took quite a razzing about her "blond brother."

Ginger, one of Terry's sisters, and her friend, Mary Lou Studer, also came to dinner but they had to go right back to St. Mary's Hospital in Minneapolis where they were in nurses' training. Alois and Terry picked up Mrs. Jolly, the mother of Terry's two women medical schoolmates (who were now interning on the West Coast), at her apartment and continued on to the Brey family home. Terry's unmarried Aunt Anne (her mother's sister) and her mother were also there, so they had a nice "homey" evening. Royall Storey, a bachelor friend who lived in another old Victorian house across the street from the Breys', came over and played cards for awhile. He hadn't met Terry's Aunt Anne before and Terry wondered if he might ask her for a date. I thought "fat chance" (Royall was very effeminate and had never married or shown interest in the opposite sex). Terry was glad they had invited Mrs. Jolly. Mr Jolly, her former husband, was in town and was having dinner at their son's home. Mrs. Jolly wasn't invited until the last minute and she felt hurt. Terry didn't think she looked well.

Rio Hato Airfield
Republic of Panama
22 November 1947

A Leisurely Sunday With The Namays; Rent Control; Housing; "Lebanese Dinner;" My Eye Examination

I got up at 8:30 a.m., had breakfast, and then returned to my room where I read EKGs until 11:00 a.m. Namay called just then and invited me to dinner. He then also invited me to go swimming. He and his wife picked me up and we went to a section of the beach that was new to me. It was a nice warm day and I even got a bit of a burn (almost impossible for me with my Lebanese skin), but the swimming was the best, deserving the description "royal," according to my friends. We took pictures, some of which I planned to send Terry and which are published here (Figures 9-11).

The Namays brought me back to my room at 2:00 p.m. and, after I showered, they picked me up again and took me to their home where we had a small lunch and then met a few of their neighbors.

I learned that one woman owned about ten small bungalows on a small plot of land, each of which she rented for $90-135 a month. The Namays were one of the renters and considered the rent to be "highway robbery." This situation was commonplace in the Rio Hato area and caused a base colonel to call a meeting of renters at which agreement was reached to move out of any house with rent exceeding $65 a month. This was his method of establishing rent control. The families were housed in vacant revamped barracks on the base if the landlords didn't respond by lowering the rent. Many of them did.

The Namays didn't participate because they found another house which they planned to share with another couple. It was about two miles from the base. We drove there about 4:00 p.m. The site was beautiful — a lovely lawn overlooking the beach with mountains in the background. The cottage was not deluxe but it was clean and the owners were very nice. They had just built a new house right beside the one into which the Nameys were moving. The new one was quite deluxe — a cozy, beautiful bungalow. The owners used it only about two weekends a month but refused to rent it at other times. It appeared they could afford it. They served us drinks and I thought how happy Terry and I could be in a setting like this — lovely house,

Figure 9- A Panamanian beach house.

Figures 10-11- Panamanian beach homes.

nice lawn, mountains behind and beautiful beach in front. But such a place was hard to obtain. We talked awhile about the history of the local area and of Panama in general. The focus of course was Henry Morgan, the Englishman, and the Spaniards. We returned to the Namay's house, had a few more drinks and then dinner. The dinner was unique for Panama. Mrs. Namay prepared yubrah, i.e., cabbage rolls. Who would have ever thought I'd have Lebanese food in Panama? That became a big joke. Mrs. Namay was Lebanese-American but was not brought up as one, i.e., she didn't know the Lebanese customs, speech, or food. She did know how to prepare the one dish she served and that she learned after her marriage. It was very good, too. Dr. Namay was just the opposite. He was brought up under Lebanese influence from infancy to adulthood. He could read and write Arabic at one time and still did to some extent — which was quite an accomplishment. The Namays met about eight months ago and were married two months later, just before coming overseas. Both had lived in Charleston, WV, all their lives but had to go to a meeting in Toledo to meet. We talked about Lebanese we knew in common. Then I told them a lot about Terry. I always enjoyed talking about her.

Tomorrow (Monday) I was to fly to the Zone for my eye examination. I doubted whether it could have any significance with respect to a discharge but, at that moment, should they have offered me one, I would have snapped it up.

As I fell asleep, I remembered that Dad, Mom, and Juanita were due back in the USA in a few days and that I'd best write them tomorrow.

Minneapolis General Hospital
Minneapolis, Minnesota
29 November 1947

N&M; Brown Eyed Susan Dishes; Christmas gifts

Terry was on call again—as usual it seemed to her. Elaine and her husband Roy were going to the interns' party tonight, so Terry was taking calls. Everything was dead as could be and she hoped it would stay that way.

Her next service was to be N&M (nervous and mental) and her partner was to be McClusky. She had planned to have two partners but the extra one (Verby) was shifted to "con" (contagious diseases) instead, so there were three on "con" instead of three on N&M. It was a little disappointing to Terry in a way, but she thought maybe it would be good for her to be busy. She didn't think the night calls would be as tiring, either, as they were in OB. She thought McClusky would be nice to work with too.

Elaine covered the OB-Gyn service while Terry shopped in the afternoon. Terry said she found shopping to be a dangerous pastime for a wife. She bought her Christmas present from me, the set of yellow pottery dishes in the "Brown Eyed Susan" pattern which she had been admiring for so long. She said she hoped I didn't mind, because she liked them so much. She'd rather have something for our future home together than anything else she could think of. She asked me to write and say it's alright with me. She said she wouldn't tell me how much they cost until I did; they were really quite expensive and her conscience had been feeling guilty ever since she made the purchase.

She also bought Christmas gifts for Elizabeth Haddy, my oldest sister, and for Gene Haddy, the husband of one of my twin sisters, whose names we got in the drawing. She bought them each a set of lovely Cannon ("that's good quality") peach colored bath towels. She had the initial "H" put on them in blue with a fancy monogram, and they were really nice. Each set came to about $5 — not up to the $10 limit, but she thought they would make adequate gifts. Easy to send, too. She hoped these gifts met with my approval.

She also shopped for bath powder and incidentals for herself. She got some false hemming so that she could let her hems down on her coat and suits. Never let it be said that her baby's wife doesn't have that "new look!"

She said, "I love you, darling. You and our marriage are most important to me and come before anything else in the world."

Rio Hato Airfield
Republic of Panama
26 November 1947

Dependency; Early "Short Arm;" EKGs; X-rays; Christmas Gifts; Pending Transfer; Potential Discharge; Thanksgiving Schedule

Two more letters arrived from my sweet Terry today. The last one was mailed on the 23rd (written on the 22nd). That letter took less than three days to get to Rio Hato, which was mighty fine time, I thought. One of her letters included comments by her male coworkers concerning "man living alone." I told her to ignore their teasing and kidding. It may not be good for a man to live alone, but I would get by as long as I had her waiting for me back home. I thought it odd that men depended so much on their wives. I guessed it was true that women can mold a man's future. Clearly, I was much stronger knowing that Terry loved me. I told her to keep telling me that, just the way she had so far. She couldn't have known how much I enjoyed reading the parts of her letter that to others would probably seem "mushy." But to me they were the most necessary things in life.

Today was mighty long, in part because of some distasteful early morning medical activity. I wasn't certain I should describe this activity in a letter, especially to my wife, but I just had to gripe and get it off my chest. I told Terry I didn't know if she was aware of how the Army checks for V.D. It was a matter of putting the men in a long line and holding what was called "short arm inspection," in Army slang (I told Terry not to show the letter to anyone — I was embarrassed to write it). I thought that was probably okay in the daytime but about once a month the medical officers get up at 4:30 a.m., descended upon the barracks, wake up the men, and hold the above mentioned inspection before the men had a chance to urinate and wash away any discharge. We did that this morning and I didn't go for it. I viewed it as degrading the dignity of the men and of the medical profession. And the hour was ungodly! I told Namay so. I also wondered at the value of it — it was pretty hard to tell a G.C. discharge from a nocturnal emission at that time of the morning (nocturnal emissions occur frequently in young healthy celibate males). Enough of that. In any event, I felt that any man who wasn't interested enough in his own well being to come to see a doctor when he had a penile discharge wasn't the patient I wanted to treat. But the Army had its regulations, I guessed.

We then held sick call. When it finally ended at noon, I was off for the afternoon. I hung around the dispensary for a couple of hours, and then went to my room and read EKGs. At 4:00 p.m. I went swimming. I really loved it. Following that I read some more and then went to dinner with Alpier. He and I spent a couple of hours in the evening reading the X-rays for the last month — mostly normals but a few fractures and pneumonias.

In my letter to Terry, I told her to handle the Christmas presents for Gene and Elizabeth herself and that I thought steak knives would be fine (note that she changed her mind and bought monogrammed towels). I also asked whether she received the letter in which I asked about the paperwork I needed for my Mayo fellowship application and I wondered what happened to the package she sent to me at Camp Kilmer, NJ, a long time ago. It hadn't caught up with me yet. I mentioned that Nunnelley had been transferred to Howard Field in the Zone effective December 1st and that Namay is thinking about taking his discharge because the Nunnelley transfer would make us a bit short handed again. For his sake, I hoped he did, for ours, I hoped he didn't. He could in fact get out under the new regulation that made anyone in before May 1946 eligible for discharge.

I was scheduled to be OD for the rest of the weekend, beginning tomorrow (Thanksgiving Day) morning. Then I would be off for the next 2-3 weekends. I was considering a trip to Costa Rica one day soon. A group of us were also discussing a fishing trip in a week or two. The Army had launches in Rio Hato which officers could reserve at no cost. Pretty nice.

I didn't send the letter I wrote Terry in the evening because it wouldn't go out the next day (Thanksgiving Day); I held it and added more the next evening.

Rio Hato Airfield
Republic of Panama
Thanksgiving Night 1947

Hectic Holiday

Thanksgiving must be my jinx day. One year ago I had 7-8 deliveries on that day at MGH and today was just as hectic. This morning I saw 10-12 patients who straggled in — there was no formal sick call since it was a holiday. The Officers Club had its Thanksgiving Day dinner at 3:30 p.m. Right in the middle of the meal, I got called out for an ambulance run to an auto accident in which a civilian was killed and a soldier injured. Then a little later a sergeant was brought into the dispensary with a fractured cervical vertebrae, which he obtained by diving into shallow water. I rigged up a traction apparatus on the litter — which incidently is quite a trick. Then I made arrangements to have all three of them flown to the Zone (Figures 12-14). It was 8:00 p.m. before all of that was completed.

The full responsibility for all this activity was mine, since all the other medics were on holiday. The appropriateness of this might have been questioned, since I was a relatively inexperienced physician just out of medical school. However, this never crossed my mind. I was full of confidence in my abilities — just as was Terry confident of hers.

Later in the evening, I got in a bridge game. Despite my fatigue, I enjoyed it very much. It had been a long time since I played the game. There was always a bridge game going either at the fraternity (Phi Chi) or around the Brey household, but that was interrupted by internship and active Army duty. Following the bridge game, I saw another patient and then went to my room. It was 11:00 p.m. and I was plenty tired. It would have been a beautiful day for a swim, but I just didn't find time. I did find time to fantasy about Terry. She was here and I was snuggling up on her shoulder and falling asleep, refusing to move for days and days. I sure loved that woman.

Minneapolis General Hospital
Minneapolis, Minnesota
30 November 1947

Another Missed Party

Terry reported that last night the OB service had a breech delivery. Dr Baker did the delivery and his wife came in and watched. They didn't get to the interns' party until about 11:00 p.m. because of it.

Elaine also went to the interns' party last night, so she was on call today. However, Terry took calls for her in the afternoon while she slept. Terry then went home to start on the Christmas cards and packages. We were sending cards to a lot of people.

One of the medical technologists told her last night that most of the medics in the Fort San Houston class behind mine received US assignments. Smith, Christianson, and Bob Rocknem (one of my roommates during internship at MGH) were stationed in Texas. However, George Lund, a classmate of mine, was to go to the European Theatre. Apparently we were just one class too early for US assignments.

Terry said everyday someone on the MGH wards tells her how much they liked me and how much fun I was to work with.

She again said she missed me and worried if I was receiving her letters.

Figure 12- Our connection to the Zone and hospital beds— the airport from a distance.

Figure 13- One of the hangars.

Figure 14- A takeoff from the base airport.

Rio Hato Airfield
Republic of Panama
27 November 1947

ANOTHER BUSY HOLIDAY; TABES; ICED TEA; FLY BOYS

I was really having myself a busy weekend and I was glad, because that made the time go much quicker — making it a bit easier to bear our separation.

Today, the day after Thanksgiving Day, was supposed to be a holiday. However, I began work at 8:00 a.m. and finished about 4:00 p.m. In addition, I saw a couple of patients in the evening. I was on duty alone, so the entire responsibility was again mine, so soon after arriving in Panama. The only thing I didn't like about it was that I couldn't get in my daily swim. But I would begin again on Monday.

I picked up (diagnosed) a case of tabes dorsalis (central nervous system syphilis), based on the history and physical examination alone. The manifestations (signs and symptoms) were classical. I was so certain of the diagnosis that, even if the blood serology and spinal fluid laboratory tests were reported to be normal, I wouldn't believe it.

The mother of a child I treated wanted to know how soon Terry would join me. Many people asked me that but this one had a definite reason. She evidently was a big wheel in the "wives club" and had Terry all slotted for membership. I guessed she liked the little extra attention I showed her kid. Of course she'll love Terry when she arrives; she's so lovable.

One of the fellows mentioned that yesterday was the first time he'd ever had iced tea on Thanksgiving. I said, "me too. We'll probably also have it on Christmas Day."

I got into a bull session with a fly boy later that evening. He told me of his wartime flight experiences while we sipped several glasses of a very unique tasting Portugal wine (it tasted a lot like a liquor to me). I was getting to know many of the people at Rio Hato better now. It made life simpler and more pleasant. One advantage of my arriving in Rio Hato first was that I would "sort of be in the know" and would be able to function as a teacher and guide to Terry. I thought I would like that.

My letter to Terry that night closed with, "Do you know that I love you more than anything — anything on earth — anything in the universe. It will always be so."

Rio Hato Airfield
Republic of Panama
29 November 1947

First Movie; Rio Hato As A Home; Photographs; "Farm Dance;" EKGs

I went to a movie this evening, my first since arriving at Rio Hato (Figures 15-17). Since I was medical officer of the day (MOD), this wasn't simple. The theatre was about a mile and a half from the BOQ so I had the ambulance driver take me to it as a special favor. It was necessary to inform several sources where I'd be if needed. I was told the projectionist would flash "MOD"

Figure 15-Movie advertisements in front of Base Theater.

Figure 16-The Base Theater.

Figure 17-Looking toward the stage in the theater.

on the screen if a need arose and the ambulance driver would pick me up and whisk me to the dispensary. Fortunately, I was able to sit through the entire movie undisturbed — which was quite unusual, I was told.

The movie was *The Hucksters* and I thoroughly enjoyed it. The theater, by the way, was quite large and all of the walls served as screens — something not seen in the States. It felt as if you were in an outdoor movie except that a roof was overhead.

My four days of continuous MOD were almost over. I had been quite busy, thank heaven. It made the time pass more quickly and the pain of separation from Terry less intense.

I hoped I was still stationed at Rio Hato when Terry joined me. I was certain she would like it here. Alone, it wasn't too much fun, but together, I thought we'd really be happy. Not that we wouldn't anywhere but a few months here would be a period in our lives we'd remember always, I thought. First, we'd have a home of our own; second, we'd swim whenever we pleased, play tennis, spend time at the club playing bridge and going to parties, etc. Most Rio Hato residents I talked to wouldn't trade it for the Zone because it was more friendly and "homey," as they put it. So I thought if I must be overseas when Terry arrives, I hoped it would be Rio Hato.

I spoke to an amateur photographer — a medic in the dispensary — and he agreed to provide me copies of pictures he took of the base and surrounding territory, for a small price. I wanted them to send to Terry. He also took a "snap" of me. I planned to send that too (Figure 18).

There was a "farm" dance — or a "barn" dance at the club last night. It looked like a lot of fun. Dancers wore "hickey" clothes and a "backwoods" type of orchestra entertained. I watched for a few minutes and then spent the rest of the evening reading EKGs and seeing patients at the dispensary.

By now, I was getting quite good at reading EKGs. Not that I was an expert but I thought my judgement in the case of cardiac patients would be right most of the time. I found it an interesting area once I got into it. The book I had was very complete and well written.

I had now been in Rio Hato three weeks tomorrow. I knew the time would eventually pass but I did wish it would hurry. I missed Terry very much and said so in no uncertain terms and in great detail in a letter to her.

Minneapolis General Hospital
Minneapolis, Minnesota
2 December 1947

Five Letters!; Photographs; Come Home Soon; Medical Meetings

Terry was at home, all bathed and in bed. She had received five letters from me today and, according to her, "all of them so very sweet." One of them contained photographs of me and there were others of the base (Figures 19-21). She thought they were "swell" and, yes, she would send some of them on to my family but not the lovely one of me standing on the dispensary steps (Figure 18). She hated to be piggish, "but no one is going to get it away from my clutches."

Earlier in the evening, she and her oldest sister Ann had seen *Green Dolphin Street* at St. Mary's Hospital. The hospital showed movies for the hospital personnel and Terry and Ann were "Ginger's" guests. "Ginger" was one of Terry and Ann's younger sisters; she was in nurses' training at St. Mary's Hospital. Terry thought it was a lovely movie, but oh, how she wished I could have been there. She said she didn't go to movies much because they made her lonesome, remembering how we used to sit and hold hands. The couple in the movie were married eight or ten years before they decided to be in love. Just think! — taking that long. She said she loved me for so long before our marriage, she thought she decided very young that I was the only one there could ever be for her. But her love had grown so rapidly since our

Figure 18-Me on the dispensary steps.

Figure 19-A view of the camp and surrounding countryside.

Figure 20- A view of the camp looking toward the headquarters' building.

Figure 21- The field headquarters.

wedding day that now she was completely dependent on me. Couldn't I please plan to come home soon?

We had earlier written about my flying back to the States in January "to attend a medical meeting." She checked several meeting schedules and sent me two suggestions:

1) A.M.A. Interim Session, Cleveland, January 5-8, Dr. George F. Lull, 535 N Dearborn St. Chicago, 10, Sec.
2) American Society for Surgery of the Hand. Chicago, January 23-24, Dr. Douglas H. Boyer, 1401 S. Hope St., Los Angeles, 15, Sec.

She wondered whether one would be suitable and promised to look for more. At the time I did not know what was suitable or possible, but I did know I would explore the regulations in short order. Terry also promised to answer all five of my letters.

Rio Hato Airfield
Republic of Panama
1 December 1947

Five Letters!; Answers To Questions; My Pay; Our Home; Liking One's Work

Today I was showered with gold — five letters from my wonderful spouse (one envelope contained two letters).

The first one was written on November 10th — a back number. It contained the newspaper clipped pictures (but not the associated newspaper article) of the MGH "Women Physician's Club," including the one showing Christine's legs (Figure 1d). I told Terry her legs were better and that that photograph should have been of her. I saw why the three women got razzed around MGH — that article did make good razzing material. The second letter was written on November 12th — another back number. It contained comments (see November 12th) on the morals of women, stimulated in part by a case of "crabs" (see November 12th). One did see everything at MGH.

The third letter was written on November 24th and contained the "blueprint" of my medical school grades. She couldn't find a photograph of me or a record of my college grades but I asked her to keep looking for them. I needed them to apply for a fellowship (residency in internal medicine) at the Mayo Clinic. I had just received an application blank from Mayo and I wanted to send the completed application to them soon. Their letter to me said, "It is expected that few vacancies will be available before the fall of 1948 or 1949. However, if you still wish to fill an application, we will complete it and present it for consideration at the appropriate time." Of course I wished to apply because that was just the time frame I wanted (I expected to spend a full two years in the service).

Terry also asked a number of questions concerning her trip to Panama (see November 24th). I couldn't answer most of them since I didn't know where we'd be stationed or what housing would be available at the time she arrived. One answer was certain, she'd need only summer clothing and a raincoat. No warm pajamas were necessary. No warm coat was necessary. Only the lightest of blankets were necessary and those were usually provided, I believe, with the housing, though I didn't know for sure. Most likely she would not bring any furniture. Yes, I could wear civvies off duty hours and yes, I did have a swimming suit. I promised to take good care of myself because I wanted to be in tip top condition for her. In turn, I told Terry to take care of herself and to not overdo the starches in the MGH cafeteria (something I said when I felt I could safely get away with it).

The fourth letter was written on November 26th and contained a letter from my sister Vernita (one of my younger fraternal twin sisters, this one lived in Cedar Rapids, Iowa, with her husband Gene Haddy). The letter indicated she was pregnant again. This surprised me because she had recently lost a young son in a tragic accident and I had wondered whether that would turn her off from child rearing. I told Terry our siblings were all getting ahead of us!

I also told Terry her letters were arriving in about four days, which I thought was good. However, the delivery at Rio Hato was not good — only four days a week — Monday, Tuesday, Thursday, and Friday — as I probably said before. I expressed my happy approval of her interest in our home to be and told her to go ahead and buy whatever she thought was appropriate.

The fifth envelope contained two letters which were written on the 27th and 28th of November. I expressed me disbelief at her inability to fall asleep and said, "You have trouble getting to sleep! Now I know you need my presence. Your letter was just as sweet as you are, dear. I love you — and especially when you write letters like that. Sentimental, that's how I want my honey. Not hard and flippant."

I was really sorry my letters weren't arriving each day but that wasn't possible because of the infrequency of the pick-up at this end. I hoped that my getting six letters today wouldn't prevent me from getting one tomorrow.

I got a month's pay today — $72 in cash and $275 sent home. My plan was to pay my club bill the next day; I would then know better how much it would cost me each month. I thought we should be able to save quite a bit if I could continue to send that much home each month.

I told Terry that I too thought it would be fun to have a home of our own. That's the only reason I wanted Terry to come to Rio Hato — I meant, I'd rather we would be together in Minneapolis — so we could give homemaking a trial. I was certain we would be very, very happy.

I also told Terry it was certainly wonderful to like one's work. I was able to keep going day and night and not get too tired. Enjoying my work was the only thing that made our separation bearable. I didn't know what I'd do if my work were a bore. Not that Rio Hato dispensary was an ideal medical experience, but it was fair. Of course, I liked medicine in any shape or form.

I thought Captain Namay had decided to leave. That was too bad. It'll mean more work, especially administrative, which I was certain I would not like.

I played some bridge at the club tonight and won. It was great fun, I found. I was glad I knew how to play; it was much easier to make friends that way.

Minneapolis General Hospital
Minneapolis, Minnesota
3 December 1947

The Low Point; No Letters; N&M

Breakfast was just over and Terry was sitting in the record room writing to me. It would be mail time in about 30 minutes, so she would be able to get a peek in her mail box before going over to "lues" (syphilis) clinic. She hadn't heard from me for about nine days and she was lonesome and anxious for a few words from me. She lived for my letters and for the day when we would be together again. She wondered if it was as difficult for me as it was for her. She thought that separation would become easier with time, but it just didn't work out that way. She missed me more every day (my sentiments exactly). Then she told me not to worry about the missing letters; she suspected they were on a ship instead of an airplane and that they would arrive very soon. She wondered whether I was getting her letters and whether she should start writing directly to Rio Hato instead of using my APO.

She thought N&M wouldn't be so bad after she got used to it. Right now she was swamped with work. There were only two interns instead of three, as there had been for the last two months. She worked under Frank Kiesler who was very nice but who wasn't at MGH very much. Her intern partner was McClusky.

She sent me a few of the Mayo fellowship application materials I had asked for. The only thing she couldn't find was my University of Minnesota pre-medicine fee statement and a photograph of me. She sent me her "own precious one that I've carried in my billfold (I hope you realize that giving it up is a sacrifice)." She said she would write the University for a fee statement and wanted to know if she should try to get more pictures of me.

Rio Hato Airfield
Republic of Panama
2 December 1947

Fatigue; My Eye Exam; Letters From Lou And Terry; Expenses; Pilot Death

I was really tired. In fact, this week was the first time I had felt fatigue from work since finishing my internship (my internship at MGH the year before had been particularly work intensive and stressful because of the 1946 poliomyelitis epidemic; at the peak of the epidemic, we did in excess of 100 diagnostic spinal taps each day). I was extra busy because the government inspectors were giving the dispensary, as well as the entire base, its biannual evaluation. Nunnelley's orders had been revoked and there was a possibility he would be back. I hoped so. That would make it easier to arrange time off to see my honey.

The report of my eye examination at Fort Clayton Hospital was returned to Namay, our chief today. He would now send it on to Washington D.C. It concluded I had several organic lesions in the left retina, the largest of which was in the macular area, that it was likely inactive, that there was a moderate central scotoma (blind spot) and that for all practical purposes I had monocular (one eyed) vision (this wasn't really the case; I had good peripheral vision in the left eye and therefore my vision was binocular, i.e. two eyed). I felt there was a bare possibility that I would be discharged — but bare.

I received a long newsy letter from Lou, one of my sisters in

Los Angeles. I learned a lot of new family happenings, e.g., Abbie Haddy had married Delores Shaheen (both related to me and to each other). This surprised me since I didn't even faintly suspect they were interested in each other. I was really behind on the news. That didn't take long when one was oversees. Lou also confirmed Vernita's pregnancy.

I also received a letter from Terry. I told her it was wishful thinking to hope she wouldn't have as much night work on N&M. I did, and plenty. I also told her that I was very happy she bought dishes for our home, that this must reflect a domestic streak in her, and that I didn't mind the cost if she was happy with them. I also told her she need not hesitate to tell me about expenditures — after all, she was half of the family and our money was as much hers as mine. I asked her whether Gene would appreciate bath towels for his Christmas present. Not very mannish! But then, perhaps married men have to expect "family-like" gifts. I told her I was sorry I wasn't there to take her to the interns' party but not to worry, we'd make up for it some day — in many ways. Finally, I reminded her of my need for the picture and transcript.

By now I had a better feel for my expenses. I paid $2 a month for room and $48 for board. Pretty reasonable! My bill this month, paid today, was $88, but this included club initiation fee, laundry, room and board for a month, and board in <u>advance</u> for December. Clearly, I would be able to send most of my paycheck home.

I was on duty again tonight (Tuesday). I would also be on duty Thursday night but then no night duty until next Monday or Tuesday.

A group of us had reserved the launch for an ocean fishing trip on Sunday. I was really looking forward to it. Since it was a "special service" activity, the cost was zero. Even the bait and tackle were free.

We experienced a real tragedy recently, the kind that always lurks in back of the minds of people on an airbase. One of the pilots whose home base was here at Rio Hato was sent to the States a month ago to learn jet planes. He was said to have been a very popular, nice, clean living, single 24 year old. He crashed the other day and was killed. His room was just a few doors down from mine and it was very depressing seeing the Chaplain and others collect his effects in preparation for sending them to his parents. I had never met him, of course.

Minneapolis General Hospital
Minneapolis, Minnesota
6 December 1947

12 Letters!; Busy N&M; Uncooperative Partner; Christmas Gifts; Baby Shower

Terry's letter surprised me. She said she had received nine letters from me on December 4th and three more on December 5th and "it was like receiving a reprieve." She had been going around for two weeks with a long face. But now she felt wonderful. She read each letter twice and said she was going to write detailed responses to each but that first she wanted to talk about a few other things and then go to bed because she was awfully tired.

She had found the N&M service to be rugged. She hadn't nearly caught up with her work yet, and it was terribly frustrating. She worked with Frank Keisler — he was very nice, but he certainly didn't spend much time at MGH. She would try to get to work a little early tomorrow so that she could do a little catching up. Maybe after that things would be better.

My father and mother called Terry from Cedar Rapids on December 4th (Thursday). They were well and happy following their trip to Lebanon and wanted Terry to visit them on the weekend. McClusky, the other intern on the N&M service, was very unobliging, much to her surprise — even after she explained the situation. So she was unable to go. She was rather shocked at McClusky's uncooperativeness. First, she didn't expect it of him, and in the second place, she thought all of the interns tried to help one another. She wondered if he would want to take a weekend off? I wondered whether his negative response reflected a male prejudice against female interns. So here she was spending Saturday night at home rather than spending the weekend in Cedar Rapids with my parents. She spent the evening wrapping two Christmas boxes for me which she hoped would reach me in time and generate "a little of the Christmas spirit." "Now mind, honey — no peeking!"

Terry, Elaine and two girls from the hospital went to a baby shower for Jane Gumprecht Tuesday evening. It was nice but it lasted "too darn late." Jane was a classmate with whom I had externed at Asbury Hospital in Minneapolis during my senior year in medical school.

Terry wondered whether her letters had been slow in reaching me and which of two addresses would be faster, my Rio Hato address (1st Lt. Francis J. Haddy 0-1766736, AAF, Rio Hato Airfield, Rio Hato, Panama) or my APO address (290th Med. Detachment Aviation, APO 838, c/o Postmaster, New Orleans, LA). She decided to use my APO address for a while and make a final decision after feedback from me.

Rio Hato Airfield
Republic of Panama
3 December 1947

Shaving Cream; Malaria; Rio Hato Village, Christmas Present; Swimming And Reading; Nunnelley's Orders; Eye Exam Sent To D.C.

While shaving, I noticed that my tube of shaving cream was almost empty, and very battered. That tube was the same one I sent Delane (Delane Shaheen was my first cousin and best man) to the drugstore (Brown's) to buy the morning of Terry's and my wedding. I told Terry I had become very attached to the tube and that when it was empty, I was going to save it. It obviously had a very special significance to me but why I had picked that item to focus upon I did not know, but I had. I guess it reminded me of the very special feeling I had the morning of the wedding and still had.

Today I spent a busy morning in the dispensary. Then right after lunch I spent a couple of hours in the laboratory looking at the malaria blood smears we had prepared from a Panamanian patient of mine who I was sure, from the clinical observations, had malaria. But I couldn't find the organisms on the smear. I looked and looked, — and finally I saw them! Extremely minute ring forms of falciparum malaria. It just again goes to show, you sometimes have to practice to see the obvious — especially in this case. Once you learn how, it's easy.

Then Namay took me for a ride showing me parts of the base I had never seen before. He also drove me into the small town of Rio Hato, three miles distance from the base. I hadn't been there before either. Just a dirty collection of wooden buildings and grass huts, I thought.

After that I went to the PX to hunt for Terry's Christmas present. I finally bought a wrist watch with a sweep second hand, something of quality and useful for a physician. I had a difficult time making this selection — most of the available items were junky souvenirs of Panama. I didn't know whether the watch was appropriate (not very romantic you see) but I was certain she would like it.

Following that, I took a short dip with a friend. I usually swam in the late afternoon, thus avoiding the hot sun. I was dark enough.

In the evening, I read the *Surgery, Gynecology, and Obstetrics Journal* in the dispensary library and found it entirely appropriate for our practice — a general practice in which we saw anything and everything and referred off the serious cases to specialists in the Zone.

Nunnelley's orders were in fact revoked and he was back with us — for how long I do not know. I still couldn't decide whether I liked him or not, and that was unusual for me. I almost always liked everyone.

My eye examination was sent to Washington D.C. today. Namay thought they might discharge me but I doubted it. I didn't cheat either, and that was the truth. I wanted a discharge but then who wouldn't in my situation.

No mail today but then I had the more to look forward to tomorrow.

Rio Hato Airfield
Republic of Panama
4 December 1947

Reflections On Life In Rio Hato And The States; Fast Letter; Swim; Dinner At The Club; Christmas Present

Life in Rio Hato was good. They say that people who have lived here want to return after a few years for a vacation. I thought I knew why. Here there was none of the fast, tense city life that was found in the States. Life was very simple and, because of its simplicity, was actually soothing — provided you didn't permit yourself to become bored. No one over-worked. There was no need to rush. There were no buses or streetcars to catch. No one complained if you were a few minutes late to work. Anytime you felt like it, you could step out for a few minutes. The day began early but always ended early. Rain or shine, the afternoon swim or tennis match went on. I told Namay that if I could get a nice house and if Terry was here, life would be ideal. I was certain Terry and I would be very happy. Then, of course, the old, ugly head of ambition would pop up and I'd want to move back to the States to "conquer the profession." Then would the difficulties of the fast, tense life start again? In a way, ambition could be bad. People, sadly enough, were never satisfied.

I received a letter from Terry written on November 30th but sent on December 1st. Today was December 4th. The letter took exactly three days (72 hours) to arrive. I told Terry that her letters were arriving regularly and then asked about mine. I was writing every day.

Nunnelley and I had another fine swim today. I again wished Terry could have been here to enjoy them with me. It was really nice to step out the door on to the nicest beach I've ever seen.

This evening Alpier, Namay, Mrs. Namay and I ate at the same table at the Club (the Namays ate there only occasionally). The Club served a very, very delicious meal of lobster, French fries, strawberry short cake, iced tea, etc. Some of the meals at the Club couldn't be beat. After dinner, we went to the movie. I didn't realize until it started that I had already seen it with Terry. It was "Slave Girl" with George Brent, Yvonne De Carlo, and the talking Camel. But I enjoyed it again.

I sent Terry her Christmas present today, registered airmail. I told her she was free to open it as soon as it arrived. I hoped she liked it and that it was appropriate, the latter always a worry when I bought presents for anyone.

I told Terry that we should be vacationing together in about two months, that I was waiting patiently but that it was so hard.

Rio Hato Airfield
Republic of Panama
5 December 1947

Bridge; More Malaria; Laboratory; Photographs; A New Way To Visit Terry

It was late before I got around to writing Terry. I played bridge at the club — and got badly trounced — until 11:00 p.m. and then listened to the championship fight. I then went to the BOQ but I couldn't find proper stationery before 12:00 p.m. — and I had to get up at 6:00 a.m.

The day was not unusual. I worked in the dispensary again and diagnosed another falciparum malaria in a Panamanian. I decided to save the slides I made which appeared to be of any teaching value. I continued to do a lot of my own laboratory work just to keep my hand in practice. The afternoons were not too busy so that's when I worked in the laboratory.

Following that, Nunnelley and I went for our daily swim.

I looked at a large number of photographic negatives owned by an amateur medic photographer. He agreed to prepare prints from the negatives I selected so that Terry could see what Rio Hato looked like. I enclosed a snapshot of me in my next letter. It showed me just outside the dispensary, with my hair uncombed (see front cover).

As I wrote my letter late at night I was actually chilly — nice for cuddling, had I had my honey to cuddle with.

Namay said this morning that a medical officer could go back to the States to take medical board examinations without a charge against leave time. Pay could continue and, he believed, the Army would even provide transportation, though he would need to check on the latter to be sure. I asked Terry to check when national boards (for licensure to practice in any state) were scheduled. Maybe that would be my ticket home to see Terry. I also asked Terry how she was coming on finding my photograph and credit transcripts which I needed for my application for a fellowship at the Mayo Clinic.

I finished my letter to Terry well after midnight. I just had to get it written cause the weekend was upon me when there was no outgoing mail after 9 a.m. Saturday morning. My letter closed, "Goodnight sweetest one. I miss you so very much. Today was especially hard on me — I don't know why it should have been worse than other days but it was. All my love. Fran"

Minneapolis General Hospital
Minneapolis, Minnesota
8 December 1947

Night And Day Dreams; McClusky — Anti-Hen Medic?; Our New Dishes; Discharge?

Yesterday (Sunday) was another busy day on the N&M

service so Terry didn't find time to write to me. She had worked all day and evening at histories and physicals, and finally caught up.

In a letter to me, Terry said, "I dreamed about you all night last night — do you suppose it was my midnight lunch, or do you think I'm going 'stir crazy' from being away from my sweet baby? It was an awfully nice dream, though, and it was so nice to see you!"

"Lately I've been dreaming — day dreaming, that is — a lot, especially during the time when I didn't get any letters for so long. I keep wishing that I'd fall and break my leg. Then I'd go into the hospital to have it reduced and immobilized, sign out against advice the next day, and immediately take the quickest plane to Panama. I couldn't work, you know, so I might just as well be with my papa. I'm sure an illness would heal twice as fast when I'm around you anyway."

Terry was disappointed that she didn't get to meet my parents in Cedar Rapids, Iowa. She was afraid they now thought her ungracious. She just couldn't figure out why her partner, McClusky, wouldn't work for her — he gave such lame excuses ("his wife didn't want him to"). She thought he must have heard ahead of time that she was hoping to take a vacation in December (it would have worked out, she thought, if N&M had remained a three intern service), and he probably thought she would try to take advantage of him (being a female, she supposed). There were a few interns at MGH who were definitely anti-"hen medic," but she didn't think McClusky was one of them.

Our new dishes arrived and Terry thought they were so pretty. She knew I would like them too. They were yellow and brown with a brown-eyed Susan design — that's a flower, you know, something like this....

About my getting out of the Army, she confessed to me that she would be tickled. Anything that would bring me home would be wonderful.

She used my Rio Hato rather than my APO address on her

December 8th letter to me and asked whether her letters reached me faster with this address.

Rio Hato Airfield
Republic of Panama
7 December 1947
(290 Med Disp, Aviation
Rio Hato Air Field
Republic de Panama)

Deep Sea Fishing; EKGs — Fini; Namay Discharge; Nunnelley In Trouble; Alligator Bags And Shoes; New Friends; Alpier's Date

I had quite an interesting weekend. I went deep sea fishing at 1 a.m. in the nicest motor launch I've ever imagined (Figure 22). It was fully equipped with the best in heavy fishing gear — all for free. We caught three big mackerel and one large "jack." When they hit your line, you really knew it. It was quite a thrill to fight them. One of them actually broke my wire leader and got away with the big spoon. I would have liked to have landed him because it takes a mighty big fish to break that type of tackle. The reel on the "fish pole" was as big as your head. I'm going again soon. If it weren't for the seashore, life at Rio Hato could be quite a bore I fear.

I went to a movie tonight, *Wild Harvest* with D. Lamour, Alan Ladd, L. Nolan, etc. It was all about wheat harvesting in the mid west and quite entertaining.

I finished the book on EKGs, all 450 pages of it! I just didn't read it, I actually studied it quite thoroughly. I'm satisfied because I think it will be of value to me some day.

I feared the Nameys would leave Rio Hato sometime in January. I hear via the grapevine that the Army may also ask Nunnelley to take his discharge. He occasionally went on quite a drunk I was told and had an odd personality to boot. He apparently got in some trouble over the Thanksgiving weekend while drinking, but that was only hearsay also. Anyway, he wasn't too well liked.

I asked Terry whether she wanted me to buy her alligator bags and shoes. They were on sale all over Panama for a song

Figure 22-Beach, motor launch, and island. The launch was the one we used for fishing. Most of the fish were caught as we circled the island.

and I personally thought they were nice. Most of the women bought several pairs of shoes. One of the nurses recently ordered eight pairs! You gave the merchant an old shoe and he manufactured them beautifully, with the finest matching bag. They also made nice shoes and bags out of snake skin.

I was chumming around with two new friends — a civilian pilot-meteorologist named Allison and another civilian civil service workman named Taylor. They arrived in Rio Hato about the same time I did. We seemed to get along quite well. They were on the fishing trip with me. Civil service workers signed a two year overseas contract with the federal government and then were given a 25% raise as compensation. Both of my friends were a bit discouraged about being sent to Rio Hato but made out all right, I think.

Alpier had a date this weekend. I took note of this because, as mentioned earlier, the process was unusual. There were single females on the post, but many of the fellows had their girl friends in the Zone. These fellows had "full weekend dates," i.e., their dates were brought to Rio Hato Saturday afternoon and taken home Sunday night. The government provided transient quarters for such a purpose. It was considered necessary and proper. As far as I could tell, there was no abuse of the system. In fact the camp overall seemed very "prissy" — except perhaps for the actions of some WACs. But this was hearsay.

Also of interest to me that little mention was made of the fact that the date was Sunday, December 7th.

Rio Hato Airfield
Republic of Panama
8 December 1947

Delayed Letters; Letters Of Reference; Photographs; Separation; More Malaria; Pretty Clothes

It was late before I wrote Terry. I played bridge most of the evening — and won most of the evening. I told her I was sorry my letters hadn't arrived regularly and that hopefully she had received a batch by now. I told her I was writing every day. The rumor was that the Thanksgiving holiday and the Christmas early mail rush had slowed up delivery to the States. Perhaps some mail was in fact being sent by boat as Terry suggested earlier. I told her that her letters were arriving regularly and that she should therefore continue using my APO.

I told her I had received her letter written on the third (not bad time) containing my photograph and medical school transcripts for my Mayo application and that I still needed my University of

Minnesota pre-medical transcript. I then asked her advice concerning letters of reference. Should I ask Dr. Raymond Bieter, Chairman of the Department of Pharmacology for a letter? Terry had worked for him for a year between her sophomore and junior years in medical school and I got to know him quite well while tagging Terry around the Department. Did she suggest anyone else? I had to have two references from medical school as well as many not from my medical school experiences. How about Cecil Watson, chairman of the Department of Internal Medicine? I did my best work in pathology and in all of the anatomy courses — nothing less than an A. Maybe E.T. Bell, chairman of the Department of Pathology or Boyden, chairman of the Department of Anatomy would be better. I asked Terry to please give me her opinion and told her that the Phyllis Brown Studios had my proofs from which additional photographs of me could be made simply and reasonably. I would probably need more as time went on and if Terry happened to be interested in having one for herself — well! However, I knew that there was a photograph of me in a brown jacketed folder in my belongings at home.

I enclosed a couple of photographs of the surrounding neighborhood. I had more and planned to send a few in each letter. Legends to the figures were written on the back. I told Terry I would like some snapshots of her and asked her to have some made and to send them on to me.

I then told Terry I understood how she felt. It was awfully difficult for me to be away from her too. It didn't get easier with time. However, the separation did teach me how much I really loved her. I probably would have never known the great magnitude of my love for her had we not been forced apart. The separation also showed me that I never needed to fear that I might be unfaithful. Thoughts of unfaithfulness did not enter my mind and for that I was thankful — both to heaven and to Terry. I had wondered how I would react to a separation. I knew now. I'm Terry's completely.

We had another case of malaria in a Panamanian citizen today.

This one was P. malariea, so I had now seen the three different type of malaria down here. I was getting pretty sharp at the microscopic differentiation these days.

I asked Terry whether she was buying those pretty clothes I wanted to see her in the next time we met. "You know, the low cut strapless evening dress, brief bathing suit, fancy undies, etc. If not do so stat!" (Stat was medical short hand for immediately). Clearly, my fantasies were getting the best of me. As would have been predicted on saner days, Terry did not respond to my question. She was not into that kind of dress.

I wondered what ever happened to that package Terry sent me while I was at Camp Kilmer, New Jersey, months earlier, and then slipped back into my fantasies. "We had a hard long rain tonight and its very cool now. Damn, another smooching night wasted."

Minneapolis General Hospital
Minneapolis, Minnesota
10 December 1947

Four Letters And My Christmas Gift; Two Critical Patients; Starches; Sentimental; On Getting Out

Terry received four of my letters and my Christmas gift, all at once. She said she got so lonesome for me; but when she heard from me, she was happy all day long. She couldn't wait to open my package, especially since I said it was alright to do so. It was beautiful! She loved it. Such a wonderful watch. It was a lovely thing, and practical, too. She said I had such a wonderful taste — I couldn't have chosen anything she would have liked better. She said she would wear it every day and think of me each time she looked at the time. Think how many times a day that would be! — in addition, of course, to all the other times she thought of me.

"Sweetheart, I love you so —." That response made my day.

She regretted that she hadn't been able to write as often as she wished. She would like to write five times a day. Instead, she didn't even write once each day. But she knew that I understood.

The N&M service was really a busy one — and so frustrating. Her resident had his primary responsibility at the University Hospital on the campus of the University of Minnesota, and he didn't have much time for MGH. At the present time, Terry had one critical patient and one patient with a brain tumor who soon was also classified as critical — and the resident hadn't seen either of them. A male patient with a supposed CVA (cerebrovascular accident) came in last night in terminal condition. Terry felt he didn't have the typical appearance of a CVA; there was no information about him available; and he had a very peculiar odor to his breath — so she called Dr. Gouze (the internal medicine resident). He agreed that the case resembled some sort of poisoning and stayed with her most of the evening. The man finally died (he stopped breathing immediately after she had given him a third cubic centimeter of picrotoxin, a respiratory stimulant), and they were unable to get a post mortem due to lack of cooperation on the coroner's part. Very disappointing. She was certainly grateful to Dr. Gouze for helping her out — and quite disgusted that she had no resident of her own to whom she could turn.

She told me she was glad I was enjoying my work and proud that I was such a good doctor and so conscientious. It was wonderful to have a husband that one could be proud of and in love with at the same time. Those attributes, together with my consideration in every way, made me the most wonderful husband in the world — and the most beloved. On reading those words in her letters to me, I truly felt that way.

She told me she was trying to stay away from starches, as I suggested, and that her weight was 128 ½ lbs. and hadn't changed since I left. "But I do love desserts, you know?"

As to my surprise at her capacity to be sentimental in her letters to me, she said I should not be surprised since I should know that she loved me more than anything in the world. My sentiments exactly about her.

She thought it would be wonderful if I could get out of the Army, but that she would not complain either way. Her only wish was to be with me. She was glad I didn't cheat on my eye examination. If I get out, we'll have clear consciences — and she hoped I did get out!

She told me not to worry about getting too dark from swimming in the Rio Hato sun. She didn't think I was too dark — she thought I had a lovely completion.

Rio Hato Airfield
Republic of Panama
9 December 1947

Pathologic Deviate; More Malaria; Detached Service; Flight Time; JSG&O; Love

Today was rather interesting. At 7:00 a.m. I was notified that I was to be the medical officer member on a review board hearing the case of an enlisted man, rank private, proposed to be discharged for mental reasons. He was a young, not too bright kid who the psychiatrist had classified as an inadequate personality. I thought he was a P.D. (pathological deviate). The proceedings were interesting in that we listened to and questioned a number of witnesses. There were two other members of the board, a major and another officer with my rank (lieutenant). The major complimented me after I brought out the fact from a witness that the young man "did not profit by his past experiences" (the sine qua non of a P.D., I thought) i.e. he continued to repeat the same mistake. I think I did better than I expected for a first time experience. Maybe I should have gone into law rather than medicine.

We picked up two more cases of malaria, both in Panamanians

who lived some distance off the post where precautionary measures were not in force. One was a falciparum and the other a vivax. I was accumulating a nice set of malaria blood slides for teaching purposes, I thought.

In my daily letter to Terry, I told her that other fellows were having the same trouble with mail deliveries. I thought the reason our mail wasn't regular related to the Christmas advance rush and that we'd just have to bear with it.

Alpier told me that medics could take 10 days per year on detached service (pay continuing and transportation provided) to further their education by attending medical conferences. I asked Terry to find out when the Minnesota or nearby state medics meet, perhaps by checking the latest Journal of the American Medical Association (JAMA, "jama"). Our copies were about two months old when we received them. It was another angle for getting home temporarily, particularly attractive since the ten days didn't start until one arrived at the meeting. The National Board angle wasn't as attractive because it involved study and stressful examinations.

Namay flew up to Haiti and then on to Puerto Rico early this morning to get his required flying time. He had to get four or more hours a month to be eligible for flying pay. He should be back late tonight or early tomorrow. I understood it was a nice trip, if only for the shopping and sightseeing.

I sent Terry a few more photographs of the area. I hoped she was getting an idea of what it was like in Rio Hato. The photographs were not technically too good but were adequate, I thought, for the purpose intended.

I spent the evening reading the *Journal of Surgery, Gynecology, and Obstetrics* (*JSG&O*). It helped pass the time. I was scheduled to be OD (officer of the day, on call) tomorrow, the first time in a week. I didn't mind because it tended to blot out my need for Terry. In my letter to her that night, I told her that being away from her was really difficult. I was particularly lonesome today — why I didn't know. Love (to hold dear, to cherish) was an odd syndrome (a group of signs and symptoms that occur together and characterize a particular abnormality). I pondered over its mysteries today while lying on my bunk. Love caused one to change completely in thought and action. The few years of knowing Terry had made her a necessary part of my soul. All of my thoughts repeatedly returned to her. Nothing else was important anymore — just her. That was not the case a few years ago. My thoughts varied. And they were big — immense. When I thought of Terry, I could actually see her and everything around her was a blur. Did that sound odd? That was actually what happened. Seriously, all I saw was Terry — clearly — in an immense vast surrounding blur. That made her the center of my universe. I didn't see where she was. Only her. If she was in a grass hut or Buckingham Palace — all I'd see was Terry. The rest would be blurred. I didn't see Minneapolis, or the MGH, or the Brey house — only Terry. And she was always so bright and shiny and very lovely. She was not moving or talking. Only smiling a little. Never looking at anything. Just a wonderful half smile. I knew true love. I told Terry to always remember that.

Rio Hato Airfield
Republic of Panama
10 December 1947

Uba Uba And The Portable Pro Station

I was at the dispensary reading in the office. Since I was OD, it was simpler to stay at the dispensary than to run back and forth between the dispensary and the BOQ or the officer's club.

I had received the sport sections from two *Minneapolis Star Journals* sent to me by Terry. I enjoyed them. Somehow keeping abreast of my favorite teams toned down the homesickness.

Allison, my pilot-weather observer friend, was negotiating for another fishing trip. He applied for the fishing launch for next weekend. We wanted to try our luck again either on Saturday or Sunday. The chef at the officers' club had prepared the last batch of fish we caught and it was very tasty.

No mail delivery today because it was Wednesday (a half work day). That meant I should receive at least a couple of letters from Terry tomorrow. It was difficult when one doesn't hear from the "one and only." The day just wasn't complete. I retracted that. It wasn't as complete as usual. It would never by fully complete as long as Terry was not here. It would not be until I had my arms around her again.

I saw some beautiful alligator luggage a WAC bought in Costa Rica. One fine looking bag cost her only $25 and I knew it would have cost more than a hundred in the States. The Costa Ricans made items to your order. For example, if you wanted alligator shoes, you gave them an old shoe and asked them to match it for size but out of alligator. I asked Terry whether she was interested. We decided to wait until she joined me next July.

The gonorrhea rate was really high the previous month, probably the highest in the Caribbean theatre. This was not hard to understand. There was a terrific shortage of females relative to males on the base, particularly at the level of the enlisted personal. This led men to risky behavior in the village of Rio Hato, which was just three miles away. The village was packed with Panamanian prostitutes from the Canal Zone who did a thriving business even though the village was off limits after sundown. The prostitutes seemed to be led by one more mature woman named (by the enlisted personal?) "Uba Uba." On the surface she appeared to be kind and benevolent but we suspected she was in fact a hard and shrewd business woman who extracted a commission from the younger and, in most cases, lovelier women. Whether she in turn paid into a central organization in the Zone I never learned. We were encouraged (ordered) by medical command to reduce the rate by any means necessary. We encouraged the personnel to come into the dispensary following intercourse in the village for a "pro" (prophylaxis, whereby an ointment, which hopefully killed the gonococcus of gonorrhea and the treponema pallidum of syphilis, was injected into the urethra via the meatus of the penile glans). However, few did and the rate thus remained high. As a last resort we decided to send a portable pro station (really a semi trailer outfitted as a little clinic, see Figure 23) right to the heart of the village, i.e., right to the village square, on the weekend in the hope that the convenience would increase compliance. The portable station did a good business on the first try so we decided to send it to the village each weekend. Unfortunately, we did not get 100% compliance; some drunken enlisted men staggered out of the prostitutes' place of business, looked at us, and then walked on by. We had no way to force compliance on them.

How quiet the camp was as I wrote my letter to Terry later Wednesday evening. It was quiet every night. The silence was occasionally broken by the roar of an airplane but that was all — except for one thing. You could always hear the breakers hitting the beach. I went to sleep with the roar of the waves each night.

Incidently, those breakers could be dangerous. Most of the time the water was fairly calm. But when the tide started coming in, the breakers really got high. As long as one stayed out in the water just past the point where the waves begin to break, a matter of ten yards from shore, there was no danger. But if you got caught in the place where they began breaking, they would break you! A lady came into the dispensary today with a severely traumatized knee, just from that action.

I sent Terry some more photographs of the area today and asked whether she would agree to send some of them on to the family in Los Angeles. When I finished writing my letter to Terry, I stayed in the dispensary reading medical journals and then went back to the BOQ and the bunk.

Figure 23-The portable “pro” station that went to Rio Hato village each weekend.

Rio Hato Airfield
Republic of Panama
11 December 1947

My And Terry's Colleagues

Thursday evening was interesting. Nunnelley took me to the homes of several of his friends. One was a prominent civilian engineer in the Canal Zone and another was an army major. The homes were very nice for Panama and all of the owners were hospitable, serving cocktails and showing us around. I just hoped that if Terry ever joined me in Panama, we could find as nice quarters.

I received a letter from Terry on December 11th which she had written on the 6th and mailed on the 7th. Not bad. I was happy to hear that all of my letters had finally arrived. Most everyone on the post had been receiving phone calls and cablegrams from parents, sweethearts, wives, and what not from home who thought their loved ones weren't writing. Evidently all the mail from Panama had been delayed because of the holidays, perhaps, as Terry said, because they sent a batch of airmail by boat. I imagined it would be irregular until after the holidays. However, Terry's mail to me had been arriving regularly and in good time, so I encouraged her to continue using my APO address.

I went swimming today but didn't stay in long because the breakers and undertow were too great. Alpier and Sandusky, one of the two dentists in the dispensary, accompanied me. To pass the time, we took a walk up the beach for about half a mile to a fishing village. It's pictured in three of the photos I sent Terry (Figures 9-11). The village was small and very primitive, made up of grass huts.

I was gradually getting to know my coworkers. Nunnelley was an intelligent fellow but I wished he weren't quite so hypomanic (hyperactive) — just like one of my medical school fraternity brothers but a little more so. He was essentially an internist and a psychiatrist at heart but didn't get along well with Namay and Alpier, who were surgeons at heart. I thought Alpier had his share of faults. He tried to "poison my mind" against Nunnelley in an attempt to get me "on his side" and Nunnelley tried the reverse. It was a poor situation and I didn't care for it a bit. I felt very uncomfortable when they "placed me in between." In addition, it was not at all conducive to the best practice of medicine. Namay, however, was all right in my estimation, a fortunate happening because he was our leader.

A WAC captain whose home was in Minneapolis and who had worked at the Board of Health on the University of Minnesota campus for a long time told me she had the *Minneapolis Star* newspaper article on women doctors of which Terry was a part. She promised to show me the entire section of the newspaper containing the article. She knew many of the physicians at the University of Minnesota, including the late Dr. O'Brien. She noticed the name "Haddy" in the newspaper article and this prompted her to mention it to me today.

I sent Terry more photographs of the area in and around Rio Hato. I hoped they were of interest to her. I told her more were coming; my local supplier took my picture in front of the dispensary today and I told Terry that I would send it to her as soon as he developed it.

I told Terry I was surprised at the attitude of her co-intern, Dr. McClusky, when he refused to substitute for her while she visited my parents in Cedar Rapids, Iowa. I added that I had come to not completely trust those who on the surface appeared overly friendly and obliging.

I also told her I was the most "in love" husband ever and that I wished she was at my side at that very moment so that I could prove my love tenderly and convincingly. And I would enjoy the process immensely.

Minneapolis General Hospital
Minneapolis, Minnesota
12 December 1947

Christmas Gifts; National Medical Boards; Bank Balances

Terry wondered whether she was ever going to get a letter written to me while she was on the N&M service. Last night produced two critical patients for her, so she was really busy.

She received my letter containing the photograph of me. She "loved it" and put it in her billfold so that she could "look at her handsome husband often." She thought I had such a thoughtful pleasant expression on my face — just the way she liked to think of me.

It was night time and she was sleepy but she was determined to write me and then Bea, my sister in Joice, Iowa, and my parents in Hollywood. My parents had sent my Christmas gift to Terry. Included in the gift were halawa (Lebanese candy), sheets of dried apricots (a favorite food of mine), and two lovely ash trays. The ash trays were from Damascus and were purchased during their recent trip to Lebanon and Syria. The ash trays were made of bronze or something like it — and they couldn't have been prettier. My mother told Terry not to send them to me, but instead to keep them in Minneapolis for me. Terry sent the other items on to me.

Terry's gifts from my parents were two 22 carat gold bracelets from Lebanon; she thought they were beautiful and that I would also like them. She had been showered with gifts recently, including "that lovely watch that keeps perfect time" and reminded her that we were getting closer each minute. She liked the note that I sent with the watch "6 months and 19 days — I can hardly wait." We missed each other more every day. And still, there was something warm inside of us that told us that we loved each other — and for that reason we were richer than any other couple in the world. Nothing could ever hurt us as long as we had the security of our love.

Terry looked forward to the pictures of Panama I promised but "believe me dear, I'll like it there, though — no matter how it looks. Isn't my baby there?" She liked my idea of taking the National Medical Board examination as a mechanism for getting home for a short visit and she promised to get the necessary information regarding dates, sites, cost, etc. (certification by the "National Boards" was in fact useful; it allowed one to practice in more states than the "Minnesota Boards" whose certification I already held). We didn't know whether this mechanism would be successful but at this point we were willing to try anything to see each other, if only for a few days.

Terry noted that our bank balance at the Farmers and Mechanics Bank in Minneapolis was $490. She didn't know the exact balance at our other bank, St. Anthony Bank in St. Anthony Park, St. Paul, but she thought it was about $200.

Rio Hato Airfield
Republic of Panama
12 December 1947

Women Doctors; Detached Duty; Photography; Recreation; Malaria; Gonorrhea

I was angry at the mail service to Rio Hato. I would get Terry's letters regularly if they would only deliver the mail to Rio Hato everyday. They got around to it three for four times a week. I told Terry to keep using my APO address. It was working fine.

My WAC captain friend in fact gave me the entire article on women doctors that appeared in the *Minneapolis Star*. I told Terry I was proud of her, even though the picture did nothing for her. Perhaps it wasn't meant to and couldn't since it showed her with a face mask in the process of being gowned.

Nunnelley was temporarily assigned as ship doctor on a trip

to Trinidad on the Northern Coast of South America. He was to leave on December 17th and return before Christmas. That was a nice break for him and I wouldn't have minded it myself. About the same time, Alpier was to fly back to the States for five to six days. A plane happened to be going up there for official purposes and he arranged to get aboard. When the proper time comes, maybe I won't have too much trouble getting there myself. However, the departure of the two of them would leave Namay and me here alone over the holidays for a week or two.

Alpier and Sandusky, one of the dentists, showed color photos they had taken in Jamaica and Peru. They projected them on a screen and they were absolutely beautiful. They were taken with an Argus camera. I would have liked one. However, they were quite expensive, as were the projector, film, and its development. I didn't get flight pay.

I sent Terry some more pictures, all of poor quality. I told her not to get the idea that it's as dusky in Panama as the pictures indicate; it was very bright and sunny!

I was playing a lot of pool with Taylor and Allison and getting to be a regular shark. Our fishing trip for this weekend fell through since both vessels were being repaired. I didn't go swimming this afternoon. I slept instead. They said that, after a month in Rio Hato, one was tired most of the time. I hadn't experienced that until today. Namay invited me for a shopping trip to the Zone tomorrow. I thought I would perhaps go since the fishing trip was off.

Malaria and gonorrhea were seen at a good clip now. We had more malaria than any other army post in the Carribean. However, the incidence was still very low and about 90% was in Panamanians living off the post.

Rio Hato Airfield
Republic of Panama
13 December 1947

Time For Relatives; Trouble Brewing In Panama!; The Future Of Rio Hato

Terry's letter of December 8th arrived today. I was pleased that she dreamed of me, particularly because she rarely dreamed. I told her so and asked her to reveal the content of her dream. I also told her not to act on her tongue in cheek scheme for coming to see me, i.e., breaking a leg to get time off from work. I liked here sleek curvaceous legs just as they were and would be angry if she changed the curves, to say nothing of adding a plaster cast.

I also told Terry not to fear my mom and dad would not understand her inability to get time off from work to meet them in Cedar Rapids. I broke them in "but good" during the years I was in medical school and interning. I wrote and visited them infrequently during that period. I felt badly about this but they soon came to understand. I thought that we medics had less control of our time than non medics but nevertheless McClusky's uncooperativeness surprised me. I thought we medics also did our best to help one another out and he had initially seemed so cooperative. However, I had noted that oftentimes the sweet, smooth friendly talking people weren't always in fact the most cooperative.

I cashed a $25 check on the St. Anthony Bank yesterday. With Christmas coming, I found myself a little short. But this was the first check I cashed since leaving Minneapolis. Pretty good I thought.

New development! All Army and Navy personal have been restricted to their posts this weekend. This canceled the shopping trip with the Namays, since we were also not allowed to go to the Canal Zone. The alert related to the USA lease agreement with Panama for the Army bases in Panama outside the Canal Zone, including the airbase at Rio Hato. Apparently the USA and Panama had been trying to settle on an agreement for a year. They finally signed an agreement a few days ago. Then yesterday Panamanian University students began rioting during a demonstration against the signing; they didn't want the USA to have the bases so cheaply. About 40 of them were injured by Panamanian police before the rioting was ended. I wondered if this development could in some way affect my stay in Rio Hato.

As usual, I got sleepy about 3:00 p.m. and went swimming. I didn't want to sleep away the afternoon! The swim was great and soon erased my questions concerning the future of Rio Hato.

Minneapolis General Hospital
Minneapolis, Minnesota
14 December 1947

Alcoholic Hallucinations; Comatose Pregnant Young Woman; Unfortunate Girls; Children Of Our Own; News From Home

One of Terry's patients over on station H (the psychiatric ward at MGH) was a retired cop who was alcoholic. He had been hallucinating like mad, and now spent his time standing at the intersection of the hall, directing traffic. Terry hadn't been able to interview or examine him. Every time she suggested it, he thought she was trying to seduce him — he had now ordered her to stay in her room. Every time she came on the ward, he walked over and fixed a baleful glare on her. She wondered what would happen when she next took a male patient into the conference room for an interview.

Terry also had an interesting but sad case on Thursday night (one of the times when she "didn't get to write to her darling husband"). She was a 24 year old girl who came in comatose. The only thing that was found then and at post-mortem was a 4 month gestation, intact. There also was evidence of an amateurish attempt to cause an abortion by cervical instrumentation, but not enough to cause coma or death. The staff supposed it to be some form of poisoning, but didn't know what. Terry was alone (of course!) with no resident covering. Dr. Thomes (from the Internal Medicine service) and Dr. McCaffrey (from the Obstetrics and Gynecology service) both came to see her — that helped. It was quite a nervous strain, however, and Terry didn't lose her headache for the whole next day. She didn't mind working over the patient all night, but she was quite annoyed at not being adequately covered in such a serious affair. She was also annoyed because one of the residents told her she was wrong not to have told the girl's boyfriend, who was there, about her pregnancy. The reason she did not speak up was because on an earlier occasion she had been criticized royally by the psychiatry resident for telling the girlfriend of a man with spirochetes in his spinal fluid that he had syphilis. She was told that the man, had he recovered (he did not), could have later sued her successfully for divulging personal information about him. This was, she was told, an issue of patient confidentiality.

She told me that she had seen so many pitiful cases on the Gyn and N&M services of unfortunate girls. She felt sorry for some and was angry with others, but they were all to be pitied. She thought that she must be an awfully lucky girl to have so much love and security as I gave her. She said I could be sure that she would never do anything to lose it. She loved me so.

Terry said that we were now receiving Christmas cards. One was from Andy and Carol Midthune. Andy (Andreen Sylvain Midthune) was a fraternity (Kappa Chi of Phi Chi) brother of mine and their card contained a picture of their first born, Paula. Carol had subsequently had a baby boy and both mother and baby were doing alright this time. Carol had a very difficult time when Paula was born. A caesarean section had been very seriously considered. I suspected that Terry gave me all of these details because she thought we were getting behind all of our classmates in the children generating department.

On the other hand, she also kept me informed of the news in other areas. For example, two of our medical school professors had died, Dr. William A. O'Brien, who established the Department of Continuation Medical Education, and Dr. Robert Meyers, a well known gynecological pathologist. At autopsy, Dr. O'Brien was found to have fresh subacute bacterial endocarditis vegetations (infection) in his heart valves. The immediate cause of death was the rupture of a mycotic aneurism (blood vessel infection and blowout). He had been thoroughly studied and had had numerous blood cultures but the diagnosis had not been made pre-mortem.

Rio Hato Airfield
Republic of Panama
14 December 1947

Panamanian Fishing Village On The Beach; Lazy Sunday Afternoon

I slept late this morning and then read a book on the heart until noon. I found the book in the small dispensary library.

In the afternoon, Taylor, Allison, and I took a walk on the beach. Allison owned a fine automatic 22 rifle which we took along and used for target practice. About a mile up the beach we came to the very interesting fishing village that I had mentioned previously (Figures 9-11). The occupants were Panamanians in their most primitive state. I had sent Terry some snapshots of the village earlier. They lived in thatched huts on the beach, ate the fish they caught, and ground their meal by hand with a large "pestle and mortar." We did not actually speak with the inhabitants but only observed from a distance. I'd like Terry to see the village someday.

The rest of the day allowed for bridge, reading, letter writing to my family in Los Angeles, and letter writing to Terry in which , at the risk of annoying her, I again reminded her that I needed the transcript of my premedicine credits at the University of Minnesota so that I could complete my application for an internal medicine fellowship (residency) at the Mayo Clinic in Rochester, Minnesota. I also enclosed a few more snapshots in the letter and told her I wished I could enclose myself. "Ah me, I can hardly wait to see you again but I guess I'll have to make out somehow."

Minneapolis General Hospital
Minneapolis, Minnesota
15 December 1947

Christmas Gifts; Religion And Prejudice; Letters Of Reference

Terry had received two letters from me today, one containing photographs of the post. My letters had been arriving pretty well; both of these letters were postmarked the 10th. She would continue writing me at my APO address.

Last night was her night off and she used the time to wrap a box for me containing some of my favorite foods — halawa (a Lebanese candy), dried apricots in sheets, and a set of nut crackers and picks (to be used on my Christmas nuts, and also in our home later). She also wrapped boxes for my parents and for Elizabeth (my oldest sister) — sets of monogrammed towels. Since I didn't think they were suitable as a man's present, she decided to get Gene (my sister Vernita's husband) steak knives after all. As I had requested, she promised to also buy something for the Albert Haddys, maybe towels for them too. She was surprised to hear of the marriage (Albert Haddy and Delores Shaheen, both relatives) since we did not get an announcement and didn't even know they were interested in one another.

My question regarding letters of reference for my Mayo Fellowship application generated interesting comments regarding religion and prejudice by my 23 year old bride. She didn't think Professor X would be a good person to ask for a reference. He probably would give me a good one — "but he's a peculiar person. He bears a strong grudge on occasions, and he's really a very depressed person underneath that pleasant exterior. He's also a religious fanatic, and I think he believes that you are influencing me against the Church. At least he resents my marrying a non-Catholic, and I know that he bears a grudge against me for it. He's also prejudiced and I think that people who are strongly prejudiced in one field are apt to be in others — and I would prefer to deal with persons who have a broad viewpoint. Now I hope you don't misunderstand me, darling, I know that everyone has prejudices — but I definitely don't think they should be encouraged."

" Now don't worry, my love, I'm not saying that I'm worried at all. I know you love me — and I love you more than anything in the world. You've made me happier than I'd ever dreamed of being, and I'm so proud that you are tolerant and broad minded."

Terry went on to say that Dr. Cecil J. Watson (chairman of the Department of Internal Medicine at the University of Minnesota) and any of the other professors I suggested would give me good letters of reference. She also said that she was waiting for our bank account to build up further before she bought clothing for herself, she was glad I had fun fishing, and she was proud that I was getting good at reading malaria slides.

Rio Hato Airfield
Republic of Panama
15 December 1947

Swimming; Seasonal Change; Rumor Of Discharge; Married Officers Quarters; Merry Christmas

Today was the usual very busy Monday. I worked very hard from 7:00 a.m. to 3:00 p.m. Then Nunnelley and I took off and headed for the beach. He was really a marvelous swimmer, a good "buddy" for me since my swimming expertise was not all that great. But I was getting better. I was also getting darker but the Rio Hato veterans said the tan one acquired in Rio Hato disappeared very quickly; a week inside would do it. I wasn't sure I believed them.

It was a beautiful cool evening with a fine gentle breeze. The dry season was on its way and I felt it too. None of the sticky humidity and stronger winds I've experienced in the past few weeks.

Alpier and I went to a movie in the evening. He was OD (on call officer of the day) and he took calls from the theatre. That worked out nicely. The movie was *Diamond Horseshoe* with Betty Grable and Dick Haymes, all about a medical student trying to crash the show business but who finally decided to go back to medical school. The movie was several years old but entertaining. It was one of Grable's better pictures, I believed.

More rumors today. These that I would be discharged from the Army. I didn't place much stock in them, however; not until I saw the orders.

I was 40th on the list for quarters in the Canal Zone. Not bad. I wondered whether Terry and I would ever use them. We wouldn't if we stayed in Rio Hato.

Nunnelley's trip to Trinidad was cancelled, allowing three of us to take calls over the holidays. Fine, I thought.

There wasn't a mail delivery today, so now I had to wait another day to hear from my honey. But it was something to look forward to — something very nice.

Christmas was very close now. I wrote, "A Merry Christmas to you darling. I wouldn't want to think it would be complete without me but a merry Christmas anyway. May we never spend another apart. I love you very, very much, sweetheart. Keep dreaming about me. It does so much for my ego."

Minneapolis General Hospital
Minneapolis, Minnesota
15 December 1947

Letters From Beatrice And My Mother; Slow On Call; Never Again

It was midnight. Terry said she had received two letters from my sister Beatrice in Joice, Iowa. The first was dated Monday, November 14, 1947. She wanted my address because she had drawn my name for Christmas. She had been in Cedar Rapids a few weeks earlier for the Albert Haddy-Delores Shaheen wedding and learned for the first time that I had visited my parents home in Los Angeles in July and August before leaving for active duty. She expressed annoyance with me for not letting her know of my whereabouts. The second letter Terry received from Beatrice was undated but was sent just after she had again returned from Cedar Rapids where she this time welcomed my parents and sister Juanita back to the USA after their trip to Lebanon. Beatrice told Terry everyone was sorry she had not been able to make the trip to Cedar Rapids but that my parents and sister Juanita looked well and were now on the way to their home in Los Angeles. Enclosed in the second letter was a letter from my mother regarding Christmas gifts for me and a short note to Terry regarding a Christmas gift for her. The gifts for me included Lebanese candy ("halawa") and dried apricot sheets from Lebanon, and ash trays from Damascus, Syria. Terry's gifts were 22 carat gold wrist bracelets from Lebanon. Beatrice again asked Terry for my address. Terry forwarded the letters and my gifts on to me and included Dr. Robert Meyer's obituary.

This was Terry's night on call and, for the first time this month, she was able to spend a lazy evening, listening to the radio, reading a love story, and knitting on her sister Ginger's Christmas mittens. The mittens were almost done — made of black yarn left over from the sweater she knitted for me.

It was midnight and she decided to write a few words to me, to say that she's been thinking of me and that I was in her mind every second and that, when she was not working, those thoughts formed more concrete pictures in her mind. And she missed me so terribly on these long leisurely evenings. She loved the picture she had before her now (see front cover). It was a really lovely one she thought, and she liked to think of me smiling just as I was in it. She said there was a program of Christmas carols tonight. It was going to be a lovely Christmas day this year. So far the weather had been perfect — there had been lots of snow, but the temperature had reached zero on only one or two occasions. "Do you know that we have never really spent Christmas together? After this year, sweetheart, that will never, never happen again. Good night, sweet dreams. All of my love to you — every last particle of it!"

Rio Hato Airfield
Republic of Panama
16 December 1947

Namay's Discharge; N&M Service; Body Weight

I was OD tonight. It was nice and peaceful so far. I hoped it stayed that way.

Namay got the final word today. He will be leaving about January 15th. Too bad. I wondered if he would be replaced or if we would continue on with only three docs. We actually didn't need a fourth but having four was nice because it left some time for reading.

I received a nice letter from Terry today, written on December 10th and mailed on December 11th. It appeared that a five cent airmail stamp on a letter with my APO address got to Rio Hato as fast as ten cent stamps with my APO address or ten cent stamps with my Rio Hato airfield address and I told Terry this.

I also told Terry that I understood when she didn't write everyday but I nevertheless felt bad when I didn't hear from her. "So try, even if its just a short note, to say hello each day." I did in fact understand her problem. I had also experienced the N&M service. It was my first service during my internship at MGH more than a year ago. George Lund was the other intern on the service and "incomparable" Gouze was the resident. We three ran the service alone for 6 weeks. We worked awfully hard but enjoyed it more then any service during our internship. That's what a good resident could do for you. Apparently Terry didn't have comparable leadership.

I was happy to hear that Terry liked the wrist watch I sent her. It was a very good Swiss make, advertised in "Esquire" quite frequently. I thought the face of the watch was pretty. Now if it only ran and kept time.

Terry's letters included her body weight! That was the first time she even actually came right out and told me her weight. I was flabbergasted when I actually saw it in writing. It was a pretty trim figure. I told her "as a special favor to your loving husband, try to stay that way (do I hear gnashing of teeth?), huh?"

I sent Terry some more photographs of the base. I hoped she enjoyed them and that they were at least giving her a rough picture of her future home.

It was now over two and a half months since I last saw my darling. To only hold her in my arms again! When that day arrived I would be the happiest and most excited husband ever, I know. That was because I loved her so.

Minneapolis General Hospital
Minneapolis, Minnesota
17 December 1947

National Boards — Say "Yes" Dear;" Transcripts And Photographs; More Christmas Gifts; Move To The Canal Zone?

Terry said the N&M service hadn't been too busy lately and that was bad because it gave her too much time to think about our separation. She hoped I could in fact arrange to take the National Board Examination somewhere in the States. Surely that would be very worthwhile in several ways and could easily be justified. Say "yes" dear. She would help. She was calling and calling Dr. Rasmussen's office, but had as yet not been able to find out when the examination would be held (Dr. Rasmussen was one of our basic science professors in medical school and he administered the basic science Part I portion of the examination). She would keep trying. "I miss you so much, honey. I think about you all day and dream about you at night. Please, don't you think you could come to see me soon? I don't think I can live without you much longer."

Terry also called the University of Minnesota record office for a transcript of my pre-med grades. She also called the Phyllis Brown Studio about the photograph of me they had on file. Both the transcript and photograph would be needed for my Mayo Clinic fellowship application.

Last night she spent her usual quiet evening at home. She wrapped my Christmas gifts to Gene Haddy (my brother-in-law) and Bonnie Haddy (my godchild). She sent Gene steak knives since I had suggested a more masculine gift than bath towels (my parents got the towels). My gift to Bonnie was a little blue stuffed horse and Terry's gift to her was a pair of pink mittens which Terry had knitted several months ago.

Christmas cards were arriving. Terry said she would bundle

all of the cards and send them to me one of these days. She also sent me a card concerning my medical license, which required my signature.

Terry's letter on December 17, 1947, contained two informational items possibly relevant to USA-Panama relations and the longevity of the Rio Hato airbase. Her brother Paul said he heard over the radio last night that all of the American soldiers in Panama are being called into the Canal Zone because the natives have been complaining. Also, the contents of the last package she sent to me had to be declared, item by item. She thought this was a little odd. "I'm not worrying, darling, but I would like to know if everything is alright. Darling, I love you so — I miss you more than I can ever say. I'm counting the minutes and seconds (by my handsome new watch, of course)."

Minneapolis General Hospital
Minneapolis, Minnesota
18 December 1947

CME For Physicians; "Hen Medics" Party; An Ego Builder

Terry received two letters from me today. She welcomed my statement that overseas officers could return to the States for a medical convention. She said she would check up on it. "How about one of the continuation center courses for graduate study (CME for physicians administered by Dr. William O'Brien in the Department of Continuation Medical Education)? Would they do? How about planning on January? I wish you could come next month."

Terry was proud of my performance on the committee that evaluated the young man with the personality problems.

She told me my letters were arriving pretty well now and she hoped that her letters were reaching me. Yes, she would share some Rio Hato photographs I sent her with my parents. She was in the process of sending out our Christmas cards. We had been getting loads of them from our relatives and friends and she would be sure to send all of them on to me. She sent me a picture of little Tommy Abraham (my sister Beatrice's first born). I agreed that he was cute and looked like a regular little devil, a darling one.

In the evening, Terry dashed away to a "hen" party at Elaine's home (women physicians were frequently referred to as "hen medics"). The party was for Robin (Roberta Follansbe), who was leaving to go to Cleveland for a pediatrics residency (she was specializing in pediatrics after finishing her internship at the University Hospital on the University of Minnesota campus). Terry chipped in $1 for her gift (a lovely gold bracelet) and $1 for the potato chips. There was to be boozing — she would send me the details.

She ended her December 18th letter to me by saying the more she sees of other men, especially doctors, the more she thanks her luck for such a wonderful husband as I am. A real ego builder!

Rio Hato Airfield
Republic of Panama
18 December 1947

High on Rio Hato; Visitations; My Coworkers; Beach Development; Terry's Need for Secrecy

I was pretty high on Rio Hato tonight and I wished Terry were here because I was absolutely certain she would like it. I hoped I would still be stationed at Rio Hato when she joined me. It was kind of a miserable place for a married man without his wife but the two together could have a very full life. Part of my enthusiasm was generated by visitations made last night, courtesy Nunnelley. He took me around visiting some of his married officer friends again. I was meeting a lot of new people through him and, incidently, getting a few ideas on homes, maids, and, in general, how to live here. Nunnelley, hypomanic that he was, had a lot of friends and most of them held quite high ranks. They all were very cordial and insisted you drink a lot when you visited them.

Frankly, there was little for the couples to do but entertain each other in their homes. This they did with "mucho gusto." Everyone was quite close, which was not the case in the Zone.

Some of the homes were very nice, others not so nice. But all of them had maids. One of the wives told me her maid worked six full days a week for $35, and did everything but the cooking. This included care of the children. Anyone could afford a maid at those prices. The maids were Panamanian citizens and many of them, especially the older ones, were very efficient, and taught you Spanish to boot. This same wife told me she paid $65 a month for the home which included all utilities. The home had a large living room, kitchen, two bedrooms, and a bath. This particular house was not completely furnished but it did have a beautiful stove and refrigerator. Most of the houses were completely furnished for that price.

We returned to the BOQ about midnight, too late to write Terry a letter. I told her I was sorry in my next letter and made it extra long. I had had about 4-5 drinks during the evening and tolerated them well, surprisingly. I was tired today, however. Oddly enough, in the Rio Hato climate, staying up past 11:00 p.m. led to fatigue the next day, i.e., most everyone felt "bushed," so they all retired early and got up early.

Nunnelley continued to display his oddity. He disliked Alpier very much and continually tried to make me feel the same way. This irritated me to no end. Alpier had his faults; he was a bit selfish and his ethics were less than perfect. But I prided myself in being able to get along with anyone, so it griped me to have someone try to turn me against him or anyone else. Many people disliked Nunnelley and many others felt he was okay. I feared the guy would blow up soon and this was no idle thought. He was a typical hypomanic. However, because of his hypomania, he worked very rapidly and fairly efficiently, only occasionally making a mistake. He had a good heart in many ways. For example, because the venereal disease was so high, he was arranging to make the beach more inviting to the enlisted men by erecting a concession stand, roping off a section of the beach, stationing a life guard there, installing a loudspeaker for beach music, etc. He was working hard to arrange this, and I felt he would probably succeed at something which was very hard to do in the Army. Incidently, I gave him some of those ideas, but I, in turn, had heard them from another person.

Nunnelley and I went swimming yesterday and again today. I really enjoyed it but not as much as I would had Terry been there. One of my favorite fantasies concerned our swimming at this beach because it was usually devoid of people. Someday perhaps.

I received three different sports sections from the *Minneapolis Star*, all three courtesy of Terry. I really enjoyed them. One of the three packages also contained the article on women doctors. I sent it to my parents in Los Angeles. I wasn't sure Terry approved of this but I did it anyway. Terry had asked me not to mention that she was a doctor to too many people here. I told her I couldn't help it. I usually had to tell in explaining why she was not coming for a few months. I got a big kick out of it anyway. It made me feel real proud and I enjoyed watching the unbelieving expression on the listener's face. Most people thought it was wonderful that she was a physician so I told Terry not to feel self conscious. Those who didn't quite understand were the envious ones anyway.

I received Terry's nice long letter dated Sunday, December 14, 1947. I answered most of her questions, e.g., yes, I knew Carol Midthune had had difficulty with her first delivery (Carol was the wife of Andreen Midthune, my medical school classmate, fraternity brother, and good friend). This new baby made quite a family, well ahead of Terry and me. Did Terry know where Jake (Lyle Jacobson) and Freddie (Fred Engstrom) were stationed (both fraternity brothers and Jake had driven me to California to see my parents in July)? I still owed each one $17.50 for the sail boat which I jointly owned with them and with a fourth fraternity brother and in which I used to court Terry on Lake Calhoun in Minneapolis while in medical school. The postmortem findings on Dr. O'Brien (undiagnosed subacute bacterial endocarditis) were indeed surprising and unfortunate since penicillin might have been of value had the diagnosis been made sometime anti-mortem. I told her I was amused by her story of the hallucinating cop on the N&M ward. Interning can become quite a strain but there was never a dull moment. I also told her that I loved her paragraph about love and security and that I loved her most when she was sentimental. I was just a sucker for flattery I guess. "Please keep flattering me," I said.

I told Terry I was trying hard to understand but from Wednesday to Sunday was a long stretch without writing to me. Just a note would do if it said "I love you."

I played bridge just before eating dinner this evening. I began to realize how nice and useful it was to know how to play that card game. It made it very easy to meet people. I t appeared that most people had accepted me as a valuable member of the team in Rio Hato and that made me happy. Bridge contributed a bit in that direction, I'm sure.

I noticed a banana tree while sitting on the club terrace today. I guessed Rio Hato was really the tropics.

After writing Terry, I read a little "heart" and then retired.

Rio Hato Airfield
Republic of Panama
19 December 1947

Use Apo Address!; Responses To Three Letters; Religion During Labor; Similar Thoughts And Opinions; Psychic Problems; My Greatest Asset

I received three letters form Terry today! One of them arrived this morning and was dated Friday, December 12, 1947. It had gone into the village of Rio Hato and had been delayed a couple of days. I got a terse note from the post Postmaster saying not to use the Rio Hato address "since we don't have a mail call in the Panamanian village." I told Terry she had better use my APO from now on and that I retracted the statement I made in my last letter about her not "writing from Wednesday to Sunday."

I told Terry I was glad she liked the picture of me (see front cover) and that I would try to send more. I also told her I was waiting patiently for the "sheets of dried apricots" my parents brought from Lebanon or Syria. That was my favorite childhood delicacy. The package from Terry marked "Don't open until Christmas" arrived today. I shook it every which way trying to decide what was inside. I wondered whether I would be able to hold out. I would try. I told Terry I was also anxious to see the ash tray and her gold bracelets. But that would also have to wait. I told Terry that the bank balance she quoted wasn't bad and that it would be reinforced by $275 again this month. We had more money than ever before!

The second letter from Terry was written on Monday, December 15, 1947. It contained the letter from my folks (my mother and my sister Beatrice). The third letter was also written on December 15th and I said to Terry "Omigosh! I just noted that the third letter was also written on the 15th. You sweet dear. Two in one day!" Dr. Meyers obituary was interesting and fairly medically accurate too. Terry's presents for Gene, Elizabeth, and the newlyweds were just fine. Clever Terry. It was nice having a clever, attractive wife to care for things of that nature.

In my December 19th letter to Terry, I commented at some length on her thoughts about religion. I said, "your discussion of Dr. X and religion was very interesting. (interruption — the sergeant here is all excited. His wife just went into labor. I examined her and she's really going strong. The water bag busted. She's now on her way to the Zone cause I hear the airplane taking off. Something, eh? Go into labor and I simply order them flown to the Zone on a big B-17). No dear, what you say about Dr. X is probably true, so I won't use him for a reference. That's the first time you have actually frankly discussed the religion problem (Terry was Roman Catholic and I was Eastern Orthodox) for a long time. I never think of it. However, I have always felt that your opinions were just about in that direction."

"You know darling, I have continually noted since our marriage — and before — how very similar our thoughts and opinions are. I'm not speaking of religion — I mean everything in general. In fact, it's amazing how well we agree on all things without discussing them. That is the basis for a long and beautiful love — just as beautiful as it is now. Oh honey, I love you so much and just ache for you when you write your sweet letters. I'll tell you a secret. You're getting more sentimental and uninhibited with each month — and I love you more for it."

I then went on and described a dream I had about us the night before last. It was a very realistic dream — one of the kind that makes you mad to wake up. I said, "I'd better shut up or I'll be going into details soon, and you'd have to destroy this (letter) just as you asked of your letter."

Nunnelley and Namay both flew up to San Hosea, Costa Rica today to do some shopping, so I took call for them tonight. I may make the trip myself soon.

We were planning another fishing trip for Sunday; it depended upon the availability of the boat. I had my fingers crossed.

I read the JAMA (Journal of the American Medical Association) tonight. I also practiced taking x-rays on our machine. Our x-ray technician guided me. He was very good, even though I believed he was a chronic alcoholic. Most of the enlisted men seemed to have some sort of psychic problem. Our laboratory technician (who tested blood, urine, etc.) was in Fort Clayton Hospital (one of the military hospitals in the Canal Zone) now under psychiatric observation. Rio Hato got on a single man's nerves after a time. But, I guessed, they must have had troubles before they came or they wouldn't have asked for duty here.

In the closing paragraph of my December 19th letter to Terry,

I returned to some of the troubling issues she raised in her most recent letters. "Listen here darling, you're the greatest asset I've got or will ever have. Not only do you stabilize me but you also give me something to really work for. I want you to be proud of me. Besides that, you have a wonderful personality and are quite socially wise. Besides that, you're beautiful. I'm always very proud to announce 'my wife is a doctor too.' As for the religion and nationality, I don't care a bit about them. I'm proud of what you are. Anyone who is narrow enough not to understand that — I have absolutely no time for and don't give a damn for. I don't want to 'get ahead' if people like that are going to be necessary in doing so. Always remember that. You're my ideal in womanhood and that's the honest fact. That's why I married you — of course I was also head over heels in love with you and will remain so until my last breath."

Rio Hato Airfield
Republic of Panama
20 December 1947

More Panamanian Demonstrations; "Yankee Go Home";Precipitant Primipara And A Congenital Anomaly; Hydrotherapy For Nunnelley; Leave For Alpier; Stage Play; First Hints Of Christmas

The Panamanian demonstrations against the US bases outside the Zone were making the newspapers, *Time*, *Newsweek*, and *Life*. The December 22nd issue of *Time* presented a fair description of the situation. The demonstrations were mainly in the Canal Zone but focused principally on Rio Hato. The demonstrations still occurred everyday and were carried out mostly by Panamanian students and women. Military personal were not allowed in any Panamanian community. We could use the road from Rio Hato to the Canal Zone but stopping along the way was not allowed. Once in the Zone, personnel were restricted to military bases. There were some demonstrations outside the entrance gates to Rio Hato ("Yankee go home") but I didn't tell that to Terry for fear of alarming her.

Nunnelley had a primipara precipitate (first pregnancy with a rapid abrupt delivery) on him in the ambulance today. He did the episiotomy (surgical incision to widen the vaginal opening) on the spot in the ambulance as it sat in front of the dispensary, delivered the infant, then took the mother back inside the dispensary and sewed her up. Unfortunately, the infant had a cleft lip and palate. I felt sorry for the parents but I also worried how we looked having a congenital anomaly in our only delivery of the year. Some of the lay members of the base didn't seem to understand that some things were beyond the control of the medical profession.

Nunnelley and I had our usual swim today. I thought these swims were especially good for him. Hydrotherapy has been used to calm overactive (hypomanic) patients in many psychiatric facilities. He was unknowingly giving himself treatment for a disorder he didn't recognize he had. He had to appear in civil court in Panama City on Monday for a drunk driving charge which he denied. He absolutely refused a drink in Rio Hato. In fact the only thing I had ever seen him drink here was ginger ale. But it was rumored that he occasionally got good and drunk when he was off post.

Alpier was leaving for the States at 2:00 a.m. in the morning, using some of his leave time for a vacation. He planned to fly to San Antonio, arriving about 12:00 noon. I sent a letter with him to mail to Terry in the States. She would probably get it quicker than the one I wrote yesterday and certainly faster than the one I planned to write tomorrow. Alpier said he would see to it that I got a flight to the States sometime in January or February. He was a flight surgeon and consequently had a little "pull."

I went to a stage play in the post movie theatre tonight entitled "The Man Who Came to Dinner" by Moss Hart and George S. Kaufman. It was put on by a drama group from Albrook Field in the Zone. Monty Woolley played in the original stage play as well as in the movie version of it. An Army band played Christmas carols between acts. All in all, it was quite entertaining, though perhaps a bit drawn out.

The first hint that Christmas was near surfaced the other day when a tree was put up in the Officer's Club. Terry's package to me (which I hadn't opened yet) and the Christmas carols tonight were the second and third hints. That was all, so I was not as yet too intoxicated with ye olde Christmas spirit.

The one positive feature of Rio Hato was that I had a lot of time to read the medical literature. But I would be oh so much more happy when Terry arrived. Based on Alpier's encouragement, I told Terry that it wouldn't be too long before I saw her for a short period in the States.

Minneapolis General Hospital
Minneapolis, Minnesota
20 December 1947

National Board Application; Hen Medic Party; Night On Call; Bridge; Christmas Again

Christmas rustle and bustle was everywhere, making Terry wish I could be there. She wondered if they celebrate Christmas in Panama and again was aware that, even though we had known each other since 1943, we had never really spent a Christmas together.

She found out that part I of the National Medical Board Examination would probably be held in February. She planned to write to the medical school office and ask them to send me application blanks. My application had to be in one month before the examination. She had a couple of question booklets. She planned to send me one.

Robin's party was quite a party but it just wasn't fun without me. There were a number of girl medical students there and a woman pediatric resident from the Mayo Clinic. Roy (Elaine McKenzie's husband) came home about 11:30 p.m. The drinks flowed freely, but Terry had only one because it made her sleepy. Elaine fixed some good canapes. There was one kind, made of a special cheese and onion mixture that Terry thought I would like a lot. One of the girls gave her a ride home so she slept at home (rather than at the hospital) overnight.

Last night was Terry's night on call. She addressed cards for awhile and then Elaine came in, so they talked awhile. About 11 o'clock they went to the hospital dining room for lunch and they were invited to play cards by Troy Rollins and Otto Brosius. Elaine and Terry really "licked the pants off" those poor boys. It was fun but hard for poor Troy to take. That was about the second time she had played bridge since I left. She would like to learn to be really good because she thought I would like that.

She had the afternoon off and planned to shop and send lots more Christmas cards. We got a card from my fraternity brother, Fred Engstom — he was going to marry a girl from Lansing, Michigan, next month. Fred had interned at Detroit Receiving Hospital and now was on active duty in the army, serving out his pay back duty, like me.

Christine Furman, one of Terry's co-interns, had chicken pox; she came in all full of spots this morning! There are a lot of hazards during internship but we don't expect to get a child's disease.

Terry ended the day listening to beautiful Christmas songs and thinking of me. That was the most pleasant occupation she had just now.

Rio Hato Airfield
Republic of Panama
21 December 1947

I Blew It!; The Benefit Of Separation

Smart Frannie pulled a stupid one. At 11:00 a.m. Nunnelley asked me if I'd take his calls while he went to the Zone to arrange for tomorrow's court proceeding. Having nothing else to do, I said okay. About ten minutes after he left, Allison and Tayler announced that they got the fishing launch. I really cussed cause I couldn't go. They caught lots of fish, too. Oh well, there would be lots of other days coming up, I guessed.

I read in a half-hearted sort of way most of the day between calls. But I spent a large share of the time thinking of Terry. I sometimes thought it was a good idea for us to be apart for these months. Terry would never know how hard it was for me to be away from her. However, it was something I would remember all the rest of my life. It impressed on me how terribly I loved her and I would never forget it. Perhaps that was what I wanted to find out by going overseas. If that was the purpose, I now knew for certain and forever that she was the only girl who could mean anything to me — anything at all. I was very happy about that because I wanted to love my wife with every fiber in my body. Now I knew I did. That was an accomplishment, indeed.

I hadn't opened Terry's Christmas package yet. I was doing fine and I told her so.

Minneapolis General Hospital
Minneapolis, Minnesota
21 December 1947

Relative Trouble; Wife Beater; Secure Love; Christmas Carols; Christmas Cards And Shopping; Mayo

Today was Sunday, Terry's day on call, and she was having the usual trouble with relatives. One patient's mother insisted on signing her out today. She had a hold order on the patient, whose behavior was markedly aberrant — so there was lots of red tape to getting her out. Terry had spent the entire afternoon dealing with the hordes of relatives — and she was tired.

Her newest patient was admitted to N&M because he beat up his wife — they were a young couple, 18 and 21 years old, who had been married only three months. They were undoubtedly both to blame and the whole affair was a very childish quarrel. Terry could have cried to see what a mess those two young kids, who really had so much, were making of their marriage. She was glad that her own dear husband was such a wonderful, considerate person — she felt so happy and secure, with his love. And even though we were far apart, she thought I must feel her love reaching out across the miles to me. She felt it so strongly that I surely must, too.

The radio had so many lovely programs now, with Christmas carols and all. Terry loved to sit and listen, but it made here feel sad. Family life was so important at Christmas time, and families should be together at that time. That meant us. I was the most important thing in the world to her and always would be. We would never be apart again, especially not at Christmas time.

Terry finished sending out our Christmas cards last night. She couldn't send any to many of our classmates (Donald Daggett, Lyle Jacobson, Arvid Eide, Jennings Peteler, and Roy Peterson) because they, like me were in the service at sites unknown to us.

She thought she could get some of the addresses from one of the girls at the hospital, e.g., Robert Rocknem, who interned and roomed with me at MGH.

She also finished our Christmas shopping yesterday. She only bought two things, but it took her all afternoon. She got Ginger (her sister) some bunny scuffs, and she bought a dozen sherbet glasses for her mother.

Dr. Gouze told her that the Mayo Clinic requires either a year of straight internship (one whole internship year on one service e.g., internal medicine, surgery, OB & Gyn, N&M, etc.) or a year of residency (one supervised year on one service) before taking a person on for a fellowship. Terry wondered if this were true. I wasn't aware of any such requirement. Were there such a requirement, I would not qualify for a fellowship/residency at the Mayo Clinic.

Rio Hato Airfield
Republic of Panama
22 December 1947

Easing Crisis?; Hospital Christmas Tree

Monday was always a very full day. I really put in a day's work on this Monday. But those days were not too frequent.

I received a letter from my mother and a Christmas card from Lou and George (Lucille Haddy was my sister and George Haddy was her husband; they lived near my parents in Hollywood). I also received two letters from Terry, a real morale booster. The first one was written on Wednesday, December 17, 1947, and contained the Midthune birth announcement and the bank signature card. I signed the latter and returned it to Terry for mailing. In my letter to her I reassured her that I would fly to see her as soon as possible; it would probably be in January or February. Whether it would be on leave status, for board examinations, or for continuing medical education (CME) I didn't know, but it would be one of them, never fear. I was glad to hear she was receiving the pictures of Rio Hato, and I thanked her for calling about my pre medicine grade transcript and sending a gift to Bonnie, my godchild.

The Panamanian "crisis" seemed to be easing. Part of Panama was put back on limits for us today. I reassured Terry that I was in no danger.

Terry's second letter was written Thursday, December 18, 1947, and contained a picture of Tommy (my sister Beatrice's first born). Cute! I put it up next to Terry's lovely photograph. I kiddingly told Terry not to take to boozing at these "hen medic" parties 'cause I would know if her one drink tolerance increased even a few drops when I next saw her.

Taylor and I saw a movie in the evening. It was a pretty poor re-showing of the "Informer," a picture made back in the NRA days, with Victor McLaughlin. It was about the Irish underground in 1922.

The radio next door was playing Christmas carols. I guessed they got it by short wave. The nurses put up a Christmas tree in the "hospital" ward (a few beds upstairs in the dispensary) today. But I had to have my honey to feel "Christmasy." Some snow would also help. I couldn't wait to open Terry's package. I thought she was mean holding me in suspense. But I wouldn't open it prematurely for anything in the world until Christmas Eve. She asked me not to, didn't she?

Minneapolis General Hospital
Minneapolis, Minnesota
23 December 1947

Panama Rejects Agreement; Will That Bear On Rio Hato?; Letter From Mother; Withdraw From Panama?!

Terry had planned on spending the afternoon writing on charts on the ward but Miss Honeycutt (in the record room) sent her a nasty note regarding work on charts in the record room. That took precedence.

In her letter dated December 23rd, she said, "Just think, it will be Christmas in two more days. I'm anxious to have time fly, and actually it goes rather fast. Guess I'm lucky that I've been able to be busy."

Enclosed in her letter was a newspaper clipping, probably from the Minneapolis Star, which said,

PANAMA REJECTS PACT
ASSEMBLY VOTES DOWN
CANAL DEFENSE TREATY
PANAMA, PANAMA

(AP)— The 51 member Panama national assembly Monday night rejected unanimously an agreement for leasing 13 military bases to the United States for defense of the Panama Canal.

The assembly's action in refusing to ratify the signed agreement came several hours after it was learned that Foreign Minister Florencio Arosemena had resigned because of his party's opposition to the pact.

Scenes of wild popular rejoicing were enacted in the capital as soon as word was circulated that the assembly had vetoed the agreement.

The agreement was under negotiation for 16 months and the United States State Department announced December 10th that representatives of Panama and the United States head signed the accord."

Terry asked "Dearest, will that have any bearing on whether or not the Rio Hato airfield is maintained?"

She also enclosed a letter from my mother in Hollywood. It was dated December 17, 1947, and was addressed to Terry. My mother said the departure from Lebanon had been sad. It was particularly hard on my father's mother who realized she would never see him again. However, the trip back to the States and then on to Cedar Rapids was pleasant. My mother was sorry Terry hadn't been able to meet them in Cedar Rapids and thought Terry's partner was unbelievably uncooperative for not substituting for her. The trip from Cedar Rapids to Hollywood by train was uneventful. They were welcomed both at the train station and at their home by children (Elizabeth, Lucille) and relatives. Friends and relatives dropped by nightly to hear of their travels and this promised to continue for some time. My mother was pleased to hear Terry had received the gifts (bracelets, Lebanese food, ash trays) she had sent. She commented on my isolation at Christmas time, the progress of her grandchildren, Tommy, Bonnie, and Sharon, and my responsibility as a godparent to Bonnie. Sharon was my brother Joe's oldest child.

Terry asked me whether I had received the package and newspapers she had sent. She said she had also sent me the "full page layout, in which we 'hens' got our pictures in the paper, a long time ago — funny that you haven't received it." She also said she had not yet brought new clothing. She felt she had spent a lot of our money shopping for Christmas and would wait to pick up a few new things (suit and coat) after the holidays when the Spring things arrived in the shops.

In response to my request for the full name of Dr. Boyden, Professor and Chairman, Department of Anatomy, she said his name was Edward A. Boyden. I planned to use him as a reference for my Mayo fellowship application. My grades in anatomy had been particularly good. She also said she had called the university and they said they had sent me a transcript of my pre-medicine grades.

While writing her December 23rd letter to me, Terry heard news about Panama! "Darling, I just heard over the radio that the US has announced its intention of immediately withdrawing our troops from Panama — is that true? It's so exciting — maybe you'll come home now."

"Sweetie, I sent you a cablegram tonight. I hope you get it on Christmas Eve. It's only a few words, dear, but all my heart is in them."

Rio Hato Airfield
Republic of Panama
23 December 1947

My Perspective On The Lease Agreement; OD Over Christmas For Nunnelley; His Girl Friend And His Fine; Unique Christmas Parties; Fishing; Reading; Terry Also Apply To Mayo; Merry Christmas

The Panamanian situation was still tense. Acceptance of the lease terms not only involved the Rio Hato airbase but something much bigger. The USA was planning on sinking billions of dollars into building a new sea level canal so that it could eliminate the locks which were very vulnerable to attack by air. However, if the Panamanians didn't want us to have airfields to protect our and their investment, Congress probably would turn down the whole deal. Daily demonstrations were still occurring in Panama City protesting US demands. The Panamanian assembly met today and I heard they refused the lease offer for the out Zone bases. I was not sure of this. In any event, everything but the US controlled bases and the roads in between were off limits for all personal and probably would be for 90 days. Many rumors were flying around, including one which said we may have to leave Rio Hato within a few days. That I didn't believe. I thought the Panamanians were foolish because they could and were growing rich by leasing the US a few paltry acres of land and could grow richer. They were very emotional and not at all well informed — a perfect setup for politicians trying to win a presidential election which was in progress at the time. I told Terry there is no danger of violence and that she shouldn't worry about me.

I was OD again tonight but had not been busy. Nunnelley wanted to have his girl friend come up form the Zone for the Christmas party so I said I would take over. Incidently, his girl friend was Catholic and, since Catholics hesitated to marry divorced persons, he was in the middle of a difficult romance to say the least. He said he would have talked the problem over with Terry had she been here.

Nunnelley was fined $100 yesterday for a drunk driving charge. I really laughed. He acted as his own lawyer and, with his gift of gab, I imagine he did very well. He said he fought the charge for two hours and was winning until he called one of his <u>own</u> witnesses — and the guy got the times all mixed up. I really laughed.

I dropped in on the Christmas party for a bit. The dance was held upstairs. The room was decorated with enormous green palm leaves, balloons, and Christmas tinsel. I declared, I never thought I'd ever attend a Christmas party decorated with palm trees.

They had a very novel Christmas party planned for the children. They planned to have Santa Claus land in a plane at the airport and then distribute presents contributed by the children's parents. The children ought to get a big kick out of seeing him step out of a real airplane.

Allison, Taylor, Dr. Namay, his wife (Virginia), and others, including me, were planning a fishing trip Sunday. I hoped it worked out because it sounded like lots of fun.

I found a book entitled *Allergy, Immunization, and Anaphylaxis* that was fairly good. I had almost finished nomenclature and diagnosis of heart disease. I was also eyeing another book on peripheral vascular disease which belongs to Alpier. Big plans.

I planned to open my gift from Terry tomorrow night (Christmas Eve). I had put it way up on the top shelf in my dry locker (closet to northerners) so that I wouldn't be tempted to tamper with it. I was real proud of myself.

I received a letter from Terry today which she wrote on the 20th. That was really good service. In my letter to her, I said I would fill out the application for the National Medical Board Examination (Part I). However, I had a feeling I would be able to get back to her without necessarily taking them. We would see. Terry's mention of a female pediatric resident (fellow) from the Mayo Clinic got me thinking to the future. I told her that if I ever had the good fortune to be appointed to a fellowship there, she should immediately apply for a fellowship there too, hers in pediatrics. Her work with A. B. Baker (neurologist) and Raymond Bieter (pharmacologist) would help her a lot in any application. Did Bieter ever publish the research on filariasis? "That's what referees like to see on an application — coauthor on an original peer reviewed paper." I also told her to keep playing bridge because the two of us would probably spend many happy hours at it during our bright life ahead, as partners in bridge and marriage. I also told her she was a devil, "you didn't have to sound happy about Christine's chicken pox."

I was really surprised to hear of Fred Engstrom's pending marriage. He did, however, tell me he had been going with a girl in Michigan the last time I saw him. Good for him. That's what he needed. I asked Terry to send me his address. I still owed him some cash (sale of one of four sailboats owned by members of Phi Chi)

I concluded my December 23rd letter to Terry with "Merry Christmas, darling. Try awfully hard to dream we are together on Christmas Eve. I'm certain I will. It'll be different on Christmases the rest of our lives, I promise you. Always remember that my love for you is not ordinary. It's very immense, dear. I never dreamed that I'd ever be capable of loving another so very much. But I do and it's such a nice feeling."

Minneapolis General Hospital
Minneapolis, Minnesota
25 December 1947

Merry Christmas; Radio Again Said We Would Evacuate Posts; *Time* Writeup; Tardy Christmas Boxes

Terry's letter wished me a Merry Christmas and a Happy New Year. She hoped my holiday season was as pleasant as possible under the circumstances. Nothing could ever be perfect for her, without me, and she hoped the same was true for me. She hoped I would not be too lonesome — our separation was only temporary.

The cablegram that she sent me the evening before last should have reached me last night. It contained just a few words but she wanted me to know she was thinking about me.

The news came over the radio yesterday that the U.S. Army was being evacuated from the post in the Republic of Panama. If true, that would certainly include me she thought. She hoped that our mail situation didn't become confusing again. Yesterday she received a letter from me that had been written on December 20th. It was postmarked in Texas on December 22nd. She asked me if I had received only one box. She had mailed four in all and she didn't recall that there was anything much in the first one. She hoped I got the others before Christmas day.

She read the writeup in *Time*, as I had suggested. None of the articles she had read said the disagreement was over money. The only reasons given were suggestions by some politicians that the communists were behind it all. Of course, somebody always had to mention communism.

Terry asked whether I really thought I could get home. She hoped so and she couldn't see any reason why not. We would have to plan her vacation carefully. She thought things would loosen up around the hospital after the new interns arrived. She thought there would be six more on January 1st.

Terry had had a nice Christmas Eve at home and she was at work now. She would write me this evening and tell me all about the events of last night.

Rio Hato Airfield
Republic of Panama
25 December 1947

We Really Were Evacuating! It Had Already Started; No Danger; Panama's Loss; My Reassignment? My Trip Home? Namay's Discharge; Christmas At Namay's; Opening Gifts; On Duty; All Ok

I imagined the radio and newspapers in the States were full of Panamanian news and , if I knew the U.S. news services, they were really playing up the situation.

I wrote Terry that on December 23rd the Panamanian national assembly unanimously voted against leasing bases outside the Zone to the U.S. Since thirteen of the fourteen bases were small weather stations, auxiliary air strips, and radar stations with only a few men each, the action principally involved Rio Hato and its 700-800 people. So the U.S. government decided to abide by Panama's decision and move everyone back to the Zone, thus giving up a vital defense chain for the Canal. That was the entire situation and there was no more.

Yesterday a token group of men and equipment left Rito Hato to let the Panamanians know we were really getting out. The rest of the evacuation would be a big job, slow and gradual, beginning tomorrow. It probably would be February before everyone and everything was gone. There was no disorder, rioting, or even hard feelings in Rio Hato between the Panamanians and us. Demonstrations took place only in the Zone and only by students, women, and radicals and these ended once they had won their point. In fact, I believe all of the Republic went back on limits for Army personnel today. So I reassured Terry that there was no danger and that she should not worry. I was going to call or cable her yesterday but both the telephone and cable services were so busy I gave up, thinking a letter was just as fast.

I believed the medics would be the last out but I didn't know for certain.

I thought the Panamanians would eventually be sorry for their action because many of them depended on the Army for their livelihood. Many worked on the base and were to be discharged immediately. Also, the many homes rented to Army personal were now going to be worthless properties. I suspected that the place would turn back to jungle and that the shops in the Zone would experience a reduction in sales to Army personnel because they didn't like the way they were treated after giving them so much. The personnel felt the Panamanians were an unappreciative people.

What would happen to me was a total unknown. I speculated that I would be reassigned to either France, Albrook, or Howard Field in the Zone. However, they could send me anywhere in the Caribbean theatre. There was even a slim — mighty slim — chance that I would be sent back to the States. It was all a matter of speculation at this point and I probably wouldn't know for some time. If I did get sent to the Zone, Terry would probably like it better than Rio Hato when she arrives. The quarters would be much nicer. However, no Rio Hato weather or beach will be found in the Zone.

My projected trip home was a bit in limbo too. I told Terry I would do my best to work something out and keep her informed.

Namay's orders arrived yesterday. They said he would sail on January 5th. They moved up the date since there won't be a need for him any longer.

I spent yesterday afternoon and Christmas Eve at the Namay's. Victoria cooked dinner and supper. She had some black Syrian olives and other delicacies that I enjoyed very much. We sat around drinking and talking about the new developments most of the time. In the evening, they opened their gifts. I opened the one Terry sent to me when I got home at midnight last night. It contained cards, food, and a book on bridge. I thanked Terry for the book and said I was certain I would enjoy it and would be a better bridge player for it. I also said I would take care of the food, that she was very thoughtful and that I loved her for it.

I went on duty for a few hours at 1:00 p.m. but business was very slow. I had Christmas dinner at the Officer's Club between 3:00 and 6:00 p.m.

There was to be a big meeting of everyone on the base in the theatre tomorrow at 8:00 a.m. I would probably have more concrete information for Terry at that time.

Both Allison and Taylor were happy about developments. Being single men, they were getting mighty bored here. I guess I was pleased too because boredom was getting to me also. Anything could happen now. That statement was so true in the Army. It wouldn't have surprised me too much if the movement orders were revoked but I doubted it.

In any event, I told Terry I thought I would probably be in Rio Hato for another month or so and that she should not worry even a bit. Everything was okay.

"Until I see you dearest baby, remember I love you now and will always love you. We'll soon be together again and life will begin anew. Think of it as if you were planning on being married. It will be so much like a marriage but nicer."

Minneapolis General Hospital
Minneapolis, Minnesota
25 December 1947

Christmas Eve At The Brey Home; Early On Christmas Duty; More About McClusky; News Of My Classmates

Terry wrote me a second time on this day. She was at work now but had spent last night, Christmas Eve, at home and wanted to tell me about it.

Last night at home was really very nice. Ann and other siblings had decorated the mantelpiece and table with greens, pine cones, and fruit. They used the candles Royall Storey (a neighbor and candlestick maker) had given them for the mantlepiece. He made them himself. The tree had been up and decorated for some time.

Ann finished covering the green wicker chairs — they both then had fresh, bright covers, and they looked very nice. While she did that, Terry decorated a Christmas cake for the Storey's and she and Paul (her brother) delivered it. Terry put on white frosting, arranged red cherries around the top, and laid green evergreen twigs around the edge of the plate.

They opened their gifts about 10:00 p.m. In addition to the wrist watch from me, Terry received a box of candy and a pair of white bedroom slippers from brother Paul, a white satin slip from my sister Elizabeth, a brown and blue scarf from her mother, and a lovely pink robe (rayon crepe) from her mother and sister Ann. She could hardly wait to wear the robe for me. She and I also received a lovely "wear-ever" aluminum cooking pan from my godchild, Bonnie Haddy (my sister Vernita's child).

Paul got skis, ski poles, and ski boots from mother Brey (Terry had never seen him so excited and pleased), Ginger (Terry's sister) received a new chenille robe from mother Brey and a photo (of himself) from her boy friend John, and Justine (another of Terry's sisters) received a set of matched luggage from mother Brey.

They all went to midnight Mass after the gifts were open. It was a beautiful, clear night, with all the trees and shrubs frosted over — she wished I could have seen it! The Mass was very impressive, but Terry was too sleepy to think of anything but bed.

Terry got up at 9:00 a.m. Christmas morning and Alois (her brother) took her to work. McClusky had asked her to come early, so she did. She thought it was a bit nervy of him to ask after his unwillingness to help her out. It wasn't good to be "catty" on this day of good will but she was afraid she didn't like him at all. She distrusted him ever since he told her about Mary McGee "killing" two of his elderly patients by giving them an overload of fluids one night when he wasn't there. In the first place, Terry didn't believe that one sub-q or IV could make that much difference. In the second place, McClusky did exactly that to one of her patients who came in while he was on call. The man was fibrillating and was in left heart failure — McClusky didn't recognize either condition; although how he could miss a cardiac irregularity, she didn't know. Well she felt better once she had all of those horrid thoughts off of her mind by telling me.

Terry had seen Bob Christianson last night and she wished she could remember all the things that he told her about my classmates. He, Smith, and Denton Engstrom were in a neuropsychiatry course in Texas; Bob liked it a lot. She thought Peteler was in the same course. Don Daggett was in Maine — he was a flight surgeon. Robert Rocknem was in Eye or ENT at Brooke Army Hospital in Texas. George Lund was on his way to the European theatre. Bob told Terry much more about my classmates, but she couldn't remember all of it.

Terry wrote that she missed me terribly. "This is the season for families to be together. You're practically my whole family, honey, at least the most important member of it. Here's to many more Christmases for us, dearest — all of them to be spent together in our own little home."

Rio Hato Airfield
Republic of Panama
26 December 1947

Terry's Cablegram; Straight Internship; All Hands Meeting; Gone By Feb 1?; Taylor's Background; An Interesting But Sad Case

Today I received a Christmas greeting cablegram from Terry. It arrived at the Balboa office of the American Cable and Radio Corporation in the Canal Zone at 6:30 a.m. and said "HAPPY XMAS AM THINKING OF YOU ALL MY LOVE. TERRY" (Figure 24). I thanked her for her thoughtfulness. I also received a card from Terry's mother signed "mother and children," and a letter from Terry which she wrote on December 21. Not a bad haul for one day. I told her that her description of the work activities on N&M, especially the difficulties with the relatives of patients, brought back not too pleasant memories of my experience on that same service a year earlier. I sympathized with her. I also told her I didn't know for certain whether entrance into training in internal medicine at the Mayo Clinic required a straight internship or not. There was no mention of it in their brochure, though I thought that it did. I would apply anyway and if they told me I needed a straight internship, I would get it. I had spoken with Dr. Watson (Cecil J., Chairman of the Department of Internal Medicine at the University of Minnesota) about this very subject about nine months ago and I think I could get a straight internal medicine internship at the University Hospital for a short period that would satisfy Mayo's requirement. I asked for Terry's advice.

Everyone on the base met in the theatre this morning. We didn't receive much new information. We were gradually pulling out of Rio Hato and most everyone should be gone by February 1st. The dispensary would soon be cut down to first aid station size with only a few corpsmen and two medical officers. They would remain at Rio Hato until everyone else was gone. I suspected

Alpier and I would stay until the end. Namay is leaving January 5th and the rumor is that Nunnelley would soon go to Howard Field in the Zone. I didn't have any idea where I would be going eventually. They were sending some men to Puerto Rico, a mighty nice assignment. That wouldn't be bad at all. I told Terry I would keep her informed.

Nunnelley and I had our swim today. It was unusual in that it rained the entire time we swam. That made it a lot of fun, oddly enough.

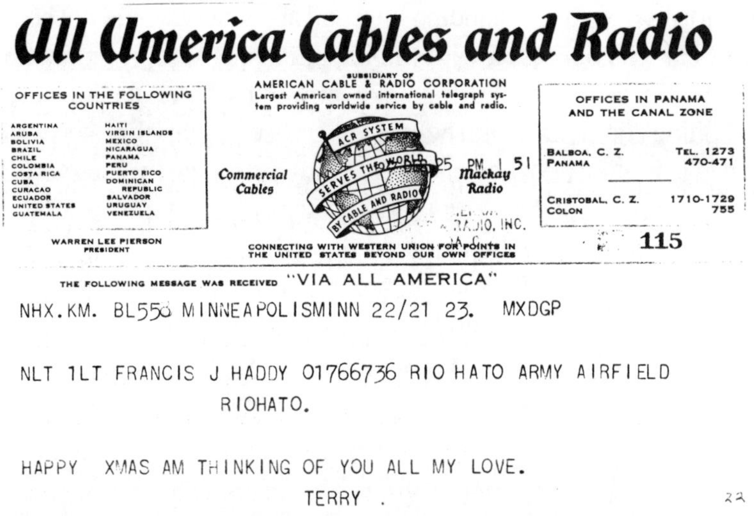

All America Cables and Radio

OFFICES IN THE FOLLOWING COUNTRIES

ARGENTINA, ARUBA, BOLIVIA, BRAZIL, CHILE, COLOMBIA, COSTA RICA, CUBA, CURACAO, ECUADOR, UNITED STATES, GUATEMALA, HAITI, VIRGIN ISLANDS, MEXICO, NICARAGUA, PANAMA, PERU, PUERTO RICO, DOMINICAN REPUBLIC, SALVADOR, URUGUAY, VENEZUELA

WARREN LEE PIERSON PRESIDENT

SUBSIDIARY OF AMERICAN CABLE & RADIO CORPORATION
Largest American owned international telegraph system providing worldwide service by cable and radio.

Commercial Cables — ACR SYSTEM SERVES THE WORLD BY CABLE AND RADIO — Mackay Radio

25 PM 1 51

CONNECTING WITH WESTERN UNION FOR POINTS IN THE UNITED STATES BEYOND OUR OWN OFFICES

OFFICES IN PANAMA AND THE CANAL ZONE

BALBOA, C. Z.	TEL. 1273
PANAMA	470-471
CRISTOBAL, C. Z.	1710-1729
COLON	755

115

THE FOLLOWING MESSAGE WAS RECEIVED "VIA ALL AMERICA"

NHX.KM. BL550 MINNEAPOLISMINN 22/21 23. MXDGP

NLT 1LT FRANCIS J HADDY 01766736 RIO HATO ARMY AIRFIELD RIOHATO.

HAPPY XMAS AM THINKING OF YOU ALL MY LOVE.
TERRY .

Figure 24- Terry's Christmas cablegram to me.

Taylor, the civil servant that I chummed around with, surprised me today. He told me he was 25 years old, was divorced, and had a three year old child. Funny, but most of the people down here have had an interesting past. Probably that was why they were here.

I had an unusual patient today, a 33 year old white female whom I had played bridge with several times. I had heard that she was divorced and it puzzled me when I repeatedly observed her coming into the dispensary for a shot of estrone (estrogen). Today she came into the dispensary quite upset and told the nurse she wanted to see me. I then got the whole story which was sad but medically interesting. She was in fact divorced and quite pretty by the way. Her first marriage was very happy. Then she noted swelling of the abdomen and long periods of amenorrhea (absence of menstruation). On consulting her M.D., she was told she had endometriosis (the presence of functioning endometrial tissue, the tissue normally lining the uterus, in places where it is not normally found, e.g., in the peritoneal cavity) and would need an operation which very probably would sterilize her. Oddly enough, her previously very understanding husband absolutely would not hear of it. He was obsessed with the idea that she was pregnant, so badly did he want children. No amount of persuasion and reasoning could make him believe otherwise. By this time she was in bad condition and they operated, doing a subtotal hysterectomy (partial removal of the uterus) and a bilateral ovariectomy (removal of both ovaries). Her husband divorced her 13 days later! They had never had a harsh word before. She immediately developed menopausal symptoms and was put on estrogen therapy. A few years later she married again, which she now thought she did out of convenience. He was in the Army and they came down here to Rio Hato. They didn't hit it off at all and she was again divorced. She returned to the US. But because of continued medical problems (estrogen therapy, removal of occasional vaginal implants, emotional difficulties), she found it more convenient to return here (no income tax, overseas pay, lower living expenses) in a civil service position. She had been having regular treatment for implants at the Gorgas Hospital in the Zone and she had received her estrone shots weekly here. Lately she had been feeling fine and had fewer emotional problems. Two weeks ago she discontinued her estrogen therapy on her own and today she noted some bloody spotting. Since this was the first bleeding she's had in the three years since the operation, she was very upset, fearing cancer and other unpleasant conditions.

I had a long talk with her and told her I thought this represented estrogen withdrawal bleeding from small, pinpoint vaginal implants of endometriosis. My vaginal examination of her verified it I thought. She's very intelligent and basically a very stable person but the constant treatment for three years and her marital difficulties seemed to overcome her today. I thought my talk calmed her considerably. Her first husband's response to her medical condition was really odd — wanting children so badly that he positively believed her abdominal swelling was due to a pregnancy. That was a pretty poor trick to play on a girl at that point. I thought the bleeding would stop if she stayed off estrogen. I sent her to the Zone for further treatment.

I told Terry I dreamed of her last night. She was angry at me for some reason but we made up beautifully. That's all I remembered.

Minneapolis General Hospital
Minneapolis, Minnesota
26 December 1947

Terry's Evening At Home With Mother; Christmas On The Homestead In Wabasso

Terry received two letters from me this morning and one this afternoon. She thought they were such nice letters, even a bit torrid in parts.

Terry spent the evening at home. Her mother was also there, home from the St. Cloud State Hospital where she worked as a nurse. She and the rest of the family were driving to Wabasso tomorrow for a Christmas party at Grandpa Daub's home (a farm outside of Wabasso, homesteaded in 1871). Terry had to work, so she did not plan to go with them.

Terry's mother opened her gifts since she had not been home for Christmas. She got 12 sherbet glasses from us, a tablecloth with 12 napkins from Justine, a photo from Ginger, and a small pressure cooker from Ann and the boys (Alois and Paul).

Terry planned to comment on my letter in detail tomorrow.

Minneapolis General Hospital
Minneapolis, Minnesota
27 December 1947

How Soon, My Dear?; What Change?; The Cablegram; Thoughts About Our Marriage; Mayo Fellowships; Other Fellowships; My Drink Capacity; My Sailboat Debt; A Bad Moment; More On Religion And Nationalities

It was Saturday night and Terry was on call. Things were dull on the N&M service and she found herself wishing to be busy. Life was empty without her husband and she only waited for the day when we would be together again. She asked me, "How soon, my dear, do you think that will be?"

The last letter she received form me mentioned nothing about any plans for evacuating the Rio Hato airfield. From radio reports she assumed that there would be some sort of change, and she could hardly wait to find out what it was. "Maybe you will come home — if only that would happen, darling, I'd be so happy! I suppose it's more likely that you'll be going to the Zone or Nicaragua or someplace — darn! Maybe I'll have a letter on Monday."

She wondered whether I had received her cablegram. She had addressed it to the Rio Hato Airfield, and then worried for fear maybe I didn't get it.

In response to my comments about where we might live, she said she was sure she could have a very full life with me anyplace but Panama would be fine. "I've been thinking — our marriage has never had a real chance to get ahead under its own steam. Mainly because we were short of money and didn't have our own place to live!"

She thought there was no reason why I shouldn't get the fellowship at Mayo that I wanted. I shouldn't hesitate, however, to apply elsewhere. She felt it would do both of us good to get a little different medical and social viewpoint from the Minnesota one. It would be good for us to be on our own. We could move back to Minnesota anytime.

Terry said, "So you held four to five drinks well! That I must see. Are you sure that you really remember how well you held your liquor?" (I had passed out once while dating her during our courtship).

She had Fred Engstrom's address and would ask him for Lyle Jacobson's address so we could pay them off our sailboat debt. "I certainly don't like to have a debt like that, especially to friends."

Interning certainly could be a strain, especially without the love and comfort provided by one's spouse. She had a bad moment a few nights ago. At 1:30 a.m. she was awakened from a sound sleep by the telephone, and a hysterical woman was put on the line without any preliminary explanation whatsoever. Terry finally found out that the woman was calling from California about a critical patient of McClusky's whom Terry didn't know at all. If she'd known his diagnosis and condition, she could have talked to her; but she didn't (the two halves of the N&M service were run entirely separately, and Terry avoided McClusky as much as possible). The woman finally said, "You're a doctor — why don't you tell me my father's condition?" At that hour in the morning, Terry was uninhibited enough to answer, "Lady, I'm a doctor, but I can't be expected to know the condition of someone I never even heard of before!" Terry guessed she could have got herself in plenty of trouble, but luckily she called again; and Miss Turner (nurse supervisor) pacified her. Miss Turner was a little annoyed with Terry, but Terry was plenty "huffed-up" herself over not having had any warning about the call.

Terry told me she knew I didn't care about her religion and nationality, and she was sure that neither mine nor hers had ever made the slightest difference between us. But we had to be sensible and admit that that wasn't true of others. Much as she admired my family, she knew they had wanted me to marry a girl of

Lebanese background. She also knew that her family did not object to my being Christian Orthodox, but they would surely want our children to be raised Roman Catholic. She cared about my love and wanted our children to have my viewpoint on life — tolerance and understanding.

Terry was lonely. She tried to work hard and get tired because then she didn't think so much — but it was difficult.

Rio Hato Airfield
Republic of Panama
28 December 1947

Gable, McDonald, And Tracy; Planters Punch; Evacuation In Full Swing; More Than I Bargained For; Tired Of Rio Hato; Practicing Medicine In The Army; Getting Cranky; Nunnelley's Friend; "GI Mess"

I was annoyed; our fishing trip was cancelled. Two boats were already gone and they were painting the third. So instead of the trip, Taylor and I went to a movie in the afternoon — Clark Gable, Jeannette McDonald, and Spencer Tracy in *San Francisco*, circa 1936 or so. It was interesting and enjoyable.

One of the more senior female civil servants threw a big "Planters Punch" party in the girls' dormitory last night. Everyone was there including the Colonel himself. Taylor and I dropped in for just a few minutes and had but one drink. I left early because I was MOD (medical officer of the day).

The evacuation of Rio Hato was fully activated. Each day several large convoys left Rio Hato for the Zone with huge loads of equipment. It would be a long slow job because there was an unbelievable amount of material to move. A medical administrative officer was to come to the dispensary tomorrow and I assumed we would then start getting our books in order to move. Aside from that, I knew little else that was new. I wished I'd hear what was going to happen to me but, knowing the Army, I expected them to hold that information until the very last minute.

It was awful without Terry. I guess I got more than I bargained for by asking for an overseas assignment. I never dreamed I could miss anyone so much. I just could not concentrate on anything for long. My mind always wandered back to Terry, no matter what I was doing. It wasn't so bad as long as I kept busy with patients, but in the Army that doesn't consume too much of the time. So I spent most of my time thinking of Terry. It was a wonderful subject to think about but I would so much rather have her to look at, to talk to, and to love. I prayed that my next move in some way would bring us together again. I vowed that I would do all I could to bring it about.

Tomorrow another week would begin. Perhaps this one would bring more concrete news. I hoped so. I was tired of Rio Hato. Nothing would make me happier than to leave. I'd like it with Terry here but without her it was just a bore. Also I thought I had gotten as much medical experience out of it as I ever would. Furthermore, I found that it wasn't always easy to practice medicine in the Army as you were taught, as you would like to practice it. For example, once I received a phone call from the Colonel's home asking me to send a laxative for his wife who was constipated. When I asked her to come to the dispensary so I could examine her, I was told in no uncertain terms that that would not be necessary. In medical school I was taught not to medicate without a history and physical, albeit brief in some cases.

Yes, I was ready to move on and meet new people and see new things. That way I would perhaps be able to live until I had my arms around Terry again.

I was getting cranky. In my letter to Terry, I reminded her that I wanted some snapshots of her and news of the family (brother Paul and sister Ginger and her boyfriend in particular). I also mentioned my army insurance premiums and a lost package she sent to Camp Kilmer many weeks earlier.

Nunnelley had a very beautiful married woman (with a new

super Buick like his) up here visiting this weekend. He said both she and her husband were good friends of his but her husband wasn't around. I was suspicious! Damned if I would let my beautiful wife visit a "good friend" over the weekend. Nunnelley was very different.

I heard the Officers' Club dining room might close on January 1st. That meant eating in the "GI mess" which was not as nice and where the food was not as good. But I guessed all would be well.

Minneapolis General Hospital
Minneapolis, Minnesota
28 December 1947

A Day Off Spent Alone At Home; The "New Look"

This was Terry's day off. She hadn't planned to spend it at home but decided to anyway since she had so many things to do. The family had gone to Wabasso, and they wouldn't be home until late. She thought I would be proud of her for staying home all by herself.

She wrote "thank you" letters to my sisters Vernita and Elizabeth and a note to the Forsleys (Lebanese friends in St. Paul). She also wrote a note to Fred Engstrom and enclosed a check for $17.50 (my debt to him concerning my quarter share of our Phi Chi sailboat). Then she wrapped a box full of Christmas cards we had received and sent it to me by first class mail. Finally, she laundered some sweaters and washed her hair.

Then the Storeys (across the street neighbors) called and invited her over for wine and tea. After returning home she took down the hems on three of her uniforms skirts. That left five more to do. "Never let it be said your wife doesn't have that "new look" while at work, too, dearest."

"Well, darling, that's my day. Now I'll say goodnight and sweet dreams to my precious husband."

Rio Hato Airfield
Republic of Panama
29 December 1947

A Big Mail Day And My Responses; Namay Received Orders; More On Nunnelley's Visitor; Packing The Dispensary; A Belated Apology

I had a big day as far as mail was concerned. I received four letters, a box containing nuts, pajamas, non-personal mail, and a sports section from the newspaper, all from Terry, and two unique Christmas cards from Royall Storey. I was mighty pleased, especially with the pajamas which I decided to save to wear the first time Terry and I got together again. The box was the second one I had received from Terry. The first one contained playing cards, a book on bridge, candy, etc.

Royall Storey, our neighbor across the street in Langford Park, was an effeminate middle aged man who worked for the immigration service. He had many artistic talents; he made beautiful candles and post cards and in addition, was a fine make up artist. The two Christmas cards I received from him were hand made by him (Figures 25-26).

I decided to respond to Terry's four letters in chronological order. The first was written Monday, December 22nd and also contained a letter from my sister Vernita. I thanked Terry for the information on medical meetings but said I couldn't plan a trip home now that we were evacuating Rio Hato. However, I encouraged her to continue sending information. I agreed with her that movies were no fun when you could not hold your honey's hand. For the first time in my life I was getting a bit tired of movies.

The second letter was written Tuesday, December 23rd and contained an article on the Panamanian situation and a letter from my mother. I reassured her that two of her packages had arrived and I was receiving the newspapers regularly. Yes, the newspaper spread on <u>women</u> (not "hen") doctors arrived and I took the liberty to send it on to my folks in Hollywood. I told her not to be so bashful about her profession. I thanked her for the information on Ginger and John and said I didn't know why I was so interested. I encouraged her to shop for clothing, "I want you to have the best and I mean it."

The third letter was short and written on Christmas day and the fourth was long and newsy and written on Christmas night. I thought her description of Christmas at home was nice, that I could just see Paul in his excitement over his new skis, and that I could hardly wait to see her in her new lovely pink robe.

Figure 25- One of Royall Storey's two handmade Christmas cards to me; one sent by air and one sent by sea.

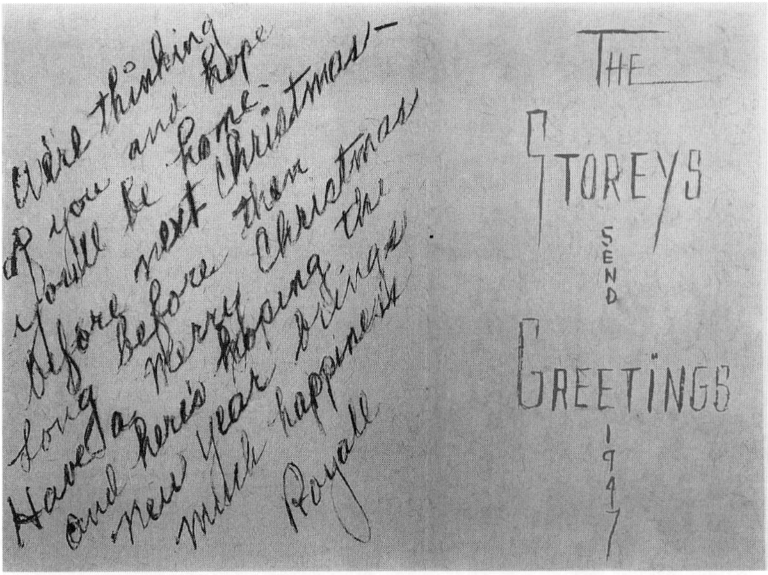

Figure 26- The second of Royall's handmade Christmas cards

I told Terry that my impressions of McCluskey were the same as hers and that she shouldn't let him tromp on her. The news of my classmates was interesting. I liked her closing "toast" — "here's to many more Christmases for us, all of them to be spent together in our own little home." I said, "They shall dear, believe me."

Namay received his orders today. He was leaving for sure on January 5th. He was not taking calls now so Nunnelley and I were working on alternate nights. This was my night and it was very quiet. I played bridge for about an hour in the evening and did very poorly. Of course it was because I didn't get the cards!

Nunnelley's visitor was still here and continued to evoke interest. She was very beautiful and had a marvelous wardrobe. All of the women — as well as all of the men — turned their heads when she passed by. She was from Hollywood and had been under contract as a starlet for about two years but had made no pictures. I didn't want to be intrusive but Nunnelley told me she was having a lot of "problems" and that there was absolutely nothing between them. She was in fact married at the time of her visit to Rio Hato. Nunnelley was very interested in psychiatry and I wondered if he wasn't trying a bit of therapy. He said he would "tell me all" soon — not that it really interested me. But if he wanted to — — .

The medical administrative officer arrived today. I thought he would have the movers start packing up the contents of the dispensary tomorrow. I hadn't heard anything new about my status and destiny. It was very frustration and trying.

My December 29 letter to Terry closed with the following apology, "I want to make an apology, honey. Remember that night we had a squabble when I was last home? It keeps popping into my head and I've just got to tell you I'm sorry. I was very immature. We don't even want to let that happen again. I love you so much darling. There, I feel better."

Minneapolis General Hospital
Minneapolis, Minnesota
29 December 1947

No Information; A Threat

Terry still had not received an informative letter from me. She was dying to hear my plans. She wrote "Honey, if you have anything to say about where you go (I'm still assuming that you'll leave Rio Hato) — and you don't ask for the US, preferably St. Cloud or Fargo — I'll never forgive you, I miss you terribly."

Dr. Brigham told her that whenever the Army moves its men, all mail was held up for a time. Or maybe Christmas rush accounted for the tardy mail.

Life was dull lately. Perhaps she would go shopping. Spending a little of my money was the most exciting thing she could think of ("I hit a new low, haven't I?").

Terry was on call and there was a pretty sentimental song on the radio. "Naturally all sentimental romantic songs remind me of you." She was ready for bed and hoped she would not be called. "I'll have a lovely dream about you tonight."

Rio Hato Airfield
Republic of Panama
30 December 1947

Filling Out The Mayo Fellowship Application Form; Asking Terry's Advice; Blushing, Eating, And Swimming; No Moving Date Yet; Namay Delayed; Packing The Dispensary

I received my premedical blueprint today, thanks to Terry, and as a result decided to start filling out my Mayo Clinic fellowship application. I labored over it most of the evening. It was quite a job, in part because what was said could mean the difference between acceptance or refusal. The application didn't even ask whether my internship was rotating or straight and I also saw no mention of it in the brochure they sent with the application blank. However, I suspected that my chances would have been better had I had a straight internship. For that reason, I was not counting on an acceptance too heavily and I was prepared to go back and take a straight internship if necessary. I didn't think I could get the application off for a few days. I couldn't decide on two of the letters of reference for my internship. I asked Terry for any suggestions. I couldn't remember the name of my Luther College instructors. I asked Terry for the name of the head of histology when we took the course in medical school. I thought I would have Boyden (anatomy) and Baker (neurology) as my medical school references. I asked Terry whether she thought it was necessary to send them a letter asking if it was okay to use their names. I thought not. I asked Mayo to send their decision to the Brey home (2239 Gordon Ave, St. Paul). I also received a transcript of my grades from Luther College that I decided to use instead of the one Terry sent me. As was typical of all church schools, they were "hurting" for cash so they charged me two bucks for it.

I received a letter from Terry today (December 30th) written on December 26th. In my response to her I said, "So you think my letter were a bit torrid. I must admit, blushingly, that's the way I occasionally feel when I think of you. That's the way it should be, I think."

I had been eating nuts and candy from the two boxes Terry sent me. I thought Terry would like it if I gained a bit of weight. I was very slender, perhaps too slender.

I had another fine swim today. That was the one thing I would miss when I left Rio Hato. The days were perfect for swimming. We didn't swim at night — too chilly and too dangerous.

No definitive news yet about my move. On December 30th, Namay heard that he wouldn't leave until January 17th. That was two more weeks than he originally thought. They started packing up the dispensary today and we closed the second floor. We would no longer admit patients to our little "hospital." Any patient with even a slightly serious problem would be flown to the Zone. They also burned a lot of expendable equipment today. I planned to latch on to some of the more useful and less bulky items. I wished I had a way to transport material because then I could equip a small office and pharmacy from the dispensary.

In my letter to Terry I said, "Well, my dearest baby, it is good night again. It would be so nice if I could cradle you in my arms tonight. Funny, we don't really appreciate things until they are gone. That is bad. We must not take anything for granted. Always remember that I love you more than anything else in the world darling. I'll always be completely yours, you can be certain."

Minneapolis General Hospital
Minneapolis, Minnesota
30 December 1947

Horrible Night On Call; No More Interest In N&M; A Roommate; Close Friends; On Call New Year's Eve

Terry didn't have a quiet night on call last night as she had hoped. Neither did she get a chance to dream. Last night, after she wrote to me, was a horrible one. The N&M service got a total of seven new patients and it had one death. Terry was to be on call again tomorrow night (New Year's Eve) and she thought that would be another busy night. She wrote, "Believe me, dear, I'll be happy to leave this service. And if I ever had any interest in N&M, it's completely dead."

Mary Teberg, a medical schoolmate, called today and said she was the only girl intern starting on January 1st. Terry believed she would be her roommate. It would be nice to have some company — maybe they would be good friends.

Terry said she had a difficult time being close friends with anyone since she met me. She was so completely involved with me that she couldn't feel close to anyone else. That was probably why she was so lonely now, she said.

Her letter to me was short because she did not feel well. She had spent the whole afternoon in bed and decided to stay at the hospital in the evening even though she was off duty.

Rio Hato Airfield
Republic of Panama
31 December 1947

New Year's Eve Dance; On Call; Malaria; Neurosis; Thankful For Terry ; Nunnelley's Proposal; Medics Out By 29 February; Where?; Payday; A New Year's Toast

There was a big noisy New Year's Eve party going on at the officer's club. I dropped by for a peek but then decided to write a letter to Terry in my quarters. It had been a long time since Terry and I had last danced. I vowed to take her to more dances when we were together again.

I was the MOD. I spent a couple of hours earlier in the evening at the dispensary working up a patient who possibly had malaria and a neurotic woman whose trouble stemmed from a fear of pregnancy and an overbearing, jealous husband. When I talked to young married women with functional problems, I was very thankful I had a lovely, stable, sensible young woman for a wife. If we had the troubles some couples did, I feared I would be most unhappy. But they created their own difficulties and a little understanding on each member's part would have done a lot to avoid them.

Nunnelley was more euphoric than usual today. His Catholic girl friend had accepted his proposal for marriage. Honestly, I pitied the poor girl. No one would long be able to live with that man. I frequently got very annoyed with him but never let on — I didn't think. His beautiful friend left earlier today.

At a meeting of the officers today, we were told the medics would be out of Rio Hato at the latest on February 29th and most likely some time before that. We were also told that about 90% of all the married officers on the base could expect to go to the Antilles group of islands which includes Puerto Rico, the Virgin Islands, Trinidad, and others. Whether I was included in this category, I didn't know. I doubted it. I had a feeling that we'd end up somewhere in the Zone.

I got paid today — $73 cash. I asked Terry to check to see that the remainder — $275 — arrived at the bank each month. I was told it was a good idea to check for at least a few months to make certain the routine was established.

There was no mail delivery today so I didn't receive a letter or package. Only two of the latter had arrived to date.

In my letter to Terry, I said, "On this New Year's Eve, I wish to propose s simple toast. 'May you and I get back together.' That's all. I purposely left out any mention of happiness because that would automatically follow in its fullest. Gee, I'm so proud of myself. To think that I convinced you to marry me! That is the most intelligent act of my entire life — past, present, and future. I love you so much darling. I don't know how I'll live if something happened to that. But nothing shall, I know."

"I think I'll jump into bed and dream of you. I hope a patient doesn't interrupt."

Minneapolis General Hospital
Minneapolis, Minnesota
31 December 1947

Happy New Year's; Part I Of NMBE; My Ticket To Terry; Application Blanks And Pictures; Forged Signature; Whiskey Sour At Richards; Roommate; New Service

Terry had a lot to tell me but, before starting, she wanted to wish me a "very Happy New Year! All the best for you and me this year, sweetheart! Meaning — may we be together as much as possible."

The news concerned part I of the National Medical Board Examination, our excuse for my getting home. Part I (there were three parts, Part I, written basic science, Part II, written clinical, and Part III, oral practical, to be taken at separate times) was scheduled to be given on February 16th, 17th, and 18th in Minneapolis. Terry encouraged me to plan on taking it and work toward that end. Dr. Rassmussen, the administrator of the test in Minnesota, said there must be six applicants or it wouldn't be given in Minneapolis. However, he was quite sure there would be enough applicants and if not, the examination would be given in Chicago. The next Part I examination would be given June 21st, 22nd and 23rd. "Darling, please come! I'm so lonesome for you that I don't think I can stand it unless I can plan on seeing you sometime in the near future."

Terry slipped away from the hospital for awhile in the afternoon to order my application pictures and pick up application blanks for me. To her dismay, she found that my picture and signature had to be notarized by Miss Smith (the head secretary in the Medical School Dean's office; she ran it with an iron hand and consequently was sometimes called "Dean Smith"). She said to send it to me airmail and have me send it back to her. Terry felt the mail service was poor, at least hers was ("no letter from my baby for a whole week") — and she thought I was either moving or going to move. So — she made a big decision. She would fill in the blanks with a typewriter and "forge" my signature so that the application would be in by January 16th (that was the rule — one month beforehand). She thought she could get the information down accurately enough for the purpose). I thought that was real dedication.

"Honey — I've been so excited all day! You can't let me down now. You'll have to come home and make my dreams come true."

Terry ordered 12 photographs of me from the Brown Studio. "Who knows, you might be doing a lot of applying." Phyllis Brown, the owner herself, waited on her. She said she remembered me and mentioned that she thought the pictures were good. She asked Terry if I was her brother — "I was so pleased to think that she thought we look alike."

Terry skipped out a second time between 4:00 and 6:00 p.m. to have a "whisky sour" with Elaine and Chris down at a new place nearby called "Richards." In fact, she had two — "and honey, I was so woozy! You'd have laughed at me, I know. It was fun, though. And I ate a whole roll of clove Lifesavers to disguise my breath." Both Elaine and Chris were leaving, and Terry would miss them.

Terry's new roommate must have moved in during the evening because Terry found lots of clothing and things in the room when she came back from the wards. She thought it would be nice to have a roommate. Maybe she wouldn't be so terribly lonesome so often anymore. Mary (Teberg) would start on N&M.

Tomorrow Terry would leave N&M and start infant pediatrics. She had one more patient to work up on the N&M service. He was a "sex maniac" who had a decided preference for brunettes in their 20's (this described Terry). He had such a gleam in his eye that Terry decided to leave him until morning.

"All my love — and so much of it. I'm so happy tonight at the thought of seeing you."

Rio Hato Airfield
Republic of Panama
1 January 1948

El Valle; The Mysteries Of Life; Rose Bowl Game; No News; I'll Pull All Strings To Get Home; Take Care Of Yourself

New Year's Day was different but very interesting. I got up at 10:00 a.m. — after several calls during the night — and dressed in civilian clothes, just to break the monotony of the Army uniform. That was the first time I had worn them since leaving Texas. I put on the brown trousers and shirt Terry helped me pick out. Taylor, Allison, and I then played pool for awhile and then after eating we were invited on a sight seeing tour by a civilian accountant who was on temporary duty at Rio Hato.

He drove us about 20 miles into the mountains to a beautiful little valley called El Valle by the Spanish speaking residents. It was very picturesque, nestled between peaks on all sides. The wealthy residents in the Zone used it as a vacation spot — their retreat, their Shangri-la. Many of the cottages were lovely, something unusual for the Republic of Panama. The natives in the valley, as elsewhere in the Republic, were backward. Their grass huts and the filth contrasted with the vacation homes. Bananas, coconuts, lemons, limes, and oranges grew in abundance. We bought bananas — large ones — for a penny apiece. Large oranges were the same price. Twelve cents a dozen was very reasonable when compared to the price in the States. However, I didn't eat a thing bought from the natives; I didn't trust the sanitation. But the other fellows enjoyed them. I gave a little boy a penny. He just couldn't believe it. He hesitated a moment, looking wide eyed at it laying in his hand, and then took off at a terrific pace for points unknown to me. I did not see him again. Very amusing. There was a fairly nice hotel in the valley which we inspected. Sadly enough, it also lacked for maintenance and cleanliness. What a haven it would have been with a little labor directed at sanitation.

The drive up and back was beautiful. From the high points we saw many more smaller mountains, all heavily clothed in green foliage. The ocean in the distance added much to the picture. I wished Terry could have seen it. I always felt bad when I saw beauty. I wanted so much for her to experience the same things I did. I felt like I was cheating — we would do a lot of wonderful things when she arrived this year.

Every time a "doc" got in with a group of guys (me and five guys today), the guys started pumping the "doc" on the "mysteries of life" — mainly venereal disease (V.D.), V.D. prophylaxis, and, always, prophylaxis against pregnancy, as well as other things. It was a little embarrassing and it was difficult to answer all of their questions because sometimes they didn't have the background to understand the situation. I always tried my best however. I asked Terry whether women ever got her in a similar question/answer session.

After returning to the base, I listened to the Rose Bowl game with immense satisfaction. Michigan 49, Southern California 0! I loved that! "Remember last year? We were in our little old apartment near MGH with some of your siblings listening to the Illinois-California game and I was happy about the results then too." That "little old apartment" was our first, and I obtained it in a most unusual way. I was interning on the Receiving service at MGH at the time and made an ambulance run to an elderly man on the first floor of an old small brick apartment building about two blocks from MGH. The man was dead on arrival (DOA). The landlord was present when I pronounced the elderly man dead and I immediately asked him for the apartment (they were hard to come by in postwar 1946). He gave me the only vacancy, one on the second floor, and Terry and I moved in after our marriage on September 21, 1946. It was a pretty "ratty" place. Terry's marriage lingerie were stolen from the wash line in the basement soon after we moved into the apartment. Incidently, one hoped that the police arrived first on these ambulance runs. I recall a run to a downtown Minneapolis bar where I found a murdered man lying face down behind the bar. The only person present was a janitor sweeping the floor. When questioned he said, "I don't know nothin', boss." It was spooky. The police arrived a few minutes later. They were supposed to arrive first on all ambulance runs.

I told Terry I had heard nothing new regarding the evacuation or a trip home. "You can count on one thing, darling, I'll do my very best to arrange time off to come and see you at the nearest possible moment. I'll pull all strings. I really think I'll be able to arrange something but what it will be I haven't the slightest idea."

"By the way, are you taking good care of yourself in that cold, cold climate? Bundle up real warm when you go out and don't catch anything from the patients. Try and get exercise — I mean like skating, etc. Eat a lot of protein and very little carbohydrates to watch your weight. I love your pretty little figure and so no matter how much it annoys you, I'm <u>always</u> going to harp on it. So there, too. That's the only thing I'll ever harp on though, dear."

"Gee, no matter how I figure it, it's always six months until we'll be permanently together again. Maybe it will pass quickly. I certainly hope so.

I ended this long New Year's Day by reading medical journals.

Minneapolis General Hospital
Minneapolis, Minnesota
1 January 1948

Loafing Away A Lonesome New Year's Day; Roommate Mary Teberg; <u>Four</u> Interns On The Pediatric Service; No Radio News About Panama

Terry loafed in the afternoon, lonesome and hoping I was getting her letters, in particular the one she wrote yesterday. It was an important letter because it described a possible mechanism for our being together for a short time in the new future, i.e., while I took the National Medical Board Examination.

Mary Teberg moved in with her and she thought they would get alone fine. It would be nice to have a roommate.

There were <u>four</u> interns on the Pediatric service. The other three were all new males. Terry didn't think they liked it so well when she didn't stay around New Year's Day, but she really thought she had a day off coming, after working Christmas Eve and New Year's Eve.

She received a letter from my parents. She didn't see how my mom found as much time to write as she did — it was remarkable how much she could accomplish. She sent Terry a silver cross and holy card which she had obtained in Syria.

She hadn't heard any more over the radio about Panama. She hoped there would be definite news soon.

Rio Hato Airfield
Republic of Panama
2 January 1948

A Belated Christmas; Sharing With The Namays; Freddie Made It; Thank You letters; A Drunk Patient; Plans For The Future; Evacuation Continues

Gee, today was really my Christmas. I received four packages and an odd assortment of mail.

There were two packages from Terry. One contained slippers. A good choice. My old ones were beginning to show wear. The enclosed card was appropriate — fireplace, pipe, and dog (Figure 27). The other package was the tardy one containing dried apricots, halvah, nut crackers, etc. I had already written and thanked my mother for the delicacies from Syria. In fact, my letter to Terry was the fifth one I had written tonight. I couldn't understand my terrific craving for dried apricots — especially when it was prepared in thin sheets. I told Terry my craving resembled that sometimes seen with certain foods in pregnant women. I was eating thin sheets of dried apricots as I wrote my letters.

Liz and John sent me a fine pair of knit pajamas — the kind with tight pant legs. Bea, Tony, and little Tommy Joe sent me white shirts, two ties, and two pairs of socks.

I also received newspaper sports sections from Terry, which I really enjoyed. Royall's second Christmas card arrived (he sent me one by airmail and one by sea). They were both hand made, beautiful and almost identical (Figures 25-26).

I called the Namays and asked them if they would like some halvah and some pressed apricots. They said, "Si! Bueno! Mucho!" or something to that effect. I delivered the next day.

I received a letter from Fred (Engstrom). He seemed very happy about his approaching (January 24) marriage and I was happy for him. I wasn't sure Freddie would ever find a wife. He was shy around women. I wrote him a letter of congratulation. He also said Annette (Eide) was pregnant and that Arvid (Eide) was happy because he had questioned whether she could conceive after having a surgical procedure. I thanked Terry for sending Fred the check and for asking Fred for Jacobson's address so we could also pay him.

I also wrote thank you letters to mom and Liz in Hollywood and Bea in Joice, Iowa. Finally, I wrote to Luther College for some data I needed for my Mayo application.

Figure 27- Terry's holiday greeting to me.

I was on call. Alpier would be back tomorrow so Nunnelley and I would get a little time off for awhile. While writing letters, I received a call from the dispensary asking me to come over and see a drunk. I almost said no but then thought better of it; you never knew when a "drunk" was really something else (diabetic, drug abuse, head injury, stroke, etc.). The examination revealed he was in fact drunk.

I received two letters from Terry today. The first was a big fat one written on December 27th. Terry got very serious at times and I liked her in that role very much. She was very sensible in addition to being a very lovely woman. I told her not to worry, from now on we'd have our own home and it would be run as she and I mutually decided, including the lives of our dear children to come. What we would decide for their religion I didn't know but it would be something that didn't cause them mental conflict. That she could bank on.

I agreed that it wouldn't harm us to see medicine as it is practiced outside of Minnesota. However, the Mayo Clinic was one application I didn't want to pass up. I would like to try it first. If that application failed, I would try something else.

I sympathized with Terry on her long distance phone call in the middle of the night. I had had a few similar experiences when I interned at MGH the previous year.

The second letter from Terry was written on Sunday, December 28th, the day she stayed home alone. I told her I would prefer that some family member be there with her. Yes, $17.50 was the right amount for Freddie and Jake each. The hems were coming down, eh? None of the women in Rio Hato had the new look as yet, but they were talking about it. Were you wearing dark nylons yet? I wondered about them.

The evacuation of Rio Hato was continuing but I had no definitive information on my own fate. Rumors continued but I decided not to confuse Terry with them.

I closed my letter to her by reminding her that I loved her and that I would always love her because I couldn't help myself — not that I wanted to help myself (I'd rather let matters take the natural course). I told her I was very much dependent on her and if she stopped loving me even one particle less, I would be devastated.

Minneapolis General Hospital
Minneapolis, Minnesota
2 January 1948

Five Letters; Devastated About My Christmas But No Longer Anxious About Evacuation; Applications And Letters Of Reference; Her Opinion Of Nunnelley; "Little Peds;" "Big Peds"

Terry received five letters from me today which cheered her up. However, she almost cried when she read about my Christmas. She felt I deserved better. She had hoped that the other three boxes would have reached me in time — but she guessed it just didn't work out that way. She was happy, though, that I received the cablegram — even if it did take three days to get there. Her thoughts were with me Christmas day, as they were every day. She missed me and didn't before realize how much her world revolved around me. Even from a distance I made her feel secure and protected, but nothing could make up for my absence. "Darling, I love you and miss you so."

She wondered whether the evacuation of Rio Hato would influence my vacation plan. Thinking about it was the bright spot in her day. She knew that meeting would be a more wonderful "honeymoon" than any we've ever had before. If she could look forward to seeing me this month or next, she would be able to keep up her spirits in spite of anything.

My five letters relieved her mind of worrying about the Panamanian situation. She was glad to have such a complete summary of it. The five letters she received today were all postmarked the 29th of December. She hoped hers got to me more regularly than mine got to her.

Terry would send in my medical license fee and also forward mail to my parents in Hollywood. They always were so thrilled to hear from me. She sent me the sports page every week, but she gathered that I hadn't received too many of them as yet.

Dr. Bieters' scientific paper on filariasis, which had included Terry's name as one of the authors, was published but she didn't know when or where (I thought it would be useful in any application she made for a fellowship). It would be easy enough to look up, however. She thought Dr. A. B. Baker (in neurology where she had worked for six months while awaiting the start of her internship) would give her a good recommendation — but she wasn't so sure about Bieter (Chairman of the Department of Pharmacology where she worked between her sophomore and junior years in medical school). He seemed to bear a terrific load of resentment toward her for some reason which she didn't understand.

Nunnelley didn't sound like a nice, clean-living kid to Terry. She was afraid he wouldn't get much satisfaction from her in regard to his Catholic girl friend (Nunnelley said he'd like to talk to Terry about their religion problem). Terry really didn't approve of divorce; and besides, she thought a girl who married him would get a poor deal. Unless she were a very unusual girl, Terry didn't think she'd consider him a particularly good risk.

Terry thought I should apply to Mayo's under present conditions. If they required a straight internship, they would let me know. And if I needed one, she knew I would not have a bit of trouble getting one.

She was glad I was moving away from Rio Hato as long as I was glad. She could easily understand my boredom. The patient with endometriosis was interesting. Terry said she was lucky to have me for a husband — she couldn't believe that I would ever be so childish or unstable (as the patient's husband). She always thought of me as being sweet and understanding of all her faults and inadequacies as a wife (the former was not always true and I didn't recognize faults and inadequacies).

Her new service at MGH was "little peds" and she was crazy about the babies — they were like little dolls! She worked with Hanson (his wife was Mrs. Hanson in the records department) and he was nice. The two new interns on "big peds," like so many medics, seemed to be a pair of jerks.

Minneapolis General Hospital
Minneapolis, Minnesota
Saturday, 3 January 1948

About Shopping; Peds Service; The Squabble; Royall; Nunnelley; Letters Of Reference; The Brey Home

Terry received two letters from me, "both just as sweet as can be." One was mailed on December 30th and the other on December 31st. One contained the Christmas letter I received from Royall Storey, our friendly neighbor. She thought Royall's letter was very nice and she would thank him for it. She particularly enjoyed one of Royall's comment about Paul, her brother, i.e., when Royall came for a visit he found Paul relaxing. Paul's laid back attitude always made people feel comfortable.

She shopped in the afternoon but didn't spend quite all of her month's check (interns' salaries at MGH were $15 cash plus room and board in 1947-48). She bought a set of 12 large and 12 small glasses with horses and unicorns etched on them, an overall and T-shirt for the Midthune's new baby, the *Adventures of Paul Bunyan*, stationery (she had run out while writing me last night), and a large envelope for my second class mail. She also bought a box of preserved fruit for me and would enclose a little pamphlet of Part I National Medical Board questions when she sent it. She hoped the sample questions would help me prepare for the examination which, hopefully, would get me home for a visit.

Tonight she was at home, and believe it or not, she had tomorrow off, too. With all the time off she was going to have on the Pediatric service, she wished I would be able to come home. She only worked every fourth night and next month on "Con" (Contagious Diseases), her next service, she expected to work every third night.

Terry thought she knew which little squabble I apologized for in one of my letters. She wanted to apologize too. She thought my visit just before leaving last time was unpleasant for me in so many ways — the house was freezing cold, nobody was home with me during the day, she had to work late so much, and — worst of all — she was so tired and cross. "You're the sweetest, kindest, most considerate husband any girl ever had. I believe that with all my heart, honey, and everyday it's impressed anew upon me — either by comparison of you on my part with other men, or by the wonderful things you say in your letters. No, darling, we don't want anything to happen again that even resembles a harsh word between us — and I know that if it does, it'll be mostly my fault."

Royall mentioned in his Christmas letter to me that he stayed home to take care of his mother. Terry said there was quite a lot of discussion in the Brey family about that. Royall felt that he had to keep hot-packing his mother's knee all day. Terry questioned whether there was really anything wrong with the knee. She was sure that Mrs. Storey could have sat by the stove and hot-packed it herself. She also could have fixed herself a sandwich at noon and let Royall go to work. Terry thought he seemed to bear a terrific load of resentment toward the grandmother who was in a rest home. Terry wondered if it wasn't really meant for his mother. Royall was a complex person in a complex situation.

Terry's comments on Nunnelley were interesting. "So Nunnelley and his friend have only a patient-doctor relationship between them. I have no doubt that he's giving her psychotherapy — probably Freudian psychoanalysis interpreted freely."

Terry thought it was proper and important that I write the men I asked for references and ask them if it's alright to use their names. She wondered why I didn't use Dr. Watson (Cecil Watson, Chairman of the Department of Internal Medicine at the University of Minnesota) as a reference. "Did I think it would hurt my chances if I wanted to fall back on him for a straight internship or residency? (The answer was "yes"). She gave me additional guidance. She suggested Dr. Gouze as a reference from my internship. She wondered if Dr. Fahr (George Fahr, M.D., a well known internist at MGH) knew me because if he did, he could give me a very valuable reference. She also suggested Dr. Ralph Anderson, Dr. Brigham (a surgeon from my internship period), and Dr. Hal Downey (a histology professor from our period in medical school).

Terry spent Saturday night at home. Justine had a bunch of friends in the large living room (the Brey family home was a large red Victorian Queen Ann house, once owned by the Pillsbury family, set on a hill across the street from Langford Park, circa 1890, perfect for entertaining) and Terry and Ann were pointedly invited to stay out. Terry decided temporarily to terminate the letter she was writing me and add a postscript in the morning.

Rio Hato Airfield
Republic of Panama
4 January 1948

Busy Day On Call; List Of Diagnoses On Sunday; Relief Now That Alpier's Back; Nunnelley's Wife To Be; My Destination Still Unknown; More Malaria; Warm Vs. Cold

I was MOD again today and the patients really kept me busy. Just to give Terry a feel for the extent of my workday, I kept track of the diagnoses of the patients I treated today. The list included appendicitis or mittleschmertz (the pain of ovulation), falciparum malaria, conjunctivitis, acute urethritis-gonorrheal (our portable dispensary in the Rio Hato village square did not reduce the incidence of gonorrhea), delirium tremens (alcohol withdrawal), sprained wrist in an infant, sting ray wound of foot, wasp sting, infantile diarrhea, and ingestion and inhalation of kerosene by a child. When I completed the list, I was again called by the dispensary, this time to see a woman with chills and fever. Not a bad variety for a Sunday. I had the malaria and the kerosine ingestion patients flown to the Zone for treatment.

MOD every other day was starting to annoy me. However, Alpier returned from the States today so we planned to put him to work beginning tomorrow. That would give Nunnelley and me some rest. I thought sick call would fall off sharply soon as a result of the evacuation. We had noticed some decrease in the numbers of patients seen already.

Nunnelley's wife-to-be was visiting him today. She seemed very nice. I still thought she was going to really have her hands full.

I thought I'd soon know my destination but to date I had heard nothing. In the words of the GIs, I was "hurtin" and still "sweatin" it out.

The woman I saw in the dispensary with chills and fever turned out to have malaria alright. That was the first white woman to have it since I arrived in Rio Hato! Well we would soon leave.

Yesterday afternoon I slept for a couple of hours and then in the evening Taylor, Allison, and I went to a movie. It was a class B murder mystery which "wasn't too hot."

Thanks to Terry, I was eating nuts, candy, and apricot sheets and enjoying them immensely. Very thoughtful. It was nice to have a wife like Terry. Thinking about it made me feel warm all over, even though she was not here.

From what I heard, the States was a cold and snowy place these days. It was hard to realize that down here in Rio Hato, with the nice warm day time sun, palm trees, swimming, deep sun tan, iced tea, suntan uniforms, etc. But I would take the cold States even so.

I hoped I would soon have some definite news for Terry. Whatever it was, I hoped it would bring us together again. I would do everything in my power to bring it about.

Minneapolis General Hospital
Minneapolis, Minnesota
4 January 1948

About Neighbors, Relatives, And Friends; My Picture In The Newspaper; Lots Of Time To Think On Peds

Terry's postscript in the morning added more about our neighbors, the Storeys. Grandmother Storey, who had been in a rest home for the last month, was taken to Anker Hospital in St. Paul a few days ago because it was thought she had a hip fracture. Well, her hip was O.K., so they returned her to the rest home.

The Brey family home was large and hospitable; consequently it had many visitors. They in fact were expecting relatives today.

Uncle Tom Taylor, married to Terry's mother's sister Helen, was said to have cancer of the toe. He was having his second series of x-ray treatments now. It must really have been cancer.

My picture was in the Minneapolis paper on New Year's Day! It was one of the drowning pictures taken while I was on the Receiving service (Emergency Room) at MGH. It was included in a review of the years events. Terry thought it was a very good picture and she said she would wrap it with the sports section she was sending me. She was also sending me this month's *Cosmopolitan* magazine because it had an article on the University of Minnesota.

Terry said that now that there were four interns on "Peds," she had lots of time to think of me — and "believe me, dear, I do."

Hollywood, California
4,5 January 1948

Letters From My Worried Mother And Father

My father and mother, recently returned from Lebanon, almost simultaneously wrote me separate letters on January 4th and 5th. Letters from my mother to me were not unusual; she had received part of her schooling in the United States and was therefore reasonably adept at writing letters in English. Letters written by my father were very unusual and written only under very special circumstances; he was a few years older than my mother when they immigrated to the Untied States and therefore he had had all of his formal schooling in Lebanon. Consequently, his letters were almost always written in Arabic, which I did not understand. His letter writing ability in English was limited and required much effort. Consequently his letters were not easily understood. When he wanted to communicate in written English, he usually dictated a letter to my mother. Only on rare and special occasions did he attempt to write a letter in English himself. This was one of those occasions. The newspapers and radio were full of news about Panama and both he and my mother were worried about me. Furthermore, my father was home recovering from a tooth extraction and had time on his hands.

My mother wrote me on January 4th. "Thank you for your letter. We were worried and wondering how the dispute will affect you. The news on the radio and in the newspapers was continuously about the Panama government and the US government. We are very happy that everything is OK with you. We are wondering if your address is going to change."

The rest of her letter concerned family and other matters, i.e., Sharon Haddy's measles; Janice Haddy's fracture; year end inventories at the two markets; the beautiful weather in California; the bitter cold in the Midwest and East; my kind friends, the Namays; Dad's tooth extraction; the photos I sent; the photos they took in Ain Arab; the halvah and apricot sheets Terry sent; other food my mother could send me; mail from relatives in Ain Arab; how sad the parting in Lebanon; weekly letters from Terry; baby sitting Sharon; letters from Beatrice and Vernita; Uncle Mike and Aunty Haddy; how important it was to write and keep them informed.

My father wrote me the next day when he was feeling better (January 5, 1948). After commenting on his tooth extraction, he said "Well old boy, how are you coming now? I hope you like it in that part of the world. Are you getting medical practice out of it? I know that it is lonesome for you away from home but, as they say, that is the Army life. We hear from Terry often. She is O.K. and working hard. I wish we could have seen her on our way home but she was not able to meet us in Cedar Rapids."

He then commented on the Lebanon trip, in particular, the emotional meeting and departure with and from his mother and brother after 37 years:

I wish you could have been with us. It was a trip we'll never forget. It would be very hard for me to explain to you the exciting meeting with mother and brother and their families. I can not describe it to you. But you can imagine; they had not seen us for 37 years. Mother and the brother and some of their children met us in Beirut. You should have seen my poor mother. She was 75 years old. She was just like a little child, so happy and couldn't believe I came back to see her. And how glad they were to see your mother and Juanita. They did not know what to do for them. No doubt your mother explained all this to you.

But I thought I would drop you a few lines myself because I am very lonesome for you. I do hope we will meet again soon. The old country has changed very much, especially in the mountains of Lebanon where some places are very modern but the small towns are about the same as when I left.

The parting with my mother and my brother was very hard, something I will never forget. They took it very hard, especially my poor mother since she knew she may not see me again.

Well son, I guess I said all I can about the trip. When I see you I will tell you more. So now I will ask you to be a good boy and take good care of yourself and do not take chances if there is any trouble in that country. There is much news about it now.

Good luck to you and God bless you.

Dad

Please write soon. I hope you can read this letter.

Rio Hato Airfield
Republic of Panama
5 January 1948

Four Letters; Assigned To A Dispensary In The Panama Air Depot In The Zone?; NMBE Trip Home In Limbo; Will Call The CO In The A.M.; Mary Teberg?; References For Mayo Application

I received four letters from Terry today. I felt bad when I learned that mine were not arriving regularly — but there wasn't much we could do about it.

I received some news today which I believed was fairly reliable. Alpier called headquarters in the Zone and they said I'd be going to the Panama Air Depot (P.A.D.). It's a large depot for air corp supplies in the Canal Zone located at Albrook Field. The work would be dispensary work again but almost solely with civilians (civil service employees) who are employed in the depot. In addition to the usual patients, they say there would be a lot of "Gyn" (gynecological) work. The transfer to P.A.D. wasn't definite but fairly likely. By the time Terry arrived in Panama in July, I should have been assigned government quarters in the Zone and the quarters there were usually very nice. However, it was much warmer there and the humidity was a bit annoying. There was more entertainment there than in Rio Hato (though I personally wouldn't need more if Terry were with me).

I told Terry not to expect certain success in my quest for a trip home. I thanked her for preparing my application to take the National Medical Board Examination. I would call Colonel Lee in the Zone tomorrow and ask him for permission to fly to the States. In my favor was the fact that patient visits were falling off rapidly in Rio Hato. But I cautioned Terry against optimism because everything was in a state of flux and definitive plans were few and far between. I didn't think I could pass the exam but didn't really care. (I did in fact take and pass the exam in February. See epilogue). That wasn't the reason for the trip.

I thanked Terry for getting copies of my photograph. I knew I would eventually use all of them. I asked her for pictures of herself.

I told Terry I didn't remember Mary Teberg, her new roommate. Please describe her. With four interns on Pediatrics, now was indeed the time to fly home.

I was still working on my Mayo fellowship application and asked Terry to suggest references from MGH. I needed two. Was Royal Grey still there? He and I got along fine. What was Superintendent Pollard's first name? I supposed I would have to use him as one of the two references. I was certain George Fahr wouldn't know me from Joe Blow.

I hoped the Colonel would be in a good mood tomorrow and that I would have good news for Terry after calling him tomorrow to ask for permission to fly to the States. I knew he would say yes if a regular Army officer asked him what I planned to ask him.

"Say hello to your mom, Ann, and the rest. Also tell yourself that I love you, cause I do."

Minneapolis General Hospital
Minneapolis, Minnesota
5 January 1948

Birthing And Circumcision; A Beat Up Intern; A Letter From Mother Describing The Hollywood Christmas

Jane and Don Gumprecht had a fine baby boy today (Jane was my classmate and Terry's friend; Jane and I roomed next to one another during an externship at Asbury Hospital during our senior year in medical school). Jane came into the hospital at 1:00 p.m. and had the baby at 3:30 p.m., almost a precipitous labor. Magee came over and Sandy gave the anesthetic (cyclopropane). Dr. Baker did the delivery, but Dr. Lang arrived in time to repair the episiotomy. Jane was very starry-eyed when Terry saw her afterwards. Poor Don spent the afternoon standing around the corridor on one foot. He looked so lost — and no one paid any attention to him.

"Honey, all these people are getting ahead of us — how does that happen?"

"I did my first circumcision today — isn't that something? Guess I'm now a major surgeon. Dr. Anderson and I had quite a discussion about the merits of the procedure. In fact, he was embarrassingly frank about his own personal preference. You and I will have to discuss the matter, sweetheart, when you come home — in regard to our sons, that is."

Terry had another happening for me. "Romanski (one of the interns who started when I did) got beat up by a patient on the N&M service yesterday. I had just left the service, you know. The patient hit him in the face with a urinal. Poor Romanski now has a contused upper lip and two missing front teeth. He looks terrible, and the worst of it is that everyone thinks it's funny." (N&M was clearly a dangerous service; I was attacked by two patients on that same service during my internship at MGH the year before. One large psychotic man broke his right upper arm when he pulled it back vigorously to strike me. As he pulled it back, his elbow struck the wall behind him and he was thus unable to render the blow, thank heaven. Another male patient burst through the door of the psychiatric floor, attempting to escape. I tackled him and we rolled down a flight of stairs together. I hung on to him as we reached the bottom of the stairs and was there rescued by an alert psychiatric aid.)

"Now tell me the truth, dearest one, would you divorce me if I had my front teeth knocked out? I'd love you in spite of anything. All my love."

Enclosed with Terry's letter dated January 5th was a letter my mother sent to Terry dated December 27, 1947. My mother asked Terry to forward the letter to me. In it she said, "We all missed you both so much during the Christmas season this year. Fran was on our minds continually because this was his first year overseas and the Panama situation had been mentioned on each news broadcast for some days. We didn't know if he would have to move or not. We hope that both of you can be with us next year."

She then went on to describe Christmas in Hollywood. All of my siblings joined my parents in their home on Christmas Eve, sang carols, opened presents, and went to midnight Mass. The next day they and others came for dinner; there were a total of 18 people, including Johnny's brother Sam and his family from Iowa and Rae's (Joe's wife) brother from Texas, who currently worked in our family store. They had a 22 pound turkey. Elizabeth and Fannie baked date nut bread and pies. Everyone got wonderful presents. They received a Christmas card and a beautiful towel set from us and a Hoover vacuum cleaner from all of the children (the old one was still good and so mother decided to give it to Lucille). They had purchased a 21 x 13 ft. oriental rug in Lebanon for their living room and planned to install it next week. Everyone was anxious to see it. They must buy accessories (drapes, couch, chairs, etc.) to go with it. They had certainly spent a lot of money this year.

While my mother was writing her letter to me, the mailman arrived with a letter written by me on December 21st and I didn't mention anything about moving. My letter did contain the newspaper article on women in medicine. Mother thought Terry looked very good in it and she planned to keep the article for herself since the rest of the family had already seen it.

Dr. Nicola came by late last night with a movie projector and showed some of the motion pictures my father took in Lebanon. Except for those taken at a wedding inside a church and others taken in a cathedral, which were too dark, the pictures were beautiful. My father planned to buy a projector of his own so that he could show the pictures to others and to himself when he got lonesome for his Lebanon family. My mother enclosed a picture of mother Mary and a cross which she had bought in the cathedral in Sadnaia, Syria. She planned to send another cross to me.

Rio Hato Airfield
Republic of Panama
6 January 1948

NMBE Trip Looks Promising; P.A.D. Is My Next Assignment; Nunnelley To Run Off And Marry; Constipation

Today I received a package from Terry containing the Christmas cards we received. I really enjoyed going through them. However, I couldn't say I remembered some of Terry's friends. I never had met a lot of them and the same was the case for her relatives.

I again cautioned Terry not to expect too much from my efforts to arrange a trip to Minneapolis to take the National Medical Board Examinations because I didn't want either of us to be disappointed — but the initial campaign for the trip to see my baby looked promising! I personally had called Colonel Lee himself today — he was head of the entire Carribean Medical Department for the Air Corps. I explained to him that "my National Boards were coming up on February 16th, 17th, and 18th and that, since business was falling off here, I think it would be a good time to go to the States and take them." He immediately told me there was an Army regulation that provided for just such a situation. He told me to prepare a regular leave of absence letter according to that regulation, have it approved by the Base Surgeon (Captain Nunnelley — that was no problem), and then by Colonel Ensign, the Base Commander. It would then arrive at his desk in the Zone for approval. He also said that ten days was usually provided for such an activity and that I should include in the letter a request for Army air transportation. If it went through like that, I wouldn't be charged leave time and my pay would continue. So I'll plan to initiate the letter tomorrow. I told Terry, "Let's both hope everyone approves it."

He also confirmed that I would be going to P.A.D. and that it probably would be in the near future. I would probably be there when the time for leave arrives. I hoped that that wouldn't complicate matters.

Nunnelley was all excited. He told me he and his girl friend were going to run off and be married by a justice of the peace or some such person because of their religious problems (his divorce, her Catholic religion, etc). However, I understood that her parents knew and approved, even though they were pretty high in the social strata in the Zone. It would be quite a jolt to the social set because they always expected large weddings of their members.

I had a number of interruptions during the evening by calls from the dispensary to come see patients. I understood that when I got to P.A.D. I wouldn't be OD but once every 10-12 days. That would be nice.

Gosh, I hoped that leave request goes through. I knew damn well I couldn't pass the basic science examination (Part I in fact covered the basic sciences) at that time, but I thought I might have a chance if I studied a bit. I again told Terry, "let's both hope it goes through — you know I'll do everything in my power to make it go through."

I told a major off today — he came in demanding a "strong laxative" for his wife. I told him I didn't give out medicine without first seeing the patient. He got mad but I stuck to my guns. I guess he went to see Nunnelley to report the "young upstart" after he left me. But of course, Nunnelley backed me up. However, I was still uneasy. I could just imagine the major going to the base commander.

Minneapolis General Hospital
Minneapolis, Minnesota
7 January 1948

Insurance; Intestinal Perforation; Freddie And Jake; "Goin' Home"; About Bull Sessions; Her Health And Her Wardrobe

Terry received two letters from me today. She thought I wrote well and that my letters left her feeling warm and close to me.

She had several things to tell me today. One was that the New York Life Insurance Company called last night and said I owe a premium for this year of $199.00 (I suspected the call came from Louis Schaller, the agent that had contacted and sold insurance to most members of the Phi Chi medical fraternity while I was in medical school). Terry told him to send her the request for payment and that she would pay with a check. She asked me whether I wanted that policy to be paid automatically by the Farmers and Mechanics Bank. If so, she would have them start with this year's premium. A notice came from the St. Anthony Bank today of a $100 deposit so she assumed that the Army was still doing its duty.

The second item concerned Dr. Schleicher, the hematologist at MGH. He was operated on a few days ago for a bowel perforation. He was said to have peritonitis. According to rumor, the cause of the perforation was not discovered. A temporary colostomy was done and no biopsy was taken. Terry strongly suspected a biopsy was taken and someone had reasons for not wanting too much known about the affair. It was possible, however, that the basis of the perforation was diverticulitis. He took this problem very poorly, she understood, and was very upset about it all. Terry hadn't been to see him.

A letter came from Freddie (Fred Engstrom, my fraternity brother and co-owner of a sailboat) today and she forwarded it to me. He thanked us for the check and enclosed Jake's address (Lt. (jg) Lyle F. Jacobson, USNR, U.S. Naval Hospital, San Diego, California) so that we could also pay him. As his address indicated, Jake stayed in the States. I don't believe that was yet certain when he and I drove from Minneapolis to Hollywood in July 1947.

Terry was at home listening to a program of lovely music part of the day. One of the songs was "Goin' Home." "It was a beautiful song and it means so much for us, dear. Home is anywhere we're together."

"Darling, I hope you soon find out where you're going. Surely you should be able to manage a short trip home out of that. Everyone asks about you. Dr. Brigham says that he thinks the Virgin Islands would be a good place for you because I'd not have to worry about you if you were there. Well, dear, I don't worry about you — and I hope you don't go to one of those horrid places you mention."

Terry then answered a series of questions I asked in my letters. The first one concerned the content of female bull sessions. "I haven't been in very many of them. Girls are a little more reticent about that sort of thing unless they know each other very well. Most of the girls I know are familiar, or they think they are, with that sort of thing through medical knowledge — so they don't ask questions."

In response to a question about her well being, she assured me she was taking good care of herself. She had had a cold during the past few days, but it didn't bother her much and it was almost already gone. In response to my question about her wardrobe, she said, no, she still hadn't bought many clothes, but she would start as soon as she thought she could wear them. She didn't have the really "new" look, but she had lowered some of her hems. Yes, she wore quite dark nylons. That was the only kind they were selling. Rumor had it that nylons were going to be less plentiful on the market, so there was quite a run on them.

She was glad I finally received my Christmas packages. She wished I could have had them at the right time. But if I enjoyed them, that's what was important.

Rio Hato Airfield
Republic of Panama
7 January 1948

Really Moving; Application For Detached Service; Fingers Crossed; A Wonderful Letter

The base was really moving. Night and day convoys left Rio Hato with heavy equipment. Most of the personnel remained, but it wouldn't be long until the number would drop off sharply. In fact, there was a party in progress in the Officer's Club now in honor of the 319th Fighter Group which was leaving this base in a few days. I had one of the free drinks that they were serving.

I told Terry I had prepared the application for detached service "to Minneapolis, Minnesota, for a period of ten days," today without much trouble. Our medical administrative officer, Captain Phillips, kindly wrote the letter for me. Nunnelley signed his consent on it and I planned to send it to Colonel Ensign, the Rio Hato Base Commander, tomorrow. I hoped he would be in a good mood and would sign it. Nunnelley said not to send it to him today because "his mood wasn't right." He had seen him in the morning. So, I held off until tomorrow. Of course, I imagined the final decision would be up to Colonel Lee, the chief medic in Panama I talked to yesterday. I told Terry to keep her fingers crossed. I had mine that way. What a terrific deal it would be if it went through! I wouldn't believe it even if it did go through.

I received the sweetest letter from Terry. It was written on Friday, January 2nd. I read it many times and it gave me the same complete, warm satisfaction each reading. In my response I said, "don't speak of your faults and inadequacies as a wife. If they are present, I haven't discovered them yet. Perhaps I'm too much in love to see them — or even care to see them. Oh, darling, if I ever get (I mean when) my arms around you again, I'm certain that it will be many, many hours before I'll let go."

Rio Hato Airfield
Republic of Panama
8 January 1948

My Responses To Her Letters; Application For Detached Service Forwarded; "368"; Study Plan; Don't Be Disappointed

I received a nice letter from Terry today, the one that was written on Saturday the 3rd and Sunday the 4th. I wondered whether she had gotten as big a bang out of the statement Royall Storey made about Paul as I did. I thought it really covered the situation well, i.e., his ability to relax and make others feel comfortable. I also thought Terry's analysis of the mother-son interaction in the Storey family meshed well with mine. I was happy to hear Terry was having a few evenings off now. It certainly made a big difference, as I recalled. I told Terry I would in fact get permission before using anyone's name as a reference for my fellowship application at the Mayo Clinic. I told her she was right about my reason for not using Cecil J. Watson as a reference; I thought I might someday want to apply to the University of Minnesota for a fellowship and it might prove embarrassing to have applied elsewhere first, using him as a reference. I probably would use Fahr and Gouze as references. I asked whether my GI insurance premiums and allotment checks (automatic salary deposits to our bank) appeared to be in order. In response to a secret message from Terry to me written in miniature script and labeled "This is written small because it's a secret," I wrote back in miniature script "Whisper to me darling, I like it." Finally, I told Terry I was surprised to hear my picture was in the newspaper and that I looked forward to seeing it.

My application for detached service went to the colonel today. I was still keeping my fingers crossed. All of the other medics seemed to think it would be approved since Colonel Lee directed me to put it in. I was hoping. Oh, it would be wonderful if it could happen.

I was on a "368" board this morning to see if one of our men, a chronic alcoholic, should be discharged. We finally decided to recommend discharge, but in the process I had to tell his defense counsel off good when he started talking a bit insultingly about the medical officers. I got real angry and really let him have it. I told him he knew nothing about medicine or psychiatry and therefore had no business passing any opinions on us — in addition to many other things — right in front of the whole board. That was the second guy I told off this week, but I thought both episodes were definitely justified. The defense counsel shut up like a clam when I was through with him. I was finding new things about myself. I didn't frequently get angry, but when I did, my mouth really became active. Surprised even me.

As soon as I got any indication that my leave would be approved, I planned to really start hitting the books. What a job that would be, because I was rusty about the basic sciences (anatomy, physiology, biochemistry, pharmacology, pathology); it had been 3-4 years since I had taken those courses.

I told Terry not to be disappointed if the trip didn't materialize because it was really a lot to expect from the system. It took a lot of nerve to get myself to call Colonel Lee and, to be honest, I was very surprised when he talked so encouragingly about it. To expect more was almost asking too much. But I was hoping just the same. If I got home, it would be all Terry's credit. I never would have called Colonel Lee if she hadn't told me she had put in my board application.

Minneapolis General Hospital
Minneapolis, Minnesota
8 January 1948

Gossip, Endometriosis, Circumcision, Pediatric Procedures

Terry visited an old friend, Audrey Arcola, in the evening. Their friendship dated back to pre-medicine days at the University of Minnesota. They had a long talk — "mostly gossip. How do you like that? I'm a ba-a-ad girl, am I not?"

Later she talked with Mary Teberg, her live-in roommate. Terry told her about my patient with the pelvic implants of endometriosis. Mary suggested that the vaginal bleeding might possibly be due to self-inflicted lesions resulting from a subconscious need to menstruate and thus prove herself a "whole woman." Of course, that's just theory; "you no doubt eliminated that possibility by doing a pelvic examination."

Jane and Don's baby was doing fine. They were wondering about having him circumcised. Don wanted it done, but Jane didn't want Dr. Anderson doing it (he was her resident when she was on Peds).

Terry hadn't heard any more about Dr. Schleicher. She assumed he was doing alright.

So far, Terry had done external jugular and femoral punctures on babies (to draw blood); no transfusions or IVs as yet. It was fun working with them, but she was afraid she got awfully attached to the little tykes.

"Honey, I love you more than anything on earth. I'm not living — only existing until I'm by your side again. I hope I'll be a good wife — at least I'll always be an in-love one."

Rio Hato Airfield
Republic of Panama
19 January 1948

No New Developments; Vanishing Dispensary; Lonesomeness; Never Again; Terry's Career

The evening was comfortably cool, as most of them were in January. To add to my comfort, I was smoking my old pipe containing tobacco Terry so thoughtfully sent. Then, of course, her letter was before me and with only her in my thoughts, I was as happy as I could conceivably be without her actual presence.

Her letter was written on January 5. I thought Jane (Gumprecht) did right well; that was a pretty short labor for a first baby. I agreed with Terry that we were being passed by (in the birthing derby) but that "just you wait until we mutually decide the time is correct — then we shall do wonders, I'm certain. However, at present, I think you are way ahead of yourself on this circumcision problems for our sons. You bet, I'll still love you if your teeth get knocked out. We'd just get some new ones for you."

There was no new development on my request for a trip to the States and home. I didn't think I would hear for a while whether they rejected or approved my proposal. But I was holding a prayer meeting nightly — and hoping awfully hard!

The dispensary was rapidly vanishing. We had to talk to our patients standing up because the chairs were gone. The upstairs hospital section, dentistry, ENT room (for routine, specialized air corpsmen examinations), and the x-ray department were closed. The dispensary was now essentially a poorly equipped emergency room. The work had really fallen off so that now I spent most of my time reading in the office. This could be helpful if I got my leave because then I'd have a lot of time to study for the National Medical Board Examination in February. I asked Terry whether she intended to take the examination if I got home (I knew the answer would be no; the time was short and an internship doesn't leave much time to review the basic sciences). I also asked whether she would take time off even if she didn't take the examination.

Namay, soon to be discharged, received a wire saying his mother had pneumonia and he and his wife hoped to be able to fly back to the States to see her on Tuesday. Nunnelley went to Costa Rica today and picked up four tailored suits he had ordered some weeks back. They were beautiful and very reasonable — $61 each. They would have cost him twice that in the States. I guess he was preparing for civilian life. I would have flown up to Guatemala this week, had he not gone to Costa Rica. I may go next weekend, just for the sightseeing.

I tried not to count to heavily on my trip to see Terry. However, I feared I would be a very unhappy boy if it fell through. The moment I got alone, I did nothing but think about her. My attempts at mental diversion weren't too successful, even though I tried very hard. But I found medical journals no match for Terry — no match at all. So my reading was necessarily very slow and somewhat forced. I feared that nothing would ever convince me that it was important enough to keep her away from me again — even her medicine. She would just have to practice and train where I did, no matter what opportunity offered itself to her (this statement did not correspond to earlier implied or spoken statements). I hoped Terry would now feel the same way about it because I didn't think I could stand having her away from me again. I needed her nearness and love so much. I asked Terry not to misunderstand. "I'm definitely not having a change of heart about your career. You know me much better than that. Also, I'm going through this separation about as I expected I would, i.e., with much lonesomeness but also with a full understanding of its necessity. But I don't want it to happen again. I love you so very much. That love is the sole reason for not wanting you to be away from me again."

Terry dropped out of medical school for nine months to work. This put her in the medical school and internship classes behind mine. Hence our current separation. This hardly cut her professional career short. She had been one of the youngest entrants to medical school.

Minneapolis General Hospital
Minneapolis, Minnesota
9 January 1948

Busy On Call On The Pediatric Ward; Frustration; About Griping; A Real Jerk; Classmates All Over The Globe

This was Terry's night on call and she was busy on the pediatric ward until 11:00 p.m. They had a five week old baby with diarrhea who needed fluids and then there were three little kids on Station I with burns, etc., who all needed watching. In her opinion, W. Anderson stunk as a resident! The man simply couldn't make up his mind about what he wanted done for the patients. Nothing got done, consequently, until very late in the day. Also, he had a rather unpleasant personality.

"Honey, have I been griping a lot lately? It's because I miss my darling husband so much that nothing seems right without you here, dear? She then went on with another gripe. "Remember my saying that I thought two of the peds interns were jerks? Well, one of them turned out to be quite nice — he's from Northwestern University. The other one was definitely a jerk — he had quit Los Angeles County (Hospital) to come here, and now he's quit MGH. Guess we go back to taking calls every third night. I'm not too sorry, though. I like to be busy and tired. It's the only way I can forget how lonely I am. Of course, I always think of you when I go to bed — but those are usually sweet, pleasant dreams."

"Honey, I'm waiting for that next letter from you. Each day I think, 'maybe I'll hear from Fran today; he'll be coming home.'"

Terry had heard that George and Jean Lund were in

Newfoundland. "Of all places! I wonder how Jean likes it?" Terry asked me where the Eides were (Arvid Eide was one of my fraternity brothers and a good friend). She wondered whether he was in Japan and whether Annette, his wife, was with him. One thing was becoming clear, the March 1946 medical school class was spread all over the globe.

Rio Hato Airfield
Republic of Panama
10 January 1948

Soft Weekend; Studying Anatomy; About P.A.D.; Hunting Pelicans; Stripping The Dispensary To A First Aid Station; To Trip News

My weekend was nice and soft. Alpier was OD, leaving me free to do whatever I liked. Yesterday afternoon (Saturday), I slept a couple of hours and then tried studying anatomy in preparation for the board examination. I had forgotten a vast amount (even though I excelled in the course in medical school, but that was five years earlier). So it seemed like an insurmountable job. However, as Terry suspected, I was not trying to get home to pass that examination (my Minnesota State Board Examination allowed me to practice medicine in Minnesota). I just wanted to see her. To be honest, I didn't think I would pass that examination. However, I did spend some more time studying anatomy this morning and again this afternoon.

Today two medics who were on the New Orleans-Canal Zone ship passage with me, and who were now stationed in the Zone, visited us during a sight-seeing trip. One was stationed at P.A.D. (where I was going) and the other was stationed at France Field (where Nunnelley was going). Both their wives had arrived and one even had his car shipped from the States. The fellow from P.A.D. described the place to me and it sounded as if it might be a fairly nice place to work.

Allison, who was leaving for his new station in the Zone tomorrow, took me hunting pelicans along the beach for an hour in the afternoon. It was fun to get a gun in my hands again. I especially enjoyed this gun because it was a 22 automatic rifle identical to the one I owned as a kid back in Kiester. It seemed like home again.

I did a lot of writing in the evening. I wrote Drs. Fahr, Gouze, and Boyden for permission to use their names as references. I also wrote my parents' home in Hollywood.

Yesterday, a group of GIs stripped the dispensary down to its bare essentials. It was definitely a first aid station now. I feared I was going to get rather bored with so little to do because this week a large part of the personnel and their dependents were leaving.

I still hadn't heard anything new on my projected trip home. If I got approval, I thought I would ask for a few days' delay en route so that I could stay home a little longer. Those extra days would come off my leave time, however. Seven extra days would be nice. I feared I was dreaming now, though.

In my letter to Terry I said, "It's time to hit the sack, honey. Always remember that besides loving you very, very much, you're my ideal girl. Not only do I love you, but I admire you. Besides, you're pretty as a new spring dress, cute as a button, beautiful as a sunset, lovely as the most delicate of flowers — and, oh yes, I love you. And gosh, I just want to hold you. Now honey, now."

Minneapolis General Hospital
Minneapolis, Minnesota
11 January 1948

Mayo Memorial Building; Dr. Anderson And IVs; Wood For The Fireplace; Wrapping Gifts; Insurance; A Long Sleep; Household Goods For Panama

It was Sunday and Terry had just washed her hair and was now sitting in the breakfast room at home writing to me. She enclosed a few application photographs of me. That left six at home in case I needed more. She decided to send one to my mother. They were old pictures, but my mother probably didn't have one. She also enclosed a clipping from the Minnesota daily paper concerning the Mayo Memorial building which would place the university's medical facilities virtually under one roof, as the central Mayo Memorial building would connect with the existing university hospital's laboratories and medical school buildings. The original plan had called for 19 stories but rising building costs forced revision to a smaller 16 story building. Work was scheduled to begin in late summer or early fall.

Friday night was quite busy. Dr. Anderson was a little bit annoyed with Terry the next morning because she had given a baby a subcutaneous infusion rather than an IV infusion during the night. He had not allowed her to give a scalp vein transfusion under supervision, however, and she had no intention of giving her first one alone in the middle of the night. Dr. Schroeder, the resident on call, didn't want to give an IV either. He felt that a sub-q would be quite adequate. "Oh me! Maybe I've been at MGH too long, but dear Warren gets on my nerves a little more each day."

Terry had yesterday afternoon off, so she went home and helped Paul get wood for the fireplace. It was cold outside, but it was nice to be getting a little fresh air for a change. Then she went to bed at 7:00 p.m.

Today she planned to wrap and send the gifts she had bought, a dozen highball and a dozen juice glasses for Delores and Albert and a little blue cotton overall and white t-shirt for the Midthune baby. The highball and juice glasses were quite nice; they had deer etched on them. Since they were also inexpensive, she thought she would get some for us.

The New York Life Insurance Company premium was $191.84, due on January 27, 1948. That was the yearly premium and she wondered how to handle it from now on. She thought the bank might as well pay those premiums for us.

"Well, dearest, I'll leave you for now. Maybe I can write a few lines this evening 'cuz it's dinner time now. I slept from 7:00 p.m. yesterday until 9:00 a.m. today. How's that? Bet you could do as well!"

"All my love forever, honey. I do hope you can come next month. In the meantime, I'm starting to make plans about household goods, etc. to take to Panama."

Minneapolis General Hospital
Minneapolis, Minnesota
11 January 1948 Late

After Midnight Communication; Romantic Movies And Radio Music; More On Trip Home And Letters Of Reference; Better To Be Busy!

It was after midnight, but Terry was still up, listening to the radio. Somehow she couldn't go to bed without again communicating with me.

She and other family members went to see "Foxes of Harrow" tonight. Like many movies, it had a very romantic theme. It reminded her so acutely how empty her life was without me. The music on the radio now was so romantic too. How much like heaven it would be if I could only be here to listen to it with her. "Believe me, my dearest, you are the most important thing in my life. I decided long ago that anything that interferes with our marriage, including my work, will have to go."

"I realize, darling, that it's impossible for you to make any very definite plans (for a trip home while evacuating Rio Hato). I'm terribly happy, though, that things look promising. Guess I'll sorta' count on seeing you for sure. It won't hurt and it will keep me almost content for a whole month."

Terry said, yes, Royal Gray was still at MGH and that he would probably give me a good reference for my Mayo fellowship application. She didn't think he had been terribly well impressed by her but that shouldn't matter. She would get MGH Superintendent Pollard's first name (his initials were D.W.). His reference should also be good.

Terry thought it was too good to be true that I could get time off with pay and free transportation. This would help a lot. "But, darling, if it cost a million, it would be well worth it."

She also thought my pulling OD so infrequently now might have its disadvantages; she would go mad if she weren't so busy. She congratulated me on not letting the major brow-beat me on medical subjects. She was proud of her dear husband and knew she would always be.

Rio Hato Airfield
Republic of Panama
12 January 1948

More References For My Mayo Application; Insurance; Schleicher; Detached Service Application Progress; Accelerated Evacuation; Allison And The Namays Left; Showing Terry's Picture

I really generated a lot of mail again in the evening. I wrote for reference permission to two hometown (Kiester) folks and to one of my Luther College teachers (Sherman Hoslett, biologist). With the three I wrote last night, that only left two to go — Dr. A. B. Baker (University of Minnesota Medical School neurologist) and another as yet unselected Luther teacher. All of these letters were in support of my Mayo fellowship application. Each of my letters turned into a fairly long document; I had to explain what I was doing, etc. to each person.

I received Terry's usual nice letter today. In response to questions, I told her to let the F&M Bank pay the New York Life Insurance premium; apparently I hadn't added that policy to the list I gave the Farmers and Mechanics Bank (F&M Bank). I suggested she check to see that it hadn't been paid twice. I thanked her for paying our sailboat debt to Lyle Jacobson and told her I was glad to hear the Army pay allotments were arriving at the bank. Dr. Schleicher's acute abdomen sounded serious and I asked Terry to keep me informed of his progress.

I heard from the Colonel's office here in Rio Hato today regarding my leave. I mean "detached service to Minneapolis, Minnesota" — ha! That office wanted to know a few details since they had never had a similar request. When I told them Colonel Lee had instructed me to file the request, they practically told me — but not quite — that their office would approve it. Everything has gone well so far. I told Terry to hold a daily "prayer meeting" please and to also hold her breath.

The "high command" in the Zone has instructed this base to hurry up the evacuation so that everything will be gone by January 31st. Maybe I would be out of here sooner than I thought.

The big envelope Terry sent with my second class mail arrived today without the brochure on the National Medical Board examination. I asked Terry whether it was coming later.

Allison was scheduled to leave tomorrow. It was soon going to be very lonesome in Rio Hato. He and I hunted pelicans on the beach again today. I was going to miss him; he has been nice to me. He brought me a big bunch of green bananas from Costa Rica on his last flight up there.

Namay and his wife left today. I would miss them, too. They

gave me some Syrian nuts they didn't want to carry with them. Good! I've been eating them all day.

Some of the women insisted that I show them Terry's picture. They wanted to see what she looked like. I showed them some snapshots of Terry and they couldn't believe that such a lovely girl could be a doctor. I agreed wholeheartedly — on the loveliness, I meant. I told Terry about this and said she should not be self-conscious because we'll be in a different place when she arrives. "Anyway, I'm not telling everybody."

I ended my day by showering, turning in my laundry, reading a bit, and then hitting the sack thinking that one month from tonight we might be in each other's arms. What a wonderful thought!

Minneapolis General Hospital
Minneapolis, Minnesota
13 January 1948

On a Pink Cloud, Witnessing My Forged Signature, Classmate Whereabouts; More Insurance; Dr. Schleicher Recovers; Circumcision; Infusions

Terry had a lovely letter all planned for me last night, but was too busy on call to write it. Her day wasn't complete unless she wrote her daily letter to me.

Terry had received two letters from me on January 13th, which said that it was pretty much almost for sure that I would be coming home. She walked on pink clouds all day — and she still was. She was told by colleagues that the Army leans over backward to have its physicians take boards. So, even though it wasn't absolutely settled, she was counting on seeing me in about a month. Terry knew that it would be hard for me to study during this month, but it was good, she found, to be busy while away from one's loved spouse. She was always hunting for work that would keep her from thinking how much she missed me. To be working was to be the happiest that she could be while I was away.

Yesterday she went over to the University of Minnesota Medical School to have "my signature" witnessed by Miss Smith in the Dean's office. Then she dropped the letter in the mailbox and went merrily on her way. She met George Gordon (a medical school classmate) in the medical school office and he gave her a ride back to MGH. He was working on a PhD in the physiology department now, and she gathered he was really studying hard. Jack McQuillan (another medical school classmate) was working there too, but he only planned to stay for a year. Harry Schragg was practicing in Elmore, Minnesota, where he and Troy Rollins will be partners. Harry was really busy, and had more than enough work to do. Troy, who will own the practice, will join him in July after he finishes his MGH internship.

Terry also stopped at the bank yesterday and was given two slips to fill out for my National Life Insurance. She enclosed them in a letter to me. The government hadn't sent premium notices for the months of December and January, so she would have to call and get the matter corrected before the bank would start paying the premiums. Such a bother!

Dr. Schleicher was now up and about, doing well. He ran around in his bathrobe and even did a little work in his laboratory.

Dr. Anderson circumcised the Gumprecht baby yesterday. Both Jane and Don stood by; Jane with a mask and gown over her robe and slippers. Terry was sure it hurt them more than the little tyke, who didn't even cry once. Terry gave the "anesthetic," she had me know — 5% glucose by mouth through a nipple.

Terry really liked the pediatric service, in spite of her lousy resident. She had done her first circumcision, and had also given a closed scalp vein infusion. She thought she would like working with the bigger children even more. In the evening, she worked quite a long while overtime, giving two intravenous infusions.

She would have really been proud if she could have heard me "telling off" that "368" board defense counsel member. She wanted her husband to stand up for his rights. She was proud, too, of my usual tact and courtesy, but she thought every man had to be aggressive at times in order to maintain his self-respect.

In her daily letter to me, Terry said she was hoping and longing for my visit home. It had to come true. She didn't think she would be able to let me go again after she next saw me and held me close. She never would have believed that anyone could be her whole reason for living. But she was happy that she was able to be so much in love with someone so sweet. Even though she was as lonesome as she could be, nothing could change the fact that she was happily married to the most wonderful husband in the world.

Rio Hato Airfield
Republic of Panama
13 January 1948

All Alone With Nothing To Do; Stripped To The Bare Walls; Leave Approved Locally; Endometriosis; Circumcision; Vanishing Wash Basins; Bargains

Nunnelley, Alpier, and I just had a fine swim. That was the entire medical department. We had absolutely nothing to do. Trucks came today and stripped the dispensary to its bare walls. The reception desk was made of packing crates now. All we had was one examining table and a few essential drugs. Our work day was over by 9:00 a.m. Here I was even writing letters in the afternoon. Non-essential functions such as routine examinations, sanitary inspections, malaria control, etc., had been stopped. We were certainly not all needed in Rio Hato and one of us, at least, would be transferred soon. I suspected it would be me, for which I would be happy. Now would be the time to go home, I thought.

My leave was approved by the adjutant on this base today, but he also stated on the application that I would be at another post at the time of the proposed leave, meaning the proposal would probably have to be again approved by the CO of my new post. It now goes to Colonel Lee, who initiated it, at my request, in the first place. I told Terry things looked good thus far, so she should keep holding her breath.

I received two letters from Terry today — written on the 8th and 9th. I told her that Mary (Teberg) may have something in her opinion on my endometriosis patient but there was no way of proving it. I still thought that the cause of her bleeding was estrogen withdrawal. I said circumcisions weren't worth making much fuss about, i.e. shouldn't generate a lengthy discussion; it was just a matter of taste and cleanliness. Daily washing of the glans was all that is necessary to make the intact foreskin acceptable. Men lived both ways. My impression of Anderson was similar to Terry's; mainly a lot of talk. Gosh, we were getting to be a couple of gossips. That had to stop. I was surprised to hear the Lunds were in Newfoundland; I didn't know we had bases there. Yes, the Eides were in Japan. I imagined Annette had joined him by now. She was pregnant, according to Freddie (Engstrom).

The guys were all griping at the moment here in the barracks. Workmen took out the wash basins in some of the rooms! Mine was still intact. I could hear the guys grousing now.

I plan to go to a movie tonight and then study a bit afterwards. I was not very excited about studying basic sciences, but believe you me, I was very excited about the prospect of seeing Terry. Just so nothing happened to spoil it.

There were a lot of bargains at Rio Hato during the evacuation. In fact, medical supplies were free for the taking. Cigarettes were always a bargain, 8¢ a pack or 80¢ a carton. That was about 1/3 of the cost in the States.

From what Terry said, it appeared that my mail reached her in spurts. Hers usually arrived at Rio Hato pretty regularly.

I told Terry that she meant more to me than life itself. I loved her. I would remind her again tomorrow and, if not in words, by my actions each day that we lived. "Always keep that foremost in your mind."

Minneapolis General Hospital
Minneapolis, Minnesota
14 January 1948

Cold Minnesota; A Dull Day At Work; Herb, Tony, Paul, And Al

It was cold as can be outside. Yesterday the temperature was -1° and today it was -14°. Of course, Terry hadn't been out very much, but she noticed that it was colder indoors. She worried about my catching cold when I came home. I had my heavy Army overcoat to wear while I was outside, and the new furnace heated the house well inside. Our bedroom wasn't too warm, but Terry said I shouldn't worry about that — she would keep me as warm as toast.

Today was a pretty dull day at work. She did another infusion and spent most of the rest of the day waiting for her resident to make up his mind about what she should do next. She switched to "big peds" on Friday noon and would have Lueck for her resident on that service.

She was home in the evening and cousin Herb (Daub), who had been in an Army hospital for so long with a lung condition, was visiting. He said he might attend school in the Twin Cities and, if so, would live with the Breys. Tony (David Goblirsch) had started General College at the University of Minnesota, like Paul, her brother, and it looked as if he and Paul were having a good time together. David roomed with Alois (Terry's older brother) and Paul roomed alone. That was to keep them from talking together all night. The Brey home was a busy place in 1948.

Rio Hato Airfield
Republic of Panama
14 January 1948

The Dry Windy Season; Movies; Inactivity; Boredom; And Depression; No Leave News; Evacuation Progressing Rapidly; Alpier Depressed Too

The dry season was really upon us. Instead of continual high humidity with numerous showers, we now had high winds and dust. However, the temperature always ranged between 80° and 90° during the day and in the 70s at night. The wind seemed to stop blowing during the night. I didn't know whether it also was windy in the Zone.

I told Terry to see the movie *Riffraff* with George Raft. I saw it last night and, besides being a good mystery, it was filmed in Panama City about one year ago. It would give her a good picture of what life would be like when she arrived in Panama.

I saw another movie tonight. It was an English war film, the *Captive Heart*. It depicted the lives of English prisoners of war during the four years they were in German prison camps. Somehow it fit my mood today. I was a bit depressed. The movie projected me into their places, I guess, for I felt like a prisoner myself, forcibly separated from my loved one — just as was the lead man in the movie.

It had been quite some time since I let depression overtake me. The inactivity of the last week was most to blame, I guessed. Wasn't it odd? I had here a wonderful vacation spot with a wonderful beach and nothing to do. Someday I would probably pay good money for a resort not half so nice. Yet I was dissatisfied because I had nothing to do. I tried to study for the medical board examination, but my efforts were not very successful, I feared. I wondered if I would ever stop wanting. I hoped so.

There were no new developments concerning my request for

leave time. As far as I knew, the request was on its way to Colonel Lee in the Zone. Nunnelley said he would call in a couple of days and boost it, if necessary.

I hadn't had a cold since my first week at Fort Sam Houston in Texas. That was in August. That was quite a record for a fellow that had one about every two months for years. I wondered what the difference was.

I received a premium receipt for my National Service Life Insurance for the month of December. I wondered whether Terry gave them my address or whether she sent the receipt on to me.

At the rate the evacuation was progressing, I was certain Rio Hato would be gone by January 31st. I had a feeling I would be gone before that. Gosh, I hoped so. I was so bored.

I suspected I in part caught my depression from Alpier. He had been home on leave at Christmas time. He said he wished he hadn't gone because now he was dissatisfied with life here in Panama — after he was reminded what life in the States was like again. However, the real reason was that he wanted to go home and marry his girlfriend. They talked about it when he was home on leave. To top everything off, he got a refusal on a residency application today. Thus the depression and it was contagious.

I thought Nunnelley was going to sneak off and get married this weekend. I didn't know for sure, but that was my suspicion.

I was watching a young married couple in the movie tonight. They didn't seem very affectionate at all. It occurred to me that if Terry were sitting at my side, I would be holding her hand — and getting such a thrill out of it. Who know where that would lead? I asked Terry whether she remembered *For Whom the BellsTolls*. I would never forget.

Minneapolis General Hospital
Minneapolis, Minnesota
15 January 1948

Lonesome And Unhappy; Heartache. No More Separations; Home Next Month; Time Off

Terry received two letters from me today. She thought I sounded more lonesome and unhappy than I ever did before — and it made her heart ache. "Please believe me, my own darling, I'll never be away from you again through any voluntary action of mine. Nothing, including medicine, is important enough to keep me from following you anywhere on earth."

"I'm very confident that you will be home next month. I'm counting on it, and it's a great comfort to me. Life is purposeless without you. In addition to being lonesome, I feel that I'm a failure as a wife — at least for the present. But just wait — after July, I'm going to be the best little wife you ever had."

Terry thought I would pass the boards with far less trouble than I anticipated. She said it would be nice if I could get home a few days before it was time to take the boards. She wondered if I wanted her to take time off while I was home. She was definitely planning to not work any nights while I was home. She was thinking, however, that she might save her actual vacation time until later — if it was at all possible that we might meet in Mexico City in April for a week. She asked whether I could manage another leave so soon?

Rio Hato Airfield
Republic of Panama
15 January 1948

Making Amends; Important Letters From Terry; A Letter From Beatrice

It was late and I was tired so I wrote Terry a short note to tell her I was still thinking lovely thoughts of her. I had just returned from a bridge party with three older ladies at the home of the major I told off about the medicines for his wife the other day. Things were a bit tense, for me at least, at first but they smoothed out well. His wife had insisted I come.

I received Terry's two sweet letters written on Sunday, January 11th. One of them contained the pictures of me I needed for my Mayo fellowship application.

I told Terry that she would never know how much her letters meant to me. I sulked just like a little kid when one didn't arrive, but when one did come that was as sentimental as the one written on Sunday night, I was the happiest person in the world. "Darling, please, please always stay that way. If you become hard and unsentimental, that would be the hardest blow I could ever receive. I want you to be completely in love always, just as I know I shall be. I want you to be cuddly — and show it — 'cause that's the way I feel at the mere thought of you."

I received a letter dated January 12th from my sister, Beatrice, who lived in Joice, Iowa, with her husband, Wadiah "Tony" Abraham and their new son, Tommy. She had recently received a letter from me telling her the Christmas packages arrived safely, albeit a bit late, and that we were in the process of evacuating Rio Hato. It was cold in Iowa , 6° above zero, and consequently their partners in the general merchandise store in Joice, George and Evaline Abraham, were vacationing in the southwest for a month. They would most likely see my parents in Hollywood. Bea and Tony planned to do the same as soon as George and Evaline got back to Joice. It would be a challenging automobile trip, because Tommy was in a very active stage of life, climbing on chairs and then up on tables, climbing over the crib side, falling on his head, etc. Bea thought it must be tough on me being away from Terry and she was, of course, right. She also mentioned her meeting with our parents and Juanita in Cedar Rapids after their trip to Lebanon and that she looked forward to seeing the movies of that trip. The Abraham and Haddy families were growing; Mrs. Abraham, Tony's mother, now had 14 grandchildren, and the Haddy family would soon have an addition because Vernita was pregnant again.

Minneapolis General Hospital
Minneapolis, Minnesota
16 January 1948

Ann's Party; An Anemic Child; Big Peds; Shopping

Terry was at home in the evening and there was lots of excitement; Ann was having a bridal shower for a friend of hers. Her mother was there and she enjoyed the party a lot. Terry didn't; she was just too tired.

Last night wasn't bad on the Pediatric service at MGH. They admitted a very sick child during the evening with a hemoglobin of 41%. There was some question about the blood picture, so they took a slide up to Dr. Schleicher. He had a room on Station E and he ran around the hospital all day with a white coat over his hospital pajamas. He was looking well now, though. He thought the child had a simple iron deficiency anemia.

Today Terry switched to "big peds" (older children). Dr. Lueck was now her resident, and she thought she was going to like him a lot. They had a peds surgery conference with Dr. Chisholm, which was excellent (Terry wondered if I had ever had Dr. Chisholm when I interned and the answer was yes). His discussion of strangulated hernias in children was absolutely beautiful.

In the evening, Terry stopped at Boutells to buy Betty (Jolly) a small gift (she was a bride-to-be). They had loads of interesting household equipment. She thought she would buy us a few pots and pans, etc., before it was time to go to Panama. She could hardly wait.

Rio Hato Airfield
Republic of Panama
16 January 1948

An Old Friend; Faithfulness; Happiness In My Marriage; The One Positive Feature Of Separation; No Serious Evacuation Accidents Yet; Mayo Application Complete

An odd happening today — a Capt. Sporer, with whom I traveled from Camp Kilmer, New Jersey, to Panama, moved in next door to me today. He was here to help convoy some of the trucks and planes to the Zone. He was a nice fellow. The Army sometimes seems like a small outfit.

I told Terry that I was very happy. The reason for my happiness? Our most wonderful marriage! Over and over again I was reminded that she and I were really in love. Each day I met married fellows and see married women who not only were completely unfaithful, but flaunt their unfaithfulness openly as if it was something of which to be proud. How empty our marriage would be if I found myself to be unfaithful — how meaningless and depressing. But knowing that I could live my love for her each day made it beautiful and so full. Each day I got a greater and greater satisfaction out of demonstrating to myself that my love for her was something large — and growing larger. Proving it over and over each day almost made our separation bearable. At least, it was the one nice thing about being apart.

I had told Terry once before that one of the reasons I wanted to leave her for a time was to see how I would react to a separation.

You could say I wanted to test my love for her. And I was so afraid of what would happen. I knew I loved her so much, but I didn't know how strong I would be. I had to find out. I had to know whether I would be stupid and weak enough to ruin the most beautiful thing that ever happened to me — our marriage. And now I know, I was strong. And my lovely, loveable wife had given me that strength.

I wouldn't insult Terry by saying I would never be unfaithful. No man could definitely say that. I had the same emotions every man did and, for example, were I accidentally put under very trying circumstances, I must honestly say I didn't know what would happen. But Terry could be very certain of this — I would never initiate unfaithfulnesss and should the circumstances accidentally arise, her boy would fight tooth and nail with old Satan. I was fairly certain I would win, too. She could be certain I would never desire anyone else even a little bit. She could be very certain, I loved her very deeply.

So that was why I was happy. Because I knew my love for Terry was real and strong. I knew I could live it. That was something to be happy for, wasn't it? And if a prolonged separation like this could demonstrate that, then it was worth it.

I was OD tonight and this weekend. We hadn't had a serious accident yet during the evacuation, so I was expecting one. With the moving of all the heavy equipment, vehicles, and airplanes, statistics predicted we should have had at least one accident.

I finally completed my Mayo fellowship application today. Compiling all of the requested information was a job, believe me. All letters were now written and all blanks were filled in. I would probably mail it in several days.

I hadn't heard anything new on my trip home yet. Perhaps I would have some definitive information on Monday. I asked Terry whether she had filed my application to take the examinations. I had almost given up hoping to pass. There were a lot of years between my basic science courses in medical school and today. But Terry was what interested me, not the tests. I would try, but would not feel too badly if I didn't pass. I wanted to personally tell Terry I loved her.

Minneapolis General Hospital
Minneapolis, Minnesota
17 January 1948

Banking Nights Off; New Dress; More On Hand Holding; Exam Questions, Insurance And Colds; Don't Be Depressed

Terry's letter to me said, "Just wait 'till you hear how hard I'm working on your visit home! First of all, here I am, on call, and it isn't even my night. I'm working for Walston tonight even though I have to work for myself tomorrow. That's because he's going to work a night for me while you're here. I'm going to start looking around for people I can work for. Then I'll have lots of persons in debt to me for when my darling husband is here. I'm going to be with you every night, darling, even if I have to lie and say I'm sick. (Let 'em check up if they want to — they'll find me in bed like a sick little girl should be.) Guess I'm getting to be a little bit risque, dear. Well, I learned it from Papa himself."

The other thing Terry did today was buy a new dress. She wasn't absolutely sure she liked it because it was kind of unusual. It was a dark brown silk print with a white design, and it had a bright green sash. It was slenderizing. It was prettier than it sounded, too. The only thing she was bothered about was whether it was worth the $35.00 it cost. She wouldn't be wearing it until I came — so she asked me to write and tell her how it sounded to me! She also bought four pairs of nylons today, totaling $5.40. She spent a little over $40.00 today. It seemed like an awful lot of money. Her conscience hurt.

Terry also bought us tickets to the nurses-interns carnival which was to be on February 19th. She asked me if we could plan to go.

Ann, her sister, also shopped for a dress today. She bought a smooth, sophisticated black number that looked very nice on her. It cost $50.00, but it looked it.

She had received two letters from me. My letters had been arriving about twice weekly — that was better than it was during the holidays. She was not complaining now. One of the letters mentioned hand holding in the movies and whether she remembered *For Whom the Bell Tolls*. She said, "How could I forget?" and that she would have no idea of what the movie was about except that she had read the book.

Terry told me that the National Board pamphlet containing practice questions was enclosed with the box of preserved fruit she sent me a few days ago.

She was confused by the National Service Life Insurance (NSLI) receipt for December which was sent to me. She wondered why they didn't send it to her. She suggested I send it back to her along with the signature slips required by the F&M Bank. She thought the sooner the bank started taking care of the premiums, the better off that policy would be.

Terry thought it was wonderful that I hadn't had any colds in Panama, but warned me about returning to Minnesota. The weather had been, and was today, extremely cold. Up until the last few days, the winter had been very nice. She hoped it was also nice when I returned in February.

She told me not to be too depressed. It made her feel bad. She loved me with all her heart and she thought about our love every moment. I was in her mind when she fell asleep and when she awoke — and all through the day, too.

Rio Hato Airfield
Republic of Panama
18 January 1948

RIO HATO WAS ONLY A SKELETON OF ITS FORMER SELF; DISAPPEARING BARRACKS; WACS IN THE DISPENSARY; MOVERS AS PATIENTS; NO WORD REGARDING TRANSFER AND LEAVE; A SUITCASE FROM COSTA RICA

I was sitting in what was left of the dispensary Sunday night writing to Terry. I thought I might as well stay in the dispensary for a while since I had been called out of the movies the last two nights to see patients. No rest for the etc....

Rio Hato Air Base was only a skeleton of its former self. The officer's club was completely closed now. Most of the personnel had left. In fact, only one mess hall was open now and it served everyone on the base. At dinner you would correctly guess only a few people remained. I ate there also. The food was definitely inferior to that at the Club, but it was wholesome.

We still had a moderate amount of work here in the dispensary since we also served the movers who shuttled back and forth between here and the Zone. They always seemed to develop problems.

The upstairs of the dispensary — formerly the "hospital" with a few beds — was now occupied by about a dozen members of the Women's Army Corps (WAC). They were to remain there a week until they were transferred to the Zone. They were in the dispensary because the wreckers began dismantling their barracks yesterday. The corpsmen were all excited, i.e. wisecracking that they needed to make bed check on them, etc. However, we had made the upstairs off limits except when going up to get prescriptions filled (the pharmacy was upstairs). Actually, I didn't think the men were too much hurt by the off-limits rule. These WACs, as most , were not what one would describe as lovely. In general, the WACs I'd seen were pretty tough characters. There were exceptions, of course.

I didn't know when I would be transferred but it probably would be sometime the latter part of the week. We were supposed to be gone by the 25th.

I thought I would hear something definite about my proposed trip home tomorrow or the next day. Let's hope for good news. I was still "pecking" sporadically at studying the basic sciences, mainly bacteriology. Maybe a definite "yes" on the trip would give me a little much needed incentive.

Too bad I got called out of that movie tonight. It was "Desert Fury" and seemed very good.

I had one of the nurses buy me a beautiful all leather suitcase on Friday. She flew up to Costa Rica, where they had genuine leather baggage — and other items — at very reasonable prices, and brought it back for me. Only $22.50. When Terry sees it, she will agree it was a good buy.

It was getting late. I decided to write to my parents in Hollywood and then call it a night.

"My best love to you darling. I do so hope I can see you soon. I know we'll be very happy. I also know we'll be very happy when you arrive here. Just you and me alone. That will be something new and nice, I'm certain."

Minneapolis General Hospital
Minneapolis, Minnesota
18 January 1948

STILL STORING UP NIGHTS OFF CALL; STATUS EPILEPTICUS; ROOMMATE MARY

This was Terry's second evening in a row on call and it hadn't been too bad. She was just as happy as she could be every time that she thought of the night off with me that she would get in return — when I came home, she meant. She planned to work for several other kids and "store up" a few nights for her darling. That would make the nights and days go faster.

"How are you, honey? Still thinking about your trip home? I am. In fact, I think of very little else. Every day I think — one day closer to my wonderful baby!"

A little girl who had extensive burns started convulsing at 9:00 a.m., and to the best of Terry's knowledge, she was still going (status epilepticus). Very upsetting — but she guessed there was nothing to be done. Of course, the staff calmed her down periodically with chloral hydrate (sedative and hypnotic administered rectally in children).

Mary (Teberg) and Terry had been relatively free of chores this evening and they had been sitting in their room talking. It was nice to have a roommate to talk to — it was a little less lonesome that way. Mary had gone over to station H now and Terry had just finished taking a bath. She hoped it would be a quiet night because she was sleepy.

Rio Hato Airfield
Republic of Panama
19 January 1948

Leave Approved! A Mood Booster; Responses To Terry's Two Letters; Mayo Application Sent!; Alpier Leaving And We Would Soon Follow

Good news! I called the Colonel in the Zone today and he said they had approved my detached service several days ago. I hadn't received official word of it yet from the personnel department, but that was good enough for me. I would be more comfortable, however, when I actually saw the orders in print. See what two people could do if they worked together?

Oh, I thought, it will be so nice to see and hold Terry again. Even though it would be for such a short time, I was certain it would do me a world of good. I had been a bit down on things recently.

I received two letters from Terry today. In response, I said in my next letter to her that I had filled out and enclosed the two bank cards. I also said I saw no reason to change my mailing address. It would only complicate things. I also sent Terry the NSLI premium receipt I received for December. She said she hadn't paid that month. I asked her to do what she could to resolve the matter; that NSLI policy was by far the best policy anyone could have and I didn't want anything to happen to it. I told Terry she was very clever in dealing with Miss Smith in the Dean's office, but that she shouldn't make a habit of forgery. I was glad she liked pediatrics and I understood the problem of finding herself on a service headed by a not too capable resident. I just couldn't imagine a temperature of -14° in Minnesota. I loved her statement "keeping" me warm as toast; as well as other sweet sentiments. I would respond in person soon!

I sent off my Mayo fellowship application today, by registered mail and airmail. I didn't even wait for answers from the persons I asked for letters of reference. I was certain they would all agree to write for me anyway — and I had become tired of waiting. I just wanted it off my hands and in Mayo's hands.

Alpier was leaving Rio Hato on Wednesday. All the rest of us were to leave on Saturday, January 24. So I would finally move on to something new, though not too much different — just another dispensary. I knew one of the physicians at that dispensary; that ought to make it easier to get acquainted with my new job.

I asked Terry whether we had any furniture in our room in the Brey home. It seemed to me she said earlier the dresser and bed had been taken away. "These are very necessary items, dear. But just as long as you are there. Do you want to reserve a room at Lowell Inn for a couple of nights? It would be nice. Was that room number 211?" (Lowell Inn in Stillwater was where we honeymooned September 21, 1946).

Minneapolis General Hospital
Minneapolis, Minnesota
19 January 1948

No Calls Last Night!; Shopping With Dr. Staub; Planning A Hen Medic Party

Last night did in fact turn out to be a very good night on call. Terry slept right on through, with no calls at all. But today was quite busy at work. Then, believe it or not, she went shopping for baby clothes with Dr. Staub, a bachelor friend! He wanted to buy a gift for a friend's baby and felt that he needed some help. The funny part of this venture was that Terry didn't know anything about baby clothes either. Hank (Henry) was an intern who came from Germany about six years previously and then went to medical school in Illinois. His mother and two sisters arrived in the spring of last year. It was said that Hank and his father spent some time in a Jewish concentration camp while still in Germany, but Terry didn't know if this was true (later it was learned this was not the case).

Chris (Christine Furman) called Terry on Sunday and suggested a little get-together. Terry invited her to come to MGH on Thursday and today she called Elaine (McKenzie) and asked her to come too. So the girls would be coming over then. Terry wondered what she should serve. "Would you mind, dear, if I bought a little hooch?"

No letter from me arrived today, but she thought that every day that went by brought us closer to that wonderful time when we'd be in each other's arms. She kept busy as a "little bee" — and with that to look forward to, she couldn't help being almost happy. She was getting tired of sleeping alone. When I came, we'll have "be kind to wives who are tired of sleeping alone" week — just for us!

Rio Hato Airfield
Republic of Panama
20 January 1948

Head Injury; Packing For The Transfer; "I Love You" Anniversary; Letter From Dr. Fahr; Ghost City

Well, we had a little excitement for a change. As usual, I was called out of the movies to see a patient but this time it was a very serious matter. A Panamanian boy had been hit by a truck and it almost scalped him in addition to breaking his arm. He remained semi-comatose after receiving plasma. Alpier rode with him in the ambulance to the Zone. He went to the Santo Thomas Hospital which was a general hospital for Panamanians. It was odd. We did all this for the Panamanians after they had kicked us out.

I started packing some of my things today. The first thing I did was to tie Terry's letters to me in a neat bundle. I just had to save them for many years. After all, they did so much to keep me happy during our separation.

I showed one of the fellows Terry's picture today. After whistling loud and low, he said, "I can see why you always act so happy." There was a lot of truth in that statement. I had much to be happy for with Terry as my wife.

In my letter to Terry, I reminded her that in two days we would have our fourth "I Love You" anniversary. I had thought about that night a lot today. Remember how poorly I said it — "Honey, I'm afraid I'm in love with you." And then you promptly answered that you loved me. Then I did better. I said, "I do love you." I don't know why I said, "I'm afraid..."

"We've done very well since then. Remember I said we had to make it last. That we couldn't throw it away. We haven't, Dear, and it has lasted. In fact, it has grown on my part each day of the four years. I know it will never stop growing. I'm 'real' proud of us. May we have many more such anniversaries as much in love as we are now — and may all of them find us together."

I received a nice letter from Dr. George Fahr at MGH in response to my request to use his name as a reference for my application for a Mayo Fellowship in Internal Medicine (Figure 28). I also received a positive response from a business man in my home town (Kiester, Minnesota). Dr. Fahr's letter reflected my comments about malaria in my letter of request to him (Blackwater fever refers to the dark urine one sees in severe cases where the parasite breaks up many red blood cells and so releases the hemoglobin to be excreted in the urine).

The camp was almost a ghost city now. They had actually started knocking the barracks down around me. Well, I would move on Saturday. I told Terry to continue using the same APO address until I notified her otherwise; the letters would reach me. I also told her we heard it was terribly cold in Minnesota and that she should take good care of herself.

Minneapolis General Hospital
Minneapolis, Minnesota
20 January 1948

"Mom, I Swallowed Something"; Death In Mayor Humphrey's Office; Bridge Party Plans; Dress A Success; Literature Search

Terry sent me two newspaper clippings today. One was about a patient she had now and the other was about a patient she had last week. The current youngster, a six year old boy, had been playing with toy automobiles at home while recuperating from a cold when he complained, "Mom, I swallowed something." Surgery at MGH removed a screw from a bronchus (air tube). He had aspirated the screw rather than swallowing it. He did well after the operation (Figure 29).

The other child, a four-month-old baby boy, died and created a crisis for the MGH. Little Arthur Jensen, as I could see from the clipping Terry enclosed (Figure 30), made headlines throughout the country. His mother brought him in with a mild otitis media (middle ear infection) about two weeks ago and announced that she planned to leave him for a month. He became well within a week, and when it came time for his discharge, the mother refused to come for him. She finally came, after being called every day for three or four days in a row, and she was furious because she had wanted the child to stay for a month. She demanded to see a doctor, but was put off by the charge nurse. Terry couldn't understand her attitude at the time because little Arthur was the prettiest, sweetest baby they had.

Last night the parents again brought the child in. He had a fever of about 101 ° and was essentially negative otherwise. Dr. Lueck sent him home with instructions to return to the OPD (outpatient department) in the morning if the child became no worse in the meantime. In the morning, the parents went to Mayor Humphrey's (Hubert H. Humphrey) office to get a slip which would enable them to admit the child directly to the hospital without going through the OPD. As the newspaper said, the child died on the way. Apparently, he developed a tracheo-bronchitis or something similar. At any rate, he was certainly not in poor or critical condition when seen in receiving, i.e., the emergency room.

Of course, the *Star-Journal* put MGH in a very bad light, and poor Dr. Lueck was sweating a little. Actually, he was not liable for anything because there were at least eight hours between the time the child was seen and his death. Also, the parents were at fault for not bringing him back to receiving when his condition changed. Terry didn't believe they noticed any change in symptoms beyond the fact that his crying bothered them. "Well, dearest, excuse me for getting steamed up — I guess I am a little."

The story also made headlines in the *Chicago Sun*, was broadcast by Cedric Adams, and also was broadcast by Lowell Thomas over a national hook-up.

Chris and Elaine agreed to come to MGH Thursday night to

play bridge. Terry bought a bottle of wine so she would have something to serve. "Do you mind if I become a wino?" It would be nice to have company, but things were never as much fun as when she did them with me.

Terry's mother was at home and would be for three days. Everyone in the family liked Terry's new dress, so she decided to keep it. They think it's slenderizing. "Get that? — slenderizing." It would be nice to have something to wear while I was there.

After finishing her daily letter to me, Terry worked on a literature search she was doing for Dr. A.B. Baker, the University neurologist, an activity initiated during her six month period with Dr. Baker between medical school and internship. The subject of the literature search was Atabrine, an antimalarial drug.

Like me, Terry spent much of her time thinking about and looking forward to our being together, particularly as the date grew nearer.

Minneapolis General Hospital

MINNEAPOLIS-15-MINNESOTA

D. W. POLLARD, M. D.
SUPERINTENDENT

January 15, 1948

1st Lt. Francis J. Haddy
290th Med. Detachment (Aviation)
APO 838
% Postmaster New Orleans, La.

Dear Dr. Haddy:

I will be very glad to allow you to use my name as a reference in applying for a Mayo Fellowship in Internal Medicine.

I wish I had your opportunity of observing malaria. I see a few cases every year but it is a small experience compared to what one gets in the tropics. Moreover, these cases are never as severe as the tropical cases so that I am very optomistic about the treatment of malaria. I have never seen a case of Blackwater fever excepting in a transfusion reaction. I imagine with the newer drugs and a better treatment of malaria, as well as better prophylaxis, we will not see as much Blackwater fever in the future as has been seen in the past.

Very sincerely yours,

George Fahr

George Fahr, M.D.

GF:FB

Figure 28- Letter from George Fahr, one of my former teachers, giving his permission to use his name and offering other comments reflecting his interest in malaria.

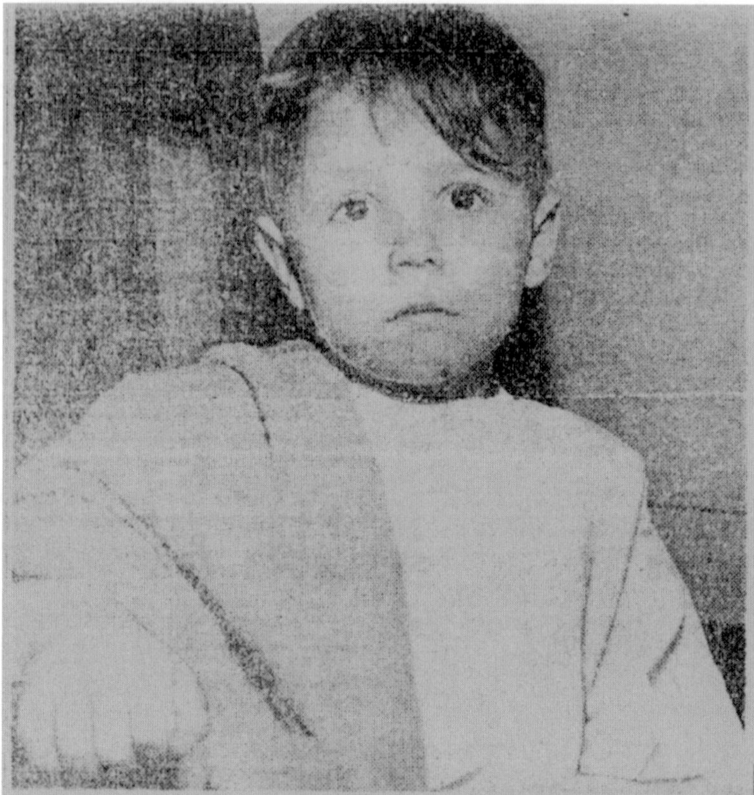

'MOM, I SWALLOWED SOMETHING'—Jerry Edlund, 6, of 2110 Fourth street N., was home with a cold Monday, so he played with toy automobiles to pass the time. Shortly after he began rocketing cars across the floor, he complained to his mother, Mrs. C. H. Carlson, that he had swallowed something. Surgery at General hospital removed a screw from his stomach. He was resting comfortably after the operation, attendants said. ← BRONCHUS

Figure 29- "Mom, I swallowed something."

MR. AND MRS. ARTHUR JENSEN GRIEF-STRICKEN AFTER DEATH OF BABY
Infant dies as parents seek mayor's assistance; investigation ordered

★ ★ ★ ★ ★ ★

Baby 'Barred' by General Hospital Dies

Death of a four-month-old baby boy, who had been sent home from General hospital after an examination a few hours earlier, started a joint investigation today by police and Mayor Hubert H. Humphrey.

The infant, Arthur Alfred Jensen, son of Mr. and Mrs. Arthur Jensen, 1716 Second avenue S., died apparently about the time his parents carried him into Mayor Humphrey's office to seek the mayor's assistance.

The baby was rushed to the hospital in a police squad car ordered by William Simms, assistant to the mayor. However, he was pronounced dead at the hospital.

Mr. and Mrs. Jensen gave this account to Police Inspector Fred Ahr:

* * *

The baby was at the hospital for about a week earlier this month, receiving treatment for an ear infection.

They took him home about Jan. 10, but he later developed a slight

They took him home about Jan. 10, but he later developed a slight **cold and fever. On Jan. 12, Mrs. Jensen took the child to the hospital's baby clinic, where he was examined.**

A doctor advised her to take the child home and keep him on a liquid diet. However, the baby's condition became worse. Late Monday, Mrs. Jensen took him to the hospital's receiving room.

* * *

She said she explained that the baby was worse and too ill to take home. The infant was given a chest X-ray and a penicillin injection.

A doctor then told Mrs. Jensen the baby was not ill enough to be kept at the hospital, and advised her to bring him back to the baby clinic today.

Mrs. Jensen pleaded with the physician but he again said she would have to bring the child to the clinic.

During the night, the infant cried considerably. In the morning, the parents took a taxicab to Mayor Humphrey's office, hoping he could arrange it so that they would not have to wait their turn at the clinic.

Mrs. Jensen said she saw her baby stop breathing as he lay on a desk in the mayor's reception room.

The Jensens told Inspector Ahr they were financially unable to place the child in a private hospital. Jensen is a self-employed gardener and landscape worker.

Dr. D. W. Pollard, superintendent of General hospital, said the X-ray of the baby's chest had been negative, and that he apparently had been suffering from only an ordinary respiratory ailment.

The child was examined by a resident doctor and a resident pediatrician called in on the case, he explained.

Both are experienced physicians, Dr. Pollard said.

He expressed confidence that they had used diligence in examining the infant.

They had been of the opinion that the baby did not require hospitalization, he added.

at the baby did not require spitalization, he added.

The hospital superintendent said that in such cases, doctors often feel that a baby is better off at home, where he can receive a mother's constant care.

Mr. and Mrs. Jensen also have a four-year-old daughter.

Figure 30-The case of Baby Jensen.

Rio Hato Airfield
Republic of Panama
21 January 1948

A Change In Assignment; Not P.A.D. But Howard Field; Not So Depressed Now; Lots Of Mail; Plans For My Visit; Last Swim And Dinner Out; Book Salvage

I had quite some news today. My new assignment was changed. While I originally was to transfer to the P.A.D. (Panama Air Depot), I was now to go to Howard Field on January 24th. Howard Field was about three miles from P.A.D. and also the same distance from Albrook Field. It was on the Pacific side of the Canal Zone. I had heard that living quarters for married personnel were pretty nice but that they were cramped for bachelor officer quarters. I was certain my new quarters would be nicer than my old ones here at Rio Hato (almost anything would be) but still far from luxurious. Of course, I wasn't concerned about what I lived in while I was alone, but I did want nice quarters when Terry arrived. Alpier's orders were also changed to Howard Field so that we would still be together.

I didn't know too much else about Howard Field, but I told Terry I would keep her informed and that, until we had further information, she should use 10¢ airmail stamps and send the letters to:

1st Lt. Francis J. Haddy 0-1766736
Base Dispensary
Howard Field, Canal Zone
Panama

Alpier planned to get a truck and have some of our gear moved to Howard Field tomorrow. I planned to do some packing tonight.

I also told Terry that I was not so depressed anymore. Her wonderful letters did so much for me. She should not feel she wasn't doing her part as a wife. Our separation was mutually agreed upon even through we didn't want it. I thought she was a wonderful wife. I would prove that when I saw her.

I received three sport sections from the newspaper and the *Minnesota Alumnus* magazine today. I got a kick out of my picture in the *Minneapolis Star* newspaper, reprinted in a year end review of activities. I showed it to everyone at Rio Hato. The preserved fruit arrived and, man, was it good. My honey took such good care of me. I also received the National Medical Boards booklet and, after looking at some of the questions, felt that I might in fact pass them with a little studying. In addition, I received three nice letters from Terry. I also got one from Dr. Edward A. Boyden (chairman of the Department of Anatomy at the medical school), saying it was okay for me to use his name as a reference. The mail did all right for me today.

In answer to some of Terry's questions, I said I thought her plan for generating nights off for the time I was home was good. "Did she think she could 'sneak' one or two days off too without ruining her vacation time? Of course she would work the days I was taking the examinations. Perhaps we could meet again in April, e.g., in Mexico City, but I 'kinda' doubted it. I thought Dr. Tague Chisholm, the pediatric surgeon, once spoke during my internship at MGH on intussusception (the prolapse of one part of the intestine into the lumen of an immediately adjoining part) and infant appendicitis, but I couldn't remember for sure. I did know that his lectures were very good. My, what a risque wife — but I loved it (see Terry's letter of 17 January 1948). However, if she used illness as an excuse, I would not be permitted to sleep with her, of course! I was very happy to hear she was finally buying herself some dresses. "Please buy some more." I wanted my honey to look fine all the time. After all, physicians must dress the part. She looked wonderful in or out of anything, but a variety of clothes was important, so I told her to please buy them. I thought her new dress sounded different, but I was certain it was very nice. "Okay, we'll go to the carnival if I am there. Let's keep our fingers crossed. Anything can happen in the Army."

Alpier, Nunnelley, and I went swimming in the afternoon, perhaps for the last time. Then Nunnelley, Phillips (the medical administrative officer), and I went out to dinner at the "Casino." That was a fairly nice restaurant on the edge of camp, one of the few in the Republic. We had a surprisingly nice meal.

Phillips declared some books from the dispensary library obsolete and said I should pick the ones I wanted. I took about ten books that were about six to eight years old, but of value — especially for studying the basic sciences.

As I wrote my letter to Terry late in the evening, I said, "Gee, the barracks are being torn down around me. Well, dear, good night and happy 'I Love You" day again. I'll be thinking about that wonderful night and you all day tomorrow."

I received a letter from my mother in Hollywood written on January 12st. She had the family, all 24 of them, over for dinner last night. They missed me at these family gatherings.

Friends and relatives still dropped by to hear about their trip to Lebanon. Dad always showed them the movies he took while there. He was asked to also show them at the "46 Club" on a Friday night. He also reprinted photos of the family in Ain Arab and some were enclosed in their letter to me. They also laid their new oriental rug, purchased in Lebanon, and my mother thought it was beautiful.

My mother asked if she should send me the apricot sheets and humus now or wait until after my move. She also said letters from Bea and Vernita indicated they were busy with their babies and, because their family was growing, Gene and Vernita had bought a larger house.

Except for Elizabeth, who had the flu, everyone was well.

Minneapolis General Hospital
Minneapolis, Minnesota
22 January 1948

Because Of Baby Jensen, Now Admitting Every Sick Child; Tracheobronchitis; Up All Night; Post Tonsillectomy Death

It was late and Terry was tired. She wrote a short note to tell me she loved me. This was our special "I Love You" day. Chris and Elaine were over tonight and they had just left. Terry didn't write last night because she was busy every moment.

Yesterday was a hectic day. Since all the unfavorable publicity, the MGH was admitting practically every child that showed up in receiving. The incident, about which she had sent a clipping (Figure 30), really made nation-wide news. She had several more clippings which she knew would interest me and which she would send on to me.

She admitted patients until 2:30 a.m. Then about 3:00 a.m. a little kid who was already in the hospital developed a severe tracheo-bronchitis. Terry thought he would die at any moment, but he pulled through. She was up until 5:00 a.m. with him.

Then of all things, they had a 12 year old post-tonsillectomy die on the ward this morning. It was really awful. Coming on top of the other big scandal, it could make a great stir; but she believed it would be pretty well hushed up. It was Terry's personal opinion that there was negligence on the part of the nurses because the patient was still under anesthesia when it happened. She had been back from the operating room about ten minutes. Terry was in the next room with Dr. Walston, and she was dead when they got to the child. (Today she would have gone from surgery to a recovery room.)

"So — things have been happening. I'll tell you all about Chris and Elaine's visit in my next letter. Honey, thank you for the sweet, sweet letter I got yesterday. I love you and miss you so much. I can hardly wait until you come."

Rio Hato Airfield
Republic of Panama
22 January 1948

Closed And Quiet; Close Call; Alpier To Howard Field With Our Gear; More On Detached Service And The NMBE; Scheduling Night Call; Discarded Supplies

Most people would really groan if they saw this place. Everything was closed and quiet. There was absolutely nothing to do. It really looked like a ghost camp. Thank heaven I would soon leave.

I held my breath today. They wanted a medical officer to stay here with a crew of men who were dismantling hangars, etc., until February 15. Nunnelley finally volunteered to stay. He almost had to since he was the Base Surgeon, i.e., the Commanding Officer (C.O.) of the medical detachment. It would have been difficult for him to order me to stay behind. Thank heaven he didn't, because it would have required a direct order to make me do it. I would have gone stark raving mad up here alone.

Alpier left today for Howard Field. I sent some of my things down with him. I hoped he had luck in finding quarters for us.

As soon as I arrived at Howard Field, I planned to complete the arrangements for my detached service. It had been approved but since I was going to a new station, I would have to clear it with my new C.O. I didn't anticipate too much trouble since the colonel (medical) in the Zone had okayed it. But, all along I said I wanted to be on the plane before drawing a first breath of relief. Anything could happen in the Army.

I studied anatomy sporadically the last few days. I had certainly forgotten a lot since taking the course in 1943. I noted in reading the National Board brochure Terry sent me that I could pass an occasional one of the tests without studying but that the rest of the tests would really ruin me. If they happened to ask the right questions, I would be alright. If not — well, I really only wanted to see Terry anyway.

I received a letter from Terry today written on the 18th. And a sweet letter it was, too. I was glad she was arranging her nights so that she would be off when I was home. It would be a sorry scheduling mess for Terry if I didn't make it. But, that was the small chance we would have to take.

I was still eating that box of preserved fruit Terry sent me. It was getting mighty slim, though. They certainly were tasty and nice looking. It was a fine wife who tries to please her husband by sending him his favorite foods.

A physician could start a nice little practice with the drugs, laboratory equipment, and surgical supplies that were being discarded. Nunnelley and I took some objects that were easy to carry for ourselves.

In my letter to Terry I said, "Panama will certainly become a much more exciting place to me when you are finally at my side. I'll be a millionfold happier and more satisfied. I've decided that you are to do just as you please when you get here — in respect to your work, I mean. You're to be a housewife as long as you like, a loafer as long as you like, or work whenever you please. I want you to know that it will be entirely your decision and whatever you do will certainly be satisfactory with me — with one exception. If you decide to be a loafer, I shall weigh you daily. To the rock pile with you the moment the scaling results are unsatisfactory."

"Happy 'I Love You' day, dear. Our marriage has been a complete success as measured by the only true scale — whether our love has grown. It has, dear. I love you more than I ever dreamed possible when I first hesitantly expressed my love for you. That's so nice."

Minneapolis General Hospital
Minneapolis, Minnesota
23 January 1948

Latest Developments In The Jensen Case And The T&A Death; We Need Malpractice Insurance!

Terry stayed at the hospital tonight because she wanted to go to bed early and catch up on her sleep. Mary, her roommate, was out with Ray (Scanlon), her steady boyfriend, so conditions for sleep were right. Terry thought her last night's letter to me "must have been sort of garbled." Things had been so hectic at MGH lately. She was collecting newspaper articles on the "big fuss" as best she could to send on to me. The inquest must have been quite exciting and she was darned disappointed to miss it.

The latest developments were that the city, MGH, and Drs. Monson and Leuck were being sued by the Jensens. Poor Dr. Lueck felt so darn bad about the whole thing. He luckily happened to have malpractice insurance. It seemed a shame that he had to be so unlucky as to get all this unfavorable publicity. Dr. Monson had been sort of a heel about the whole business, throwing the whole blame on Lueck. Actually, Monson was fully as responsible as Lueck. In fact, he had the final say because he was in charge of receiving. Last night, news casts on the radio said that telegrams were pouring in to the family from all over the States with condolences, urging them to sue. This noon, Kate Smith mentioned the incident, putting MGH in a very unfavorable light in her discussion of it.

There were also new development in the T&A (tonsils and adenoids) death. The father, who had previously been on station H with suicidal tendencies, went berserk and had to be put back on H. He banged his head against the wall and tried to break a few bones. Luckily, none of this made it to the newspaper.

"Now dear, there's at least one thing to be learned from this.

You and I need malpractice insurance. How about that, dear? Will you get yourself some? It costs $25.00 a year."

Terry also again mentioned my National Service Life Insurance. What should she do about it? How in the world did a receipt for the December premium get sent to me in Panama? She didn't remember paying it.

Terry's mother insisted on paying for her new dress. It was nice of her, didn't I think? "In that case, maybe I should get another."

"Honey, I just know you charmed all of the ladies playing bridge at the Major's home. They couldn't help recognizing what a wonderful person you are." (This was the home of the Major who snapped at me for not giving his wife a laxative without seeing her; she was in my bridge foursome).

"Did I tell you what my cousin Herb said about you? He thinks you have a wonderful personality. And he said that lots of people who met you at Wabasso (Herb's and Terry's hometown) last year thought you were very nice."

"Honey, your letters were so very sweet. I love you so very, very much — there's no danger of my ever becoming unsentimental about you. I'm happy, too, in our marriage. I'd rather be married to you than do anything else in the world."

She reassured me that she had in fact put in my application to take the National Medical Boards and that she was expecting me home with all of her heart. My visit home and our second honeymoon was all she could think about these days.

Rio Hato Airfield
Republic of Panama
23 January 1948

Rio Hato Swan Song

Because they took the plumbing and electricity from our dispensary today, Nunnelley had our "first aid station" moved to a cottage on "WAC Hill" which was formerly used to entertain generals and other high ranking persons. It was a nice little summer cottage on a cliff overlooking the Pacific Ocean. The view was terrific. Since Nunnelley was such an avid and wonderful swimmer and since he had to stay until February 15th and probably would have nothing to do, he was going to take his calls from the beach. Three honks of his car horn and he would come up. We tried it today and it worked fine. Gosh, I hated leaving that beach behind, but as to the rest, good riddance.

I had most everything packed now and was sitting in my absolutely barren room with only the crickets and an anatomy book to entertain me. I was leaving the first chance I got tomorrow.

I had had enough of Rio Hato, especially since everything closed down. All the corpsmen were scheduled to leave for Puerto Rico in the morning. Since they had very little to do the last couple of days (we had most of the dispensary moved for a week), they were half high on beer that was selling for 50¢ a case.

I received a letter from Dr. Gouze authorizing me to use his name in my Mayo fellowship application. I was surprised to find he had left the MGH but I guess Terry had in fact mentioned it in one of her letters to me.

I also received a letter from Terry. In response to her questions about buying liquor I said, “You bet you can buy hooch for your projected party. I suggest you drink a toast to our coming reunion. I’m all in favor of the ‘be kind to wives who are tired of sleeping alone’ week. Let’s make it a ‘...wives and husbands...’ week, though. I’m very tired of this solitary confinement myself.”

I planned to write again (to both Terry and my parents) tomorrow night when I would know much more.

Minneapolis General Hospital
Minneapolis, Minnesota
24 January 1948

Terry Receives My Letter With The Good News

Terry received my letter saying my detached service to take the National Medical Board examination was approved. She said "Such wonderful news — that my baby is coming home. How wonderful it will be — and darling, what a wonderful thing to look forward to. It'll do me a world of good, too. I need you so much!"

She also said she was glad my Mayo fellowship application was in. "You can't help being successful."

We had her mother's set of furniture in our bedroom in the Brey family home. Terry would have it pretty well fixed up by the time I arrived. We also had our new chair, too, which she hoped I would like.

Terry said she would be happy to reserve a room at Lowell Inn, "but when are you coming? Do you have any idea when it will be?"

Howard Field
Canal Zone
25 January 1948

Transfer To Howard Field; Tours Of The Dispensary, Night Clubs, Canal Zone, And Living Quarters

A lot had happened since I last wrote Terry and I was determined to tell her all about it.

I was chauffeured from Rio Hato to Howard Field in a jeep yesterday (January 24th). We left about 1:00 p.m. and arrived here about 3:00 p.m. I immediately checked in at the Officer's Club and was given a bunk on the third floor. I feared I would have to stay there until there was an opening in the BOQ. It was a nice building, but a bunk in a large room with about thirty other men was not too adequate. I immediately called the dispensary and found that the medical officer of the day was Bannister, a fellow with whom I traveled on the boat to Panama. He took me to the dispensary. It was a really nice, relatively new, 110-bed hospital. However, they didn't use the beds but shipped all hospitalized patients about seven miles to Fort Clayton Hospital. It was too bad, because the building was fine and just going to waste.

Counting Alpier and me, there were now about ten physicians at Howard Field; far too many. I couldn't imagine what they would do with all of us. Three of the medics came down on the same boat I did, so I already knew a good portion of the dispensary personnel.

Last night, Alpier, Sandusky (the dentist formerly with us in Rio Hato), Rimer (came down on the boat with me), Hume (a newly met medic), and I met Sporer (flyer who came down on the boat with me and whom, as I mentioned, moved into a room next to me for a few days recently up at Rio Hato) driving around in a newly bought car. We all climbed in to tour the night life in Panama City. We looked at most of the night clubs, found we hadn't missed much, and then went home. There were only about two nice clubs in the whole town. The rest were pretty much "dives."

The same group of guys, including me, have been eating our meals together here at the Club. I was paying about $1 a meal, but won't have to pay for quarters, of course, since what they provided was deemed unsatisfactory.

Sporer again took us on a tour this afternoon. We really examined the Pacific side of the Canal Zone and in the process, saw most everything, including the residential districts, the Canal, the beaches, and Gorgas Hospital. I also went with them to the BOQ where they live. The rooms were quite nice; two persons to a small suite of rooms. Of course, everything looked luxurious after being at Rio Hato. I would probably eventually live with them, which would be my first pleasant quarters since induction into the Army.

I also saw the government quarters for married officers. They were duplexes and I was certain Terry would approve of them if she ever saw them and if we ever got one. I thought I should have one lined up by the time she arrived in Panama.

Howard Field was a permanent base, so of course all of the buildings were much nicer than at Rio Hato. There was no beach, but I understood that they had just finished building a beautiful new pool that should open soon. All of the buildings were stucco with red tiled roofs and were two or more stories high.

I was told that sand flies were a terrific nuisance, causing much slapping and many bites. They did not, however, carry diseases as do other species in other parts of the world. Always something — mosquitos in Rio Hato and sand flies at Howard Field.

The medics at Howard were very dissatisfied with Army life. Gad, they should have been at Rio Hato. The army would never keep medics until they learned to treat them according to their station in civilian life, pay them better, institute some kind of teaching program, etc. Medics bitched more than anyone. And rightly so. This was an awful way to waste a group of doctors.

There was a major at the head of the dispensary at Howard Field. I was told he was about 52 years old and was applying for regular Army. That put him on my short "do not like list" right away. In my view, any physician who applies for regular Army was a "traitor" to our profession. I was to report to him tomorrow and then spend the rest of the day going around checking into the field's various departments — a chore the Army requires on coming to and leaving from a station. I would also try to pick up the loose ends of my detached service application. Changing stations just now was going to make the arrangements for that trip a little more difficult.

They said I might be placed in charge of the laboratory here. Maybe I won't even see patients for a while except when I am OD I wouldn't mind that too much for a while. I would like to try culturing some fungi out on Sabouraud's media.

Hume interned with Dave Barron (a medical school classmate) in Pittsburgh. Dave now had a one year deferment for a psychiatric residency. He just recently had a paper published in a psychiatric journal on "Symbols" — about 30 pages long. I would like to see it.

Minneapolis General Hospital
Minneapolis, Minnesota
25 January 1948

Baby Nelson And Separation Depression; The Case Of "Boarding Baby"

Today was a lazy Sunday at home. It was cold outside, but the fire was warm inside. And oh, how she wished I was there. Tonight she was writing a bunch of letters, including payment of my New York Life Insurance policy premium ($191) and the January and February National Life Insurance policy premiums. She would be glad to get those changed so that the bank automatically paid them.

We received a letter from Donna and Bob Clark (Bob was a classmate and Phi Chi fraternity brother). Enclosed in it was a front page from the *Chicago Herald* which carried the story of the Jensen baby. Terry was sending it on to me along with other newspaper articles she had collected.

Terry was awfully depressed about this baby business. She guessed most everyone at MGH was, too, especially Dr. Lueck. He was right behind the 8-ball. Terry believed the family would sue. Part of her depression was related to our separation. "I'm kinda depressed 'cuz I'm so lonesome for you, too. I love you more than anything in the world. You come before everything, baby, including medicine. Believe me, we'll never again be separated if it's within my power to prevent it."

"When do you think you'll come? Will it be before the 16th?

That would be nice because you could study at home while I'm gone during the day. Think what a nice Valentine I'm going to have this year! Darling, how long do you think you can stay? Do you want me to arrange to have day time off too? If so, let me know so that I can arrange it."

Among the newspaper clippings Terry enclosed in her letter to me was one about a little patient of hers who had been a "boarding baby" twice at the MGH, because he had been abandoned. Poor Dr. Lueck got in trouble about him, too. The first time the baby left the hospital was when the mother just took him and walked out with him — not even bothering to sign an "against advice" slip. Dr. Lueck was on call, so he was held responsible. Now the child came in again under the same circumstances as the first time. The newspaper article said "Police Play Papa to Cute Baby" and "change diapers." They had been dispatched to a home where a baby had been screaming and crying for four hours. There they found a four month old baby boy "exercising his lungs in the bedroom." "His diapers need changing, seems if," said one of the officers. The two officers became sitters for the next hour, waiting for the return of the parents. When they didn't show up, the baby was taken to MGH and Terry. The 24 year old mother turned up at the hospital at 6:00 a.m. to claim her son. She said she had been away from the apartment longer than she expected and didn't think she needed a "sitter." The case was referred to thc wclfarc department.

Howard Field
Canal Zone
26 January 1948

Detached Service — All In Order With A Delay En Route; Laboratory Officer; Civilian Sick Call

Golly, I felt better than I had in ages. Everything went right today. Here's why. I now knew that I would leave on detached service for Minneapolis on February 10th or 11th. That was for sure now. Not only that, but I would probably be home for 15 or 16 days instead of ten! Not only that, but I was assigned a job at the dispensary which I thought I was going to like a lot. Instead of becoming mess hall and sanitation officer, as I might have, I was given charge of the laboratory, with a secondary job of taking civilian sick call.

Here's how it all happened. Major Van Eter, the dispensary chief, started my day by taking me to the colonel and formally introducing me. From there I started a full day's job of checking into the field. The first stop was the personnel section. I found them very cordial and when I mentioned my pending detached service, they immediately tracked it down for me in a manner very efficient for the Army. I was afraid my application had been lost in changing fields, but they called Colonel Lee at Surgeon Headquarters. He said it had been approved and sent to Howard Field earlier to await my arrival. Sure enough, it had arrived. We then contacted Van Eter, my chief, again and he heartily approved. Not only that, but he suggested I take a delay en route "to give you more time to see your family." I plan to apply for that extra time tomorrow. Wasn't that nice? Of course, they had more docs than they knew what to do with, but still it was nice. I had about five to seven days' leave coming and I planned to add that onto the detached service. The delay en route would be charged to my leave time but not the detached service. I thought, "I had better get my winter uniforms cleaned now."

It looked as if I was going to be sanitation inspector this morning. We had some instruction in this area of activity in Fort Sam Houston and from that experience I knew doing that day in and day out would be boring. But Alpier, since he had only three months left in the Army, graciously volunteered for the job in addition to being flight surgeon. That gave me the laboratory officer's job. There was a fine laboratory in the dispensary because it was originally built and used as a hospital but it wasn't equipped to do much. The laboratory corpsmen seemed willing, so I planned to start some new tests such as blood sugar and fungus cultures on Sabouraud's media. It would take a few days to get set up for them, though. Van Eter seemed to have been disappointed in the function of the laboratory in the past, but today told me to whip it into shape and develop any procedure I felt would be useful. After a time I would also be taking civilian sick call which I thought would be more interesting than seeing only GIs because there would be more variety, i.e. pediatrics, gynecology, prenatal care, etc. So I was so far satisfied with my new position. Van Eter said I should "get the lab in shape before I left on detached service," so I would.

"So that's why I feel so fine. Be seeing my baby soon, gee!"

I bought shoes, soap, toothpaste, and many other small items today. I ran out of everything in Rio Hato after the PX closed there.

I told Terry to get a lot of sleep because we were going to do a lot of things while I was home. I doubted whether I would be able to get another furlough, especially since I would take a delay en route. Perhaps Terry should arrange a few days off while I was home but I would leave that up to her.

Gee, I felt clever arranging all of this. But I could not forget that Terry gave me the extra boost, the incentive, to call the colonel when I needed to.

I was given a P.O. box today. I told Terry to use a 5¢ stamp and send the letter to:

1st Lt. Frances J. Haddy 0-1766736
Box 429, Howard Field
Canal Zone, Panama

I was certain the letter would reach me using this address.

Minneapolis General Hospital
Minneapolis, Minnesota
26 January 1948

Slightly Quieter Today; Cold In Minneapolis; Another Dress; Happy In Panama

Terry received two letters from me today and used my new address (Howard Field, Base Dispensary) for the first time. "Honey, I'm so pleased that you remembered our anniversary of 'I Love You' day. I thought of it too, darling, all that day."

She thought the letter I received from George Fahr was friendly and nice and she wouldn't be surprised if he gave me a very good letter of recommendation. She said she would keep the letter because I might want it someday.

I was so right, it was cold in Minneapolis. Terry had a miserable ride to MGH on the street car this morning. She heard that it was -5° to -10° today, and it certainly seemed that cold. She hoped that it would be warmer when I was home because she didn't want me to get cold. She was taking good care of herself and had only had one cold this winter, and she didn't intend to have another.

Just imagine, it was only afternoon, and here she was in her room, writing a letter. Pediatrics had been slightly quieter today for a change. She was going shopping this evening. She thought she might possibly break down and buy another dress since the other one didn't cost us anything. She would also stop at the F&M Bank.

Mary was in the room, too, and they were talking. They planned to see the movie "Jane Eyre" at the Lyceum on Wednesday or Thursday.

Terry responded to my description of Panama. She said, "Darling, my love for you has grown to such greatness that it completely overshadows everything else. No discomfort will be excessive if I can only be where you are. To be with you now is my only plan for the future. I'm going to be such a contented little housewife!"

Howard Field
Canal Zone
27 January 1948

First workday at Howard Field; The Clinical Laboratory; Seven Days Leave; Clean Uniforms; Studying; Bridge

This was my first working day at Howard Field and I rather enjoyed it. Fortunately, a couple of the enlisted men (corpsmen) working in the laboratory seemed rather interested in their work. That was unusual. We ought to have some interesting experiences.

I made up some Sabouraud's media today. It hadn't hardened when it was time to leave the laboratory, so I put it in the ice box after sterilizing it in slanted test tubes. I hoped it would set by tomorrow morning. I also made about seven plates of chocolate blood agar just to try culturing GCs (gonococci) instead of guessing on smears. I forgot to check the pH of the media before I sterilized it, but I believe I it would be okay (especially since I used my own blood to prepare the media; I was certain those devilish bugs would thrive on it — ha!). We also mixed all the solutions used in measuring blood sugar, but were still looking for some methyl orange indicator for titrating some of the acid solutions. I guessed I would buy some myself in a Panama City drug store because I was certain it would take days to get it through the regular Army supply channels. I thought we would have a lot of fun doing the procedures even if they were of no value to the dispensary.

I had the secretary type an application for seven (7) additional days' delay en route. The more leave time I took, of course, the longer I would have to stay in the Army. You see, in two years, I would earn 60 days leave time. If I took no time at all, I could get out two months early, i.e., in 22 months rather than 24 months. I didn't think I would get paid for those two months if I took them at the end (terminal leave), but would if I took them now. Well, seven days wouldn't make much difference in the long run but a week more with Terry was everything to me at the present time.

I took my winter uniforms to the dry cleaners today. I told Terry, "See how I'm getting prepared for the trip. Nothing less than another war can stop it now."

I studied a little anatomy today. I guessed I could pass anatomy and bacteriology now if they didn't make tougher examinations than previously. I planned to now start on physiological chemistry, physiology, and pharmacology. I decided not to study pathology at all because I thought E.T. Bell's course, which I took my second year in medical school, was good enough to carry me through.

Another officer and I got into a bridge tournament last night here at the Officer's Club. It was duplicate bridge, i.e., all couples played the same 22 hands once each, which aims to increase fairness. We didn't do well at all, mainly because we didn't quite understand the mechanics of the new system (to us at least). We made mistakes, too. Guess I'll have to read more in the bridge instruction book Terry sent me.

I turned in early; it was tough getting to work at 7:00 a.m. each morning. "Good night, darling. All I can think of is that I'll soon be with you. Nothing is more important or exciting to me than that. My clever baby has me completely in love. It's so nice."

Minneapolis General Hospital
Minneapolis, Minnesota
27 January 1948

A Strapless Formal Dress; Insurance; Cold In Minnesota

It was only a little more than two weeks until I arrived in Minneapolis, but Terry didn't know exactly when. She said, "can you give me any idea of just when I can expect you?"

She also had another matter on her mind. "Well, dear, here's something I could hardly wait to tell you. I did it! I bought a smooth, white, brocade, sophisticated, strapless formal dress! Honey, it's really beautiful. The top is very plain, but the skirt is full. That strapless formal represents a big step in my life. I know mother will disapprove of it, but I think you'll like it. It's quite acceptable, however, and after all — I'm now a matron of 1½ years. And I think I can choose my own clothes (if it's alright with my dear husband, that is)."

Terry did a lot of shopping last night. She bought new underclothes and stationery, also some green whipcord material (like that on the chest she covered) for the dressing table chair in our room. She also took my signature cards for the National Service Life Insurance to the F&M Bank so that the bank would now pay the premiums. I could turn over my New York policy to the bank when I was home next month — there was no rush about that. It would be a relief not to have to worry about them any longer.

She spent a very quiet evening at home last night. She was spending an evening at work tonight — she hoped it would be quiet. Since W. Anderson was her resident, however, it probably wouldn't be. That man got under her skin just a little more every day.

Howard Field
Canal Zone
28 January 1948

My View Of The MGH Scandal; Another Dress; Puttering In The Laboratory; Sperm Tests; A Meeting At Gorgas Hospital; Just Two Weeks

Three of Terry's letters caught up with me today. I also received one from my sister, Juanita, and another from my mother containing photos of my father's family in Lebanon.

Terry's discussion of the current MGH scandal was interesting but depressing. It seemed something of that nature must occur periodically to take the enjoyment out of life. Wasn't it odd how some lay persons cried for medical aid and, as long as results were satisfactory, praised it. However, as soon as the inevitable bad result occurred, in spite of the fact that the medics had done their best in both instances, they pounce on them like wolves. "Little people" always delighted in proving the "big man" not so big. I too felt sorry for Dr. Leuck. I agreed with Terry that we would eventually need malpractice insurance, in my case as soon as I left the Army; in her case, as soon as she finished interning. We didn't need it until then. They don't sue Army doctors. They might court martial me, but they won't sue me.

I told Terry I was surprised to hear she was still working on the neurology paper with A.B. Baker (she had worked with him during the six months preceding her internship). I encouraged her to buy another dress with all of the accessories. "Seriously now, I want you well dressed. And don't say we can't afford it because we can. Do that for me, please. If you don't have at least one more dress besides the one you already bought, when I get home, I will be disappointed."

I was having a lot of fun puttering in the laboratory. Today I mixed diluting fluid and stain for doing sperm motility tests, counting, and stains for abnormal forms. I ran one specimen and found it not too difficult. I was branching out a bit.

In the evening, Alpier, another medic, and I went to the Gorgas Hospital for a medical meeting. They had them each Wednesday night. We got there too late for the lecture, but we did meet a lot of physicians. We decided to join the medical society and attend the weekly lectures. The membership was transferrable to one's home society upon return to the States (without reapplying), I heard.

I was still living out of my suitcase at the Officers' Club. I hoped I would get quarters soon because this was inconvenient.

"Well, darling, less than two weeks now. Oh, my, how I'm looking forward to seeing you. I'll be home for Valentine's Day.

My heart will certainly be where it belongs on that day and that's as close to you as possible."

Minneapolis General Hospital
Minneapolis, Minnesota
29 January 1948

Wonderful News; Banking Nights Off; More On The Big "Blow;" Athlete's Foot Of One Toe; Aggressive Parents; An Occasional Nice Letter

Terry received three letters from me yesterday and one today. Today's was the best of the lot because it contained the wonderful news of my coming. If I left on February 10th or 11th, did that mean she could expect me on the 12th or 13th? Yes, she would plan on taking some time off. She would see about applying for vacation time as soon as possible. If they refused to give it to her, she would say she was sick!

Last night was really a busy one. She didn't get to bed until 3:30 a.m. It would be worth every bit of it, though, if it gave her more time off while I was home. She now had two interns owing her nights, and she planned on getting a few more in debt to her before I arrived. She was sorry, though, that she didn't find time to write to me.

The pediatric service was kind of miserable these days — in a way. They admitted every child with a cold — the climax came today when they admitted a little girl with athlete's foot of <u>one toe</u>. One of the physicians in charge, Dr. Bosma, hit the ceiling when he heard of it. The big "blow" about Baby Jensen had far from died down. Many of the parents who brought their children in for 'nursemaid' care were downright obnoxious and aggressive. It made one a little bit disgusted with people.

Terry sent me a clipping from the newpaper *Times* about the Jensen case — "the only two 'nice' letters I've seen." One was from a nurse who defended MGH saying, "The emergency facilities, medications and treatments received there are prompt and excellent, despite some of the obsolete equipment which has to be tolerated!" The other was from a *Times* reader who said, "I feel sorry for the young doctors for the publicity they are getting."

Minneapolis General Hospital
Minneapolis, Minnesota
29 January 1948

Here She Was Again; Still Excited About Today's News; Planned To Be A Housewife For A Time

Here she was again. Mary and she had seen the movie *Lured* with George Sanders and Lucille Ball earlier in the evening. They were both home now, "all clean and ready for bed."

Terry was glad I was happy with my new work at Howard Field. She was sure civilian practice would be interesting and that I would do a wonderful job with the laboratory and set up all sorts of new procedures. She thought it was gracious of Nunnelley to volunteer to stay at Rio Hato. She hoped we would get nice quarters at Howard Field. It would be our home, and she did want it to be pleasant. She was planning to be a loafer and housewife for a least the first few months. The thought of sleeping a lot, puttering around a house, and best of all — being a real wife to me — appealed to her greatly. She thought she could probably pick up some sort of work later. We would probably need the money by that time.

"Good night for now, my beloved husband. Thinking of your coming will keep me completely happy until then. I'm so excited over today's letter from you that I won't be able to go right to sleep. (Tomorrow's my regular night on call — I hope I find time to write at least a little note.)

Howard Field
Canal Zone
29 January 1948

Studying Pharmacology; More And More Medics; Our Love

I went to a movie tonight and then studied a little pharmacology. I found a pharmacology book written by Harold N. Wright, one of our pharmacology professors in medical school and one of the professors in the Department of Pharmacology where Terry worked in the nine months between her sophomore and junior years in medical school. I found the book concise and easy to digest.

It was warm and humid the last few days. Rio Hato definitely had a better climate than Howard Field, but in general, Howard Field was much nicer, in particular for a married couple.

I did a sperm count, motility, and stain on a pilot with but one testis resulting from an orchitis (infection of the testis) secondary to mumps. He was happy to hear that my findings were normal.

Two more medical officers arrived today. What were they going to do with all of us! Fort Clayton Hospital was short on 'medics,' I heard. I would love to get transferred there but the chances of that happening were mighty small.

I received a sweet sentimental letter from Terry today — the type I never tired of reading many times. I missed her so much. I didn't know what I would have done had my trip home not been coming soon. Our love was so unbelievably wonderful and I prayed it continued that way forever, for who could ask for anything more than being the happiest man in the world for that long period of time.

I told Terry to drop "Base Dispensary" from my address and just use "Box 429, Howard Field, Canal Zone, Panama."

Minneapolis General Hospital
Minneapolis, Minnesota
30 January 1948

Disappointing News; Only Two Interns, Not Three; Needs Specific Dates; Lowell Inn?; An Invitation To Dinner

Terry had some rather disappointing news for me. She was feeling so doggone sorry for herself tonight. She had just found out that there will only be two interns on the Contagion service where she will be next month during my visit — after there had been three for months! Much of her planning for time off was based on three rather than two interns. She was awfully sorry for herself when she first heard it. However, after thinking it over, she might be able to work it out. She thought she could get a lot of kids to work for her, and maybe Elaine would work for her for a few days. But she needed more information from me, i.e., a pretty accurate idea of what days I would be home. It would help a lot in arranging her time off.

She thought of all the wonderful things we would do that we like to do together — and the things I like to eat. Yes, she would love to go to Lowell Inn (the site of our homeymoon). In fact, she dreamed of our being there together.

The letters she got from me yesterday, on the 29th, were postmarked the 27th. That was darn good time.

Terry was invited to Bill Schulze's home Saturday night for dinner. Bill was a resident in medicine. Fay Tichy (a neurologist Terry knew from her period with Dr. Baker) and her husband, David, would be there. Terry thought it would be fun — they had two children. Unfortunately, Terry had to work on Sunday! This was to have been her week-end off.

Howard Field
Canal Zone
30 January 1948

SNAFU #1

I wrote Terry urgently requesting her to try to straighten out a wrong examination site for me. I received a letter from the National Board of Medical Examiners in Philadelphia today. Enclosed was a receipt for $20, a schedule of the examinations, a letter, and a card containing my number and where to take the examination. I sent the card and the letter to Terry because the card said I was to take the examination in New Orleans! (How the hell did that happen?) I asked her to call Dr. Rasmussen or Miss Smith immediately and ask whether it made any difference where I took the examination. I also asked her to save both items for me because I would need to take them to the examination. Finally, I told her not to worry; this "snafu" wouldn't stop me from coming home and I wouldn't take the examination in New Orleans.

My orders for the flight were issued yesterday. Today my letter applying for seven extra days went forward. Things were lining up fine "but try to straighten out this other little matter for me, baby. Hell, I don't want to go to Tulane. My baby isn't there."

Minneapolis General Hospital
Minneapolis, Minnesota
1 February 1948

NEW SERVICE — CONTAGION; SHOPPING; THE SCHULZ DINNER; A LETTER FROM MAYO

Terry received two letters from me yesterday. One was postmarked January 29th; indicating a very short travel time. My letters had been arriving regularly and she found it wonderful to hear from me so often. She found the letters interesting and she was proud of the work I was doing in the laboratory. "Do you really think the 'devilish little bugs' will grow well in your blood? Well, I'm sure they couldn't find better blood anywhere."

She was disappointed to learn that she would have to work every other night this month. Since there was only one other intern on her new service (Contagion), she couldn't take time off and leave him with all the work. She thought, however, that she could get an outside intern to come in and work for her. Hank (Henry) Staub knew one at Swedish Hospital that wanted to take a week or two at MGH on Contagion. If she couldn't get him to work for her, she was almost certain that she could get Elaine. She was still "housewifing," Terry believed. She had finished interning and had not yet started practice. Contagion would be a fairly easy service, she thought, even though there were only two interns — at least the recent interns weren't busy. (On the other hand, the service was unbelievably busy when I served on it in 1946 because of a large poliomyelitis epidemic).

Yesterday, Terry stopped at Dayton's department store on the way home and bought panties and nylon stockings. They were having a sale and they really had some bargains. Her stockings just weren't lasting because she caught them on the chairs at work. She thought she would shop tomorrow night for a few minutes again. Her beautiful evening gown needed a fitting, too — she needed to do that this week. "Such an extravagant wife you have, darling."

She got home from MGH yesterday just in time to change her clothes and start out to Schulze's. It was quite a dinner. Fay and David were there, and another couple who weren't married. Bill and Mary Ann Schulz had two children, five and two, and Mary Ann was about two months pregnant now. They served Manhattans, followed by a spaghetti dinner with wine. It was an excellent dinner and everything was very nice. "I spent the entire evening thinking about you, though, and about how much I missed you. Everything I do with you is fun, darling, but everything I do without you is only a reminder of how wonderful it would be to have you doing it with me. Life is empty without you, dear. My only enjoyment is in thinking of the day when we'll be alone together. I can hardly wait until we have our own little home."

Terry enclosed a note from Carol and Andy Midthune thanking us for Steve's gift and also a letter from the Mayo Clinic in Rochester, Minnesota (Figure 31) suggesting I travel to the Clinic for a personal interview in support of my application for a fellowship in internal medicine. Terry strongly felt that I should plan on that personal interview; she would love to fly down to Rochester with me. "We could plan to take a trip through the Clinic and go on down to visit your sisters in Iowa." She felt my personality would impress the interviewers at the Mayo Clinic (a bit biased, perhaps?).

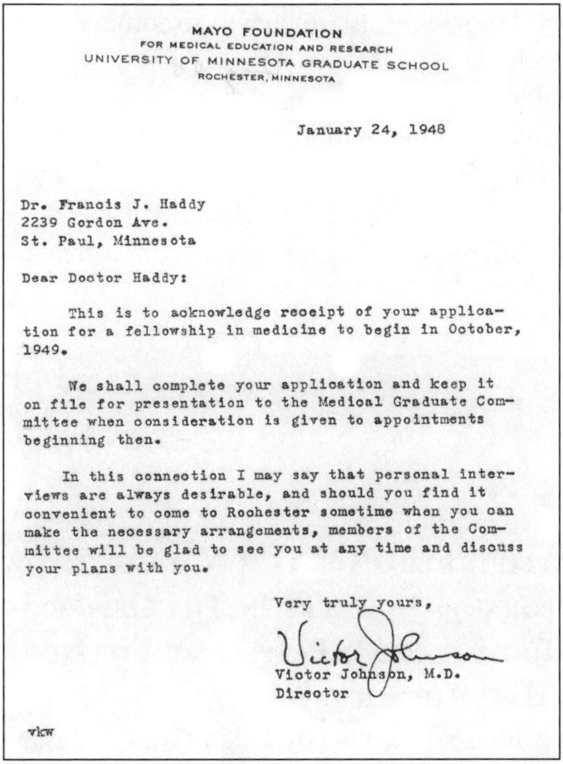

MAYO FOUNDATION
FOR MEDICAL EDUCATION AND RESEARCH
UNIVERSITY OF MINNESOTA GRADUATE SCHOOL
ROCHESTER, MINNESOTA

January 24, 1948

Dr. Francis J. Haddy
2239 Gordon Ave.
St. Paul, Minnesota

Dear Doctor Haddy:

This is to acknowledge receipt of your application for a fellowship in medicine to begin in October, 1949.

We shall complete your application and keep it on file for presentation to the Medical Graduate Committee when consideration is given to appointments beginning then.

In this connection I may say that personal interviews are always desirable, and should you find it convenient to come to Rochester sometime when you can make the necessary arrangements, members of the Committee will be glad to see you at any time and discuss your plans with you.

Very truly yours,

Victor Johnson

Victor Johnson, M.D.
Director

vkw

Figure 31 - Letter from Victor Johnson acknowledging receipt of my Mayo Fellowship application.

Minneapolis General Hospital
Minneapolis, Minnesota
1 February 1948

A Wonderful Date; Arranging Time Off; Dream Of Lowell Inn

Terry thought this date was wonderful; it was the first day of the month that was going to bring her "precious" husband home. So she wrote a second time.

She spent a very quiet afternoon, napping a little and then listening to the radio. She hoped the Contagion service remained quiet.

Terry called Elaine and she agreed to work a few days for her while I was home. She also invited us to come over during that period.

This afternoon Terry dreamed that we were back at Lowell Inn (the site of our honeymoon in September 1946). "I wish I could tell you, dearest, how much you mean to me. I wish I could express even a fraction of my love to you. My only desire is to be with you again — you're by far the most important thing in my life."

Howard Field
Canal Zone
1 February 1948

On Or About February 11th; Not Long Now; Still In Temporary Quarters In The Officer's Club; Texan Roommate; My Preference For Non-medics; Medics Hate The Army

I was getting to be a dull boy. I didn't want to do anything but lay around and think of seeing Terry. Weekends were very trying without her to make them interesting. But it wouldn't be long now.

My orders stated that I would leave Panama "on or about February 11th." That wasn't very definite for Terry's planning, but I told her she could expect me at least before the 13th. That was as exact as I could be. I didn't know if I would get that extra seven days but I was hoping like everything.

My days were spent reading — an attempt at study for the Board examination — seeing movies, playing pool, and shooting the bull with some of the fellows.

Right now I was living in a temporary room (I moved into one of the four rooms on the third floor of the Officer's Club several days ago; I had been in the dormitory on the third floor until that time). It was small and definitely inadequate, especially since I have a roommate. He was an approximately 30 year old Texan air corps captain named Hugh who just arrived from the States. He was very nice and friendly.

I noted that, since arriving in the Army, my friends were generally non-medics. Oddly enough, most fellow docs didn't attract me too much. Perhaps I hadn't met the right ones, but I was fairly certain I wouldn't become too close to the ones at Howard Field. They were nice enough fellows, but just not my type. Perhaps I felt they were not too interested in medicine. I didn't know.

I asked Terry to try and arrange for some days off too, beginning after the Board examinations were over. I realized I would be leaving home shortly after I finished the examinations if my requested seven days of leave weren't approved, but I asked her to think about it nevertheless. The probability that I would get the extra time was good, so she wouldn't be taking too much of a chance. The Lowell Inn idea was wonderful; a credit to both of us.

I told Terry that she would never know how much physicians hated the Army. I griped much less than the rest, but even so spent a lot of time at it. I hated having my time wasted. Army life would of course be oh so much more bearable when Terry arrived. The Army had not yet realized how to treat physicians. Until it did, it would never keep them.

"Good night, darling. The only news I know is that I love you more than I ever dreamed possible. My whole life is you, darling, and I love it just that way. It is very soon now, dear."

Minneapolis General Hospital
Minneapolis, Minnesota
2 February 1948

Easy Night On Call; Correcting Snafu #1; Maneuvering Time Off; News Of Friends; Pharmacology; Lab Work; Valentines

Terry thought the Contagion service was wonderful. At least it had been so far. Last night she washed her hair, her underwear, and her stockings, took a bath, wrote to my parents and my two sisters in Iowa, and slept the whole night. If it only kept up like that! She told Bea and Vernita that she hoped we could visit them while I was home.

"Congratulations on having such a clever wife, dearest! I've already (I think) taken care of your little problem with Tulane U." Terry received two letters from me today (the mail service had been extremely satisfactory recently) and one of them contained my identification card for the National Board Examination. She immediately called Dr. Rasmussen at the medical school and he said the boards would definitely be given here in Minneapolis and that she should write to the board of examiners right away, telling them you wanted to take the boards here. So she thought she would send a night letter tonight. It wouldn't be very expensive.

Terry had also started on her problem of maneuvering a little time off while I was home. She met this Dr. George Shimkus from Swedish Hospital today — and he seemed to be interested. She even offered to pay him, so she would see what comes of it. Elaine also said that she would work for her. She would rather not ask her, however, if she could get someone else. She wouldn't ask Elaine for more than four to five days, but she could safely ask Shimkus for ten days. "Oh, darling, I'm so anxious for everything to work out alright!"

Today Dr. Brigham (a surgeon who had been stationed in Panama) asked all about me — lots of people asked every day. He showed Terry a picture of his little four month old boy — just as cute as could be — didn't look at all like him. Terry also gossiped with Wally Anderson for a while, too. She asked him if there would be any parties at Phi Chi (my fraternity next to the medical school) this month. He didn't know. He did say that Morrie Johnson was spending a year working in the Department of Physiology as a basis for his surgery boards later on (one year in a basic science could be used to satisfy one year of the three year formal training requirements for specializing in internal medicine, an option I'd choose later on). Wally also said several of our medical schoolmate friends were moving right ahead with marriage and parenting. I was sure Terry thought we were falling behind.

Terry said she was proud of me for studying pharmacology and that she was sure I would pass the examinations with flying colors. She thought the book by Dr. Wright (from the Department of Pharmacology where she had worked between her sophomore and junior years) I mentioned was a widely-used nurses' text. She thought it would be a nice book for us to have and keep. She also said she was proud of all the things I was doing in the dispensary laboratory. She bet I was making a simply wonderful impression on everyone in the dispensary. She thought it would be useful to tell my interviewers at Mayo about the laboratory procedures I had developed — she knew they would be impressed with me for going ahead on my own.

Terry again reassured me about the Tulane matter. "They have to know where you'll be taking the exam because they send your identification there. We'll get it all straightened out, though, right away."

"Darling, your trip home is going to be the most wonderful

thing that ever happened to me — except our actual marriage. I love you so much!"

Enclosed in her letter were three miniature Valentines that Terry received from one of her patients. Terry said, "Honey, these valentines came from a nine year old admirer on the pediatric service, addressed to Mrs. Haddy. Aren't they cute?"

Howard Field
Canal Zone
2 February 1948

First Civilian Sick Call; Source Of Boredom; Bridge; Cleaning; Love Will Find A Way

I received two stimulating letters from Terry. In addition, I received an envelope of newspaper clippings concerning the Jensen baby. The clippings were very interesting and illustrated how quickly one incident can bring public disfavor upon a physician. The public quickly forgets the good a physician does routinely each day and almost delights in knifing him/her following the inevitable occasional bad outcome. The public seems not to recognize that a negative result will sometimes occur even when the best medicine is practiced. Dr. Leuck was a good conscientious physician and didn't deserve the criticism.

I took civilian sick call this morning for the first time. It was very light and went smoothly. I believe we had more pathology (serious cases) in Rio Hato than here at Howard Field. No wonder physicians become bored in the Army.

Another fellow and I got into another bridge tournament tonight. We had the tournament won until we made some silly mistakes near the end. As it was, we ended with an average score — out of the money.

My winter uniforms arrived back from the cleaners today. I was really preparing for my visit with my baby.

I told Terry that I was sorry to hear there would be only two interns on the Contagion service during February. We would work something out, I was certain. "Love finds its methods, you know. We've got the love, I'm certain the methods will follow." I also told her that I bought her a small valentine present today. "No, I won't tell you what it is. I hope you like it, though."

I was still sweating out my request for a seven day extension of my leave. But I was fairly certain it would be approved, so I encouraged Terry to plan on my being home until about the 25th or 26th.

Minneapolis General Hospital
Minneapolis, Minnesota
3 February 1948

Just A Little Over A Week! Preparing Our Room; On Call Every Other Night; Post-pertussis Pneumonia

"Isn't it wonderful? In just a little over a week, my baby will be coming home! I'm so excited about it all. I go around glowing all day long."

Last night Terry covered the dressing table chair in our room with the same green material that was on the chest. She wanted our room to look nice when I came home. She was anxious, too, to know what I thought of the chair she bought. She stopped uptown before coming home and bought two extra cups for our set of yellow dishes — in case of breakage, you know.

She was on call again — every other night now. However, this service promised to give her lots of time for extras. (This was not the case when I was on the Contagion service in 1946. In mid-July of 1946, a polio epidemic began to cause concern about public gatherings; 4-H officials called off preliminary judging and high school bands began backing out of performance commitments to the state fair because parents refused to let their children participate. The 1945 State Fair had been cancelled due to gas rationing, so plans called for a 1946 celebratory "Victory Fair." The fair was to open August 24th. On August 14th, the state health board recommended cancellation. About 360 new polio cases had been reported in Minnesota the previous week, bringing the year's total to 983. The opening of most schools was also postponed about two weeks that year. Panic gripped citizenry and admissions to MGH accelerated. On a peak day over 100 diagnostic spinal taps were done in receiving. There were some surprises among them, e.g. hysteria and tetanus (lock-jaw) masquerading as poliomyelitis. Eventually most of the hospital beds were filled by patients with polio and one floor was fully devoted to the bulbar variety where breathing was accomplished with the assistance of an iron lung and nutrition was accomplished with tube feedings. Complications were frequent, e.g., electricity outage stilling the iron lungs and an emergency caesarean section in a dying mother. All of this made for a busy time where I was on call two nights out of three, first call the first, and second call the second night.)

It would be wonderful to get in a bath now and then, and also write her baby.

Time out — she had to go look at a little kid now. He had post-pertussis (whooping cough) pneumonia, and his temperature wouldn't come down.

Here she was, back again. She guessed the little kid would be alright.

"Time for bed now. I'll take a bath and tuck myself in. How I'd love to have you tuck me in, dear — or better still, tuck us in together. It won't be long now, will it? How wonderful it will be when we can be together always — forever!

Howard Field
Canal Zone
4 February 1948

Snafu #2

I was OD yesterday, my first at Howard Field, and catastrophe struck. The entire story was told in a long letter to Terry, and it is here reproduce in its entirety.

Wednesday Night
February 4, 1948

Dearest Terry,

I'm sorry I didn't write you yesterday, but I was so angry and depressed that I didn't dare risk putting anything on paper. No dear, it has nothing to do with my coming home. At least I don't think it will affect it. Those orders are already made out. It could possibly affect my seven day extension, though.

First of all, I don't claim that my ideas are always correct. However, as a doctor, I am entitled to my own opinions and another doesn't have the right to impose his upon me, even if he does hold a higher rank.

I imagine you're wondering what I am driving at. Well, as I told you, there is an older man, perhaps 52, a major and doctor, who is head of the dispensary here. I got in a nasty argument with him and the final result was that he threatened to transfer me if I didn't obey his order. What kind of a doctor is it that would pull his rank on another over a medical difference of opinion? I'm not going to tell you all of the details 'cause it would be too lengthy and I don't care to discuss it. I'll tell you all about it when I get home.

No, I won't be transferred and the major told Alpier this morning that 'he was afraid he hurt my feelings but that he still thought I was wrong.' The argument occurred yesterday morning.

They have a policy here of sending drunken soldiers up to the dispensary for a sobriety test to be given by the medical officer. The medic is supposed to write an affidavit and sign it stating the degree of sobriety of the soldier in question. I was OD yesterday — my first — and the provost marshall sent two soldiers up to me with the request of "determine whether they are drunk or not." Knowing nothing of the policy, I sent them back with a note saying in brief that "since no one can define sobriety or drunkedness and since the condition is relative, I cannot comply with your request." I know I should have asked first and not have sent the note without going through channels. I admit that. The provost marshall immediately brought the note up to the major like a tattletaling school boy. The major called me in very angrily and wanted an explanation of the note. He didn't speak to me as one doctor should to another, but as a damned army officer reprimanding a Pfc. I maintained that no man can tell for certain how intoxicated a man was, whether he can perform duty, etc., or whether he had even been drinking, since there are no objective tests for it [this was before blood alcohol levels]. *I also maintained that writing out an affidavit as to his condition and signing your name was a very foolish and dangerous thing. He did not agree and told me so in no indefinite terms. I asked him, since it was against my teaching and especially against my belief as a doctor, to not ask me to perform that one duty but to have someone else do it who doesn't believe the way I do. He said it was my duty as an officer and that if I refused to follow orders, he would have me transferred. It progressed no further, but I did not say I would follow his orders. I wonder what will happen when the next one is sent to me when I'm OD I think he feels he dealt a little harshly with me from what Alpier says today.*

To me it is a matter of principal. I don't think I have to sign anything I don't want to. As a doctor, I am entitled to my beliefs and opinions, even in the Army. If I am doing something I don't believe in, I am living a lie. I don't claim I'm right. I just claim I have a right to my own belief and no one can force theirs upon me.

You know, dear, I'm learning a lot about doctors in the Army. My primary interest in life — aside from you of course — is medicine. I love it and I want to practice it the way <u>I believe</u> and the way I have been taught. I'm not saying my way is right. But dear, most of the fellows I've met, including the major, will do most anything, even though they don't believe it's right, just to please someone else who is in a position to criticize them — a little higher in ranks. They live a lie. They'll permit themselves to be pawns just so they'll get an okay from someone else who is in a position to make their lives a little fuller — fuller of the material things in life.

Damn, I intend to live the way I believe. I'd be so ashamed of myself if I didn't. Even if it means bringing the wrath of every damned brass hat in the Army down on me, I'll live by the way I believe. Gee, baby, maybe I'll make life difficult for us both by being so stubborn in that matter. Maybe I'll botch my trip home to you — and other trips, advancements, and material things throughout life. Maybe I'll botch it all. Maybe I'm being dramatic. Maybe it's the P.D. (pathological deviate) coming out. But dear, would you respect me if I gave in, became a pawn, just to polish the apple with my "superiors?" I'm certain you would think less of me if I didn't stand up for my beliefs.

Honey, while I was arguing with him, my leave papers were laying on his desk. I saw them. I thought what I was doing to your hopes and my hopes by stirring his anger. He can refuse to sign my extension, at least. But I didn't hesitate to argue right on 'cause I felt certain you would tell me to under the circumstances, even if it meant cancelling our trip. I thought of all that while I was arguing.

Am I too idealistic? Am I creating a lot of trouble

unnecessarily? Are one's beliefs that important? I think they are.

I work harder than most of the other officers — because I'm interested in my work. That's more than I can say for most of the other medics. The major realizes I do good work. He told Alpier that. He also said, "he didn't realize my beliefs were that important to me" — to Alpier. I had a fine record in Rio Hato. But I lay you ten to one that I'm going to find lots of difficulty living my beliefs in the Army. This organization is like that. They expect you to do as they do — change your ideas to conform with theirs — just so that the higher ups will be satisfied. There are many selfish people, I find. Anything is alright as long as it makes good appearances. Then we'll all advance up the material ladder.

Grr! I'm mad

I received three nice big sweet letters from you today and also a letter written by Mom and one by Dad. I'm happy to hear you are taking care of the days off and also the examination difficulty. Don't change any of your plans because of the above. The major can't keep me from going home. He's not that bad a guy, anyway. Yes, dear, I'll have an interview at Rochester.

I bought several articles for my baby today that I think you'll like. Now if I can get them home with me.

This is a fine type of letter to write to my honey. I had to get it off my chest. I should be telling you of my love for you. Oh, you just wait 'till I get home. I've saved so many endearing phrases for you — I'll whisper them in your ear each day over and over again.

All my love,
Fran

Minneapolis General Hospital
Minneapolis, Minnesota
4 February 1948

Postscript Of An Old Patient

No mail from her baby today, even though she was sort of expecting some. Maybe there would be three letters tomorrow! She wondered if I was receiving her letters and whether she was addressing them to the right place.

There had been no new progress on her hoped-for vacation. She was still working on it. She hoped Superintendent Pollard would approve it after she got it all arranged.

She wondered whether I remembered M.B. He was a patient I saw in the examination clinic just before I left MGH. I found a black tarry stool (stools that look like tar suggest bleeding high up in the gastrointestinal tract), but the occult blood studies (chemical test for blood in the stool) were negative. He proved to have a cancer of the esophagus, however, and he also had a displaced aorta. He refused surgery when it was first discovered, but he was operated on later — and the cancer was declared inoperable. At postmortem today, the cancer was found to have eroded through the trachea (wind pipe), and he had a large empyema (infection in the pleural space, the space between the lung and chest wall). Terry thought I would be interested because that first observation I made on physical examination was pretty astute, to her way of thinking.

It was only afternoon and here she was writing a letter to her husband. Pretty soft service, this Contagion. "Honey, how I love you — with all my soul and being. You're the center of my life, the most wonderful thing I know!"

Howard Field
Canal Zone
5 February 1948

Surprise! This One Positive

This day initiated a swift end to my military career in Panama. The story was told in a long letter written to Terry on the night of February 5. It was the last letter I wrote to Terry from Panama and it was sent via AIR MAIL, SPECIAL DELIVERY (5¢ stamp plus 3¢ stamp). The letter is here reproduced in its entirety.

Thursday night
February 5, 1948

Dearest baby,

Prepare yourself for a big surprise, dear. Things are happening very rapidly.

Honey, I'm being discharged! That's right, discharged from the Army. Immediately! The major called me into his office this morning and asked me if I had a friend in Washington. When I looked blank, he said, "You mean you don't know?" I said, "Know what?" Then he told me. It's a medical discharge for my eyes, the result of that examination I had a couple of months ago. He suspected I had a senator pulling for me but when I explained this was still action on my August entrance physical, he began to understand. When he heard what my vision was, he agreed that I should legally be released. Can you imagine anything as inefficient as the Army? It took them six months to decide if they wanted me and much expense to the government to get me here. Now they are sending me out.

The thing that surprised me most was the major's reaction to it. He was extremely friendly and was all set to protest the discharge with all his means <u>if I wanted</u> — 'cause he "liked *my work very much. Just when you are getting that laboratory running right, they take you away." He asked me if I wanted to get out. I said not especially. He reached for the phone to call the bigwigs to see if I could stay in. I grabbed his arm and said, "Leave it. I'll take the discharge." Isn't that odd? He actually wanted me to remain very badly. Perhaps sticking up for one's beliefs does leave an impression. I guess he isn't too bad a fellow after all.*

I'm off the subject. I'll probably leave here on Monday or Tuesday — and probably by plane. I won't know for certain until my orders come out. The orders probably will be issued tomorrow. My detached service, of course, is automatically cancelled. The port of embarkation for the air corp is Brookly Field in Mobile, Alabama. That's probably where I'll land. They usually send one to the nearest Army post — airfield in this instance — to the man's home for separation. Where that will be, I don't know. Perhaps Illinois, or I might be separated at Mobile. Separation usually takes anywhere from 5 to 20 days. So I guess I won't be able to take the National Boards.

It's a shame that all of our plans have to be junked. I'm almost certain I won't make it in time for the exams — though anything can happen. It's also a shame all of your arranging of time off is now made so uncertain. If it happens that my separation takes a week or more to accomplish, it would be nice if you could meet me at my particular separation point. We could have a wonderful time. We'd take a nice hotel room, etc. So don't junk your plans until you hear from me for certain. I know it's putting you in a very difficult situation not knowing for certain, but just leave things dangling. I imagine we'll be out the 20 bucks for the exam fee.

In a couple of ways, I'm not too happy this occurred just now. First of all, we'll feel the lack of money for a while. I'll probably get $200-$300 upon separation, however. Secondly, I did so want you to get in some traveling and rest. I wanted you to experience the experiences I have and to live in a nice *home of our own here for a while away from everyone we know. Thirdly, this has caught me flatfooted and I have nothing definitely lined up in the way of work. Those are the disadvantages.*

Now listen to the advantages. 1. I'd never be satisfied in the Army. I don't like the medicine, the brass, and a lot of the people. You'll be spared my griping on that subject. 2. We'll be together from now on. Isn't that wonderful? As soon as I get situated in something, you and I are going to find a little home of our own and spend the rest of our lives building on our great pile of love. Don't you worry about money 'cause papa will arrange all one way or the other. 3. Where there's a will, there's a way. I'll find a satisfactory position. I'll go to Rochester and have my interview. I'll ask them to set the date of my application up some (I applied for October, 1949). If they want, I can get a straight internship in the meantime. If Rochester doesn't pan out, there are other residencies and I can be a general practitioner someplace for a while until I make connections. Don't worry, honey, that will work out okay. 4. Instead of degenerating, medically speaking, for the next year and a half, I can build — if it's in me and I'm lucky to hit what I want. I'll be much more satisfied, I know. That will be a year and a half nearer my boards if things work out right.

All in all, I'm very happy about the timing even tough it is going to make things difficult for a time. My poor honey went to all that trouble to arrange things and now we still don't know. But let's plan on your meeting me at my separation point. I'll let you know as soon as possible.

At first, I was going to surprise you. Just come home presumably on detached service and then stay on saying I was going AWOL. My, wouldn't you get excited. Of course, after thinking about it, I couldn't, 'cause you've got a few things to straighten out now that our plans are changed.

Gee, are the other medics envious. They all hate the Army

and would give anything to be in my shoes.

I've been having some work done on my teeth again. Seven or eight new cavities! I'll try to get it done tomorrow before the Army kicks me out. They developed since last June. Gad!

I received an interesting letter from Baker saying it was okay to use his name. When I wrote to him, I discussed my ideas on IV oxygen with him. He wrote me a nice letter saying they seriously had considered using it in polio, but were hampered by mechanical difficulties and dangers to the patients in its use.

I was really enjoying myself in the laboratory. I received a lot of compliments on my work. That's another small reason I don't like to leave now — but mighty small! The Army isn't for me. You are.

Gad, it's sticky in this Zone. Not much of a place for having my baby. But I still wish you could have seen the place. Some day we shall make a trip together. But I'll be damned if I'll ever leave you again.

If I'm held for separation for a while, let's really try to make an effort to have you meet me. It would be so much fun and so much nicer. I think we should be alone for a while when we meet, don't you? Just like a honeymoon. You could bring your lovely new evening gown and we'll do the town, too. I'll inform you just as soon as I know.

When we learn for certain I can't take the exam, maybe you could notify Rasmussen for me.

Here's to a happy and successful future for us, darling — always together. I love you so very much.

Good night, darling,
Fran

I wrote no more letters because I was frantically, packing, separating, and traveling. But Terry continued to write four letters through February 8th, two of which were returned to the Brey home from Panama.

Minneapolis General Hospital
Minneapolis, Minnesota
5 February 1948

Admissions — Scarlet Fever And Measles; NMBE Admissions Card — The Right One; A Visit With Elaine And Roy; Still Cold

Terry spent the morning resting at home and then arrived at work about 2:00 p.m. when she went on call. She had two admissions in the evening — a scarlet fever and a measles. She hoped there wouldn't be anymore.

I received another admission card for the National Medical Board Examination February 16-18. This one was right! It was for the University of Minnesota. Terry said, "How's that for fast work."

Last night, Terry and Ann stopped over to see Elaine and Roy. They were fine, and Elaine was still a housewife. Terry thought she probably would end up by getting her to work a few days for her.

The weather was still horrid — almost always below zero. She was so afraid I would catch a bad cold when I came. She did want me to have a lovely time. This visit meant so much to her. She knew it would be a lovely memory, and she wanted it to be for me, too. How she was looking forward to my visit. It would be the most wonderful thing in the world that could happen.

My letter written February 2nd came today (February 5th). She thought she would stop writing on about the 9th. She urged me to let her know when I was coming.

Minneapolis General Hospital
Minneapolis, Minnesota
6 February 1948

Women In Medicine; Male Medics Felt Threatened; My Internship Grades

Terry received the letter in which I said I had a valentine for her but wouldn't tell her what it was. She said she was dying to find out just what it was, but all she could think of these days was my visit home. It would be heaven to have me here.

This morning, Terry went with Dr. Seigal to the University for grand rounds by the Department of Pediatrics staff (discussion focused on a subject with illustrative patient). She enjoyed it a lot. Bob Good, a classmate in medical school, presented a case and "did a lot of talking." She saw her friend Audrey (Arcola) there, too. Seigal was a "nice fellow and she really liked him" but he spent all the way back to MGH telling her how he couldn't understand how any woman could go into medicine, implying that our children were going to be neglected. He said no woman should be a doctor unless she was very unattractive, deformed, or had no intention of marrying. Terry got a little "hot under the collar" at that, as I could readily imagine.

"Honey, I'm so thankful that you're the wonderful, considerate, sympathetic person you are. I'm glad that you have enough ability and truc sclf-confidcncc so that you nccdn't feel threatened by the women, especially your wife, who are in your field. In short, I'm very, very proud that you're my husband — and I hope I never forget how lucky I am."

"Here's something else that happened today to make me proud — I stopped by Dr. Fahr's office to dictate an N&M death summary, and his secretary showed me your grade report (from my internship the previous year). She was extremely impressed, saying that yours is really exceptional. You got almost straight 95's with a few 93's. That will be used in your [Mayo] letter of recommendation, which will surely be a good one. You're wonderful dear." Surely a biased wife.

Terry's mother was home so she planned on going home tonight. She was writing to me in the afternoon, something she found time to do on the Contagion service.

Minneapolis General Hospital
Minneapolis, Minnesota
7 February 1948

Supportive Wife

Terry received my "sweet, sweet letter about your little blow-up with the major" today. As usually she was supportive. She said, "Honey, I think you were absolutely right, and I'm glad you defended your principles. I'm sure that the major was favorably impressed with your professional integrity, even though he was unreasonable." She thought it was too bad I was meeting so many people now who weren't sincere about medicine. It had been her feeling that many doctors, often renowned ones, were only shams as far as their real principles were concerned. There were, of course, many honest, conscientious, hard-working doctors in the U.S. and we would learn to know them. "Don't forget all of the good friends you made, dear, during your medical school days."

"Honey, I wish I could tell you how I love you and how much I miss you. Anticipating your coming is like looking forward to Christmas day, Easter morning, and spring — all rolled into one delightful day, the day when you arrive. And then there will be two wonderful weeks of seeing you every day, after that."

"I think I must have loved you almost from the first time I saw you, although I didn't realize it right away. This love is very strange. Even before I knew you well, I knew that you were very important to me and that I was terribly happy with you. I keep learning new things about you every day, though, and they're all good. They say love is blind. If so, I've been blind for 4½ wonderful years —

'cuz I can't see that my honey has any faults."

"Baby, I'll stand behind you in anything that involves ethical and moral principles. I think you're absolutely right. If you were wrong, though, I'd still back you up with all of my ability. Don't forget that you can count on your wife, dear!"

We received a letter from my sister, Bea, addressed to Terry. She was responding to Terry's suggestion that we might visit Joice while I was home. Bea said that she, Tony, and little T.J. would probably leave for California on February 20th. Terry thought that ruled out our visit, since I wouldn't be able to leave for Joice until after the 18th. That would catch them right in the middle of packing.

Terry, Ann, and Mother Brey visited some family friends last night. The 13 year old son had a cleft palate repair. Although his family handled the handicap well, the boy was obviously very sensitive and shy. I could have cried for him. He collected stamps. "Darling, could you bring a variety of them from Panama — for him?"

Minneapolis General Hospital
Minneapolis, Minnesota
8 February 1948

Last Letter

Terry came off call at noon, wrote me a short note, and then headed home, intending to ask Mrs. Jolly to go to the movies. She still did not know I had been ordered discharged from the Army and that I was in the process of separation. She intended to write me once more on the next day, Monday, February 9th, and then expected to see me shortly thereafter, based on my "need" to take the National Medical Board Examination. I would, in fact, arrive home at about the same time, but now for an entirely different reason: release from active duty.

Keesler Air Force Base
Biloxi, Mississippi
13 February 1948

SEPARATION FROM ACTIVE DUTY

The separation process moved much more rapidly than I anticipated. I quickly packed, leaving heavy items, e.g., books, behind, picked up a carved camphor wood Chinese chest (for $20) from a soldier who had won it in a raffle, checked out of Howard Field, flew to Keesler Air Force Base in Biloxi, Mississippi, on 12 February 1948, and reverted to inactive status "not by reason of physical disability" on 13 February 1948. I was given a lump sum payment for twelve (12) days of accrued leave.

I quickly arranged air transportation and then flew to Kansas City, where I wired Terry to meet me at the Minneapolis airport (Wold-Chamberlain Field) at 11:30 a.m., Saturday, 14 February 1948 (Figure 32). As the plane broke through the clouds over the Minneapolis airport, bright sunlight glinted off flurries of snowflakes. Terry was waiting on the ground.

CLASS OF SERVICE
This is a full-rate Telegram or Cablegram unless its deferred character is indicated by a suitable symbol above or preceding the address.

WESTERN UNION (16)
JOSEPH L. EGAN
PRESIDENT

SYMBOLS
DL=Day Letter
NL=Night Letter
LC=Deferred Cable
NLT=Cable Night Letter
Ship Radiogram

The filing time shown in the date line on telegrams and day letters is STANDARD TIME at point of origin. Time of receipt is STANDARD TIME at point of destination

KA9 PD=MP KANSAS CITY MO 14 741A

FEB 14 AM 8 38

THERESA B HADDY MD=

MINNEAPOLIS GENERAL HOSPITAL MPLS=

MEET ME AT AIRPORT AT 11:30 AM TODAY SATURDAY. LOVE=

FRAN.

11:30 AM.

THE COMPANY WILL APPRECIATE SUGGESTIONS FROM ITS PATRONS CONCERNING ITS SERVICE

Figure 32- Self explanatory.

EPILOGUE

I took and passed Part I of the National Medical Board Examination on schedule.

Except for Terry's $25 per month salary, we now had no income. Furthermore, our meager savings were impacted by an Army request to return my $300 uniform allowance. In order to make ends meet, we continued to live in the Brey family home and I substituted for a vacationing general practitioner ("locum tenems") in Minneapolis for a short period of time.

My application for a Mayo Foundation fellowship in internal medicine was successful but, as I originally requested, did not start until July 1, 1949, some 15 months after my discharge from the Army. However, I learned that one year in research could be substituted for one year of clinical training in satisfying the three year formal training required by the American Board of Internal Medicine, the body that determined requirements for specialization in internal medicine. I had liked E.T. Bell and his pathology course in medical school, so I asked Dr. Bell to take me on in the Department of Pathology as a post-graduate student in pathology. However, all positions were filled, mostly by veteran physicians returning from service with the intent to refresh and extend their training. That, of course, was my intent also, but they beat me to it.

I then went to see Dr. Maurice Visscher in the Department of Physiology (see *Hypertension*, my forty-three years with *in situ* small and large blood vessels, 17: 814-825, 1991). He took me on as a research assistant and subsequently as a teaching assistant, and here began a long and influential relationship which whetted my appetite for the basic sciences, a hunger that first surfaced in the laboratories in Panama and one which led to a career change toward physiology and eventually away from clinical medicine.

Terry finished her internship at MGH and, when we learned that my Mayo application was successful, she also applied for a Mayo Foundation Fellowship, this one in Pediatrics. Her application was also successful and she was given a starting date of July 1, 1950. However, when the Foundation was told she was pregnant, the fellowship was withdrawn even though the baby would be and was born in January 1950, well before the projected starting date (this wouldn't happen today). She then applied for and served a residency in Pediatrics at the University of Minnesota and I terminated my fellowship at the Mayo Clinic after two years rather than after the usual three years so that we could be together again (I had worn out an automobile traveling back and forth between Rochester and the Brey home in St. Paul) and because my research time in physiology substituted for the third year.

I had very much enjoyed my research experience with Dr. Visscher during 1948 and 1949 and, after leaving the Mayo Clinic, I rejoined him, this time as a Research Fellow of the American Heart Association. These two periods in the Department of Physiology resulted in two additional degrees (M.S. and Ph.D. in Physiology), a number of publications in peer reviewed journals, and many oral presentations before medical research societies, wetting my appetite for the world of medical investigation. It was during my second period in physiology that I met Earl Bakken, founder of Medtronics. He was a technician for the Sanborn Company at the time and he helped me adapt a blood flow meter to a Sanhorn recorder so that I had a continuous record of blood flow in the limb of the dog. I credited him for this in my Ph.D. Thesis. He impressed me and I subsequently invested in his company.

When Terry finished her residency in pediatrics, we moved, now with two children (Rick and Carol), to Chicago where I accepted the positions of Assistant Professor of Internal Medicine and Physiology (a somewhat unique joint appointment) and staff physician at the Northwestern affiliated VA Research Hospital (which paid my salary). Here started a long career in cardiovascular research, independent of a mentor. Terry went into the private practice of pediatrics, initially alone in Arlington Heights, Illinois (a suburb of Chicago), and subsequently together with two other women pediatricians in Des Plaines, Illinois (another Chicago suburb).

About the time we were getting on our feet financially and professionally, the Korean conflict stimulated the Army's need for physicians and, after several years, the Army succeeded in drafting me (I hadn't served a full two years to satisfy the pay-back provision for my medical school education; somehow the eye problem for which I was discharged in 1948 was now not important). I therefore served another two years in the Army, first at Fort Jay on Governors Island, New York, as an internist in the station hospital there, and subsequently in a research position in the Army Medical Research Laboratory in Fort Knox, Kentucky. Terry stayed in Arlington Heights (so much for our Panama pledge never to be separated again) with our then two children. From Fort Knox, I traveled home each weekend by rail, leaving the laboratory noon Friday and returning to the laboratory about 9:00 a.m. Monday. Terry and I often met with the local Arlington Heights' physicians on the weekends, planning the funding and construction of a medical office building for their and our use. Monday, Tuesday, Wednesday, and Thursday nights were spent at Norton Memorial Infirmary, about 20 miles from Fort Knox in Louisville, where I took night call. Nevertheless, I was very productive in research in the laboratory because by then I had developed many ideas to explore and the manpower and equipment resources at my disposal in the laboratory at Fort Knox were unlimited. I also found time to study for and pass the board examinations for certification in internal medicine in 1955.

When I was discharged from the Army in 1957, I returned to my old positions at Northwestern Medical School and the VA Research Hospital in Chicago. I published the results of my research at Fort Knox and the VA Research Hospital in peer reviewed journals and spoke frequently about the findings at medical research meetings. As a result, I soon started receiving job offers from other medical schools, particularly from basic science departments. In 1961, after much soul searching, I accepted the chairmanship of the Department of Physiology at the University of Oklahoma

Medical Center in Oklahoma City (Professor and Chairman, Department of Physiology and Associate Professor, Department of Medicine). Thus, Terry and I moved with our now three children (Alice was born in 1958) from Illinois to Oklahoma, and Terry also entered the world of academic medicine (teaching, research, service), via the vehicle of a fellowship in pediatric hematology/oncology, thus allowing more time with our children.

We stayed in academic medicine for the rest of our careers. Subsequent teaching institutions in which I was employed included Michigan State University and the Uniformed Services University (Bethesda, Maryland). Subsequent institutions employing Terry were Michigan State University, National Institutes of Health (NIH), and Howard University. I chaired departments of Physiology at the University of Oklahoma, Michigan State University, and the Uniformed Services University. I was elected President of the American Physiological Society in 1981. Terry became certified by the American Board of Pediatrics and the sub-board of Pediatric Hematology/Oncology.

Some years after leaving Rio Hato, I saw an air view of the base in the newspaper; it had been almost completely overgrown by foliage.

Terry and I moved into the Charter House in Rochester, Minnesota, in March of 2001.

Short Resume

Francis J. Haddy, M.D., Ph.D.

Dr. Haddy has published over 150 papers in peer reviewed journals. He's also published 112 reviews, and 367 abstracts. These publications concern cardiovascular physiology and cardiovascular disease, particularly the roles of sodium, potassium and digitalis-like substance in low renin hypertension. He taught 45 classes of medical students and chaired three departments of physiology (Oklahoma, Michigan State, Uniformed Services University). He has been on the editorial boards of a number of journals, including the *American Journal of Physiology*, *Circulation Research*, *Hypertension*, and the *Journal of the American College of Nutrition.* He has served on advisory committees for NIH, NASA, and the American Heart Association, and chaired one of these committees for NASA. He has served as a member of the Boards of Trustees for the National Hypertension Association (NHA), American College of Nutrition, American Association for Accreditation of Laboratory Animal Care (AAALAC), and Federation of American Societies for Experimental Biology (FASEB). He has made Liaison Committee on Medical Education (LCME) site visits, including one to the Mayo Medical School. He is a past president of the American Physiological Society. He was selected as a 2003 recipient of the Mayo Foundation Distinguished Alumnus Award.

Dr. Haddy currently administers the grant application peer review program in the cardiopulmonary, integrated physiology, and clinical areas for NASA and consults on NHA research.

Short Resume

Theresa Brey Haddy, M.D.

Dr. Haddy had her undergraduate and medical education at the University of Minnesota, where she was one of five women in a class of 104 medical students. She served an internship at the Minneapolis General Hospital and trained in pediatrics at the University of Minnesota. She spent eight years in the private practice of pediatrics in Illinois. After a fellowship in pediatric hematology/ oncology at the University of Oklahoma, she entered the field of academic medicine and taught at the University of Oklahoma, Michigan State University, and Howard University in Washington, DC. She became an emeritus professor from Howard University and subsequently worked as a researcher in the Pediatric Oncology Branch of the National Cancer Institute.

She is at present an academic advisory staff member of Children's National Medical Center in Washington, DC. Her current research interest is concerned with the late effects of treatment in survivors of childhood cancer.